THE CON

LEOPOLDO GOUT

genius
THE CON

FEIWEL AND FRIENDS
NEW YORK

A FEIWEL AND FRIENDS BOOK

An imprint of Macmillan Publishing Group, LLC
175 Fifth Avenue, New York, NY 10010

Our books may be purchased in bulk for promotional, educational, or business use. Please contact your local bookseller or the Macmillan Corporate and Premium Sales Department at (800) 221-7945 ext. 5442 or by e-mail at MacmillanSpecialMarkets@ macmillan.com.

Library of Congress Control Number: 2016953574

ISBN 978-1-250-04582-9 (hardcover) / ISBN 978-1-250-12340-4 (ebook)

Endpaper credits: Eye photographs © JR-ART.net; illustrations © James Manning; brick wall © Shutterstock/Dan Kosmayer

Book design by Liz Dresner and Sophie Erb

Feiwel and Friends logo designed by Filomena Tuosto

First Edition—2017

10 9 8 7 6 5 4 3 2 1

fiercereads.com

To all the daughters, mothers & immigrants.
Those who dream big will change the stars.

August 8, from Boston field office to New York:
FEDERAL BUREAU OF INVESTIGATION
Precedence: HIGHEST LEVEL
Case ID #: 281M-TF-164629 (Pending)
Title: U.S. COURTS—VICTIM; COMPUTER INTRUSION—OTHER;
DATA THEFT—BANKING, GOVERNMENT(S); FLIGHT—OTHER;
POSSIBLE UNSUB(S)

Between August 1 and August 8, the two dozen government and private
institutions on the attached list were accessed utilizing stolen log-in
information. While a forensics team is analyzing the scope of the intrusion,
it is estimated that nearly 560 terabytes of information were stolen—
this includes personal information (passcodes, identifiers) and classified
documents. The stolen data has emerged on the black market via deep-
Web sites.

The FBI has identified three individuals as being directly involved with
this intrusion: REX HUERTA, 16—a computer prodigy from Santa Cruz,
California; TUNDE ONI, 14—a self-taught Nigerian engineer; and an
UNSUB identified only as PAINTED WOLF, possibly 16, from Shanghai,
China.

All three have been linked to an online "white hat" hacking cell
dubbed the LODGE. The LODGE was present at the recent "GAME"
held by OndScan's CEO and founder, KIRAN BISWAS. Mr. Biswas claims
that Rex Huerta utilized an experimental quantum computer to run a
program—identified in police communications as "WALKABOUT"—
to perform the intrusion. After the Game, Boston PD took Mr. Huerta
into custody. He was subsequently released into the custody of an Unsub
claiming to be his lawyer (Painted Wolf is strongly suspected) and fled
Boston.

Mr. Huerta is assumed to be working in congress with Mr. Oni and
Painted Wolf. They were last spotted boarding a southbound train to New

York City. All units are to be on highest alert and parallel activity with NYPD. Airports across the region are on alert, and facial recognition software has been updated with the most recent images of Mr. Huerta, Mr. Oni, and Painted Wolf.

As REX HUERTA, TUNDE ONI, and UNSUB identified as "PAINTED WOLF" are wanted in connection to multiple counts of computer intrusion and data theft, Boston field office requests that the NYPD work in conjunction with NY field agents to locate and hold them.

PART ONE

SURFACE TENSION

1. TUNDE

Omo, please take my advice: Never jump from a moving train.

Outside of the physics related to falling and landing and rolling, there are a number of ridiculous hurdles one must overcome. The speed at which the train is traveling, the conditions of the ground onto which you are landing, the angle of your descent, these are only but a few. This is why the people who risk life and limb to jump from trains do it in a heartbeat. It is one of the few things in life in which the brain needs to be rerouted.

If you think about it, you will not do it.

It is *na beanz*, my friends.

So my advice to all who know me is, always use your brain.

After Painted Wolf and I broke my closest friend, Rex Huerta, from federal custody, we took the first train out of Boston and headed for New York. I will tell you, I was very anxious. I was sitting, in the very literal sense, on my own future.

The jammer, the piece of machinery I believed would save my family and my dear Akika Village, was just under my seat. My father told me at an early age that there is only one way to ensure you do not lose your most prized possessions—you must always have one hand on them. And so it was that I kept my hand on the jammer for the brief time we were on that commuter train.

Yet as this train rounded a bend and slowed to a manageable fifteen miles an hour, we pulled the emergency release on the hydraulic doors and jumped out into the midmorning cold.

One of my favorite concepts in physics is the first law as conceived by Sir Isaac Newton. It is very simple to understand and yet that is why it is so elegant.

Simplicity is always the hardest skill to master!

The first law is this: An object that is in motion will continue in motion at the same speed and in the same direction unless it is acted upon by another force.

In our case, the other force was the ground.

I landed with the jammer slamming up against my back. Painted Wolf was the most graceful. Rex *don sakoro* before he tumbled head over heels in the pea gravel just beyond the tracks. We were up and moving before we could feel the bruises.

Our timing was excellent. Only a half-mile distant we could see the by-now-familiar blue and red strobe lights of police vehicles. They were waiting for us at the next station. Seeing those cars instantaneously brought our actions into focus. The police wanted us, and we were running!

Running!

My friends, never in my life had I broken the law. I say this with confidence. I was an honest person, an upstanding member of my community. To break the law went against everything I believed and yet here I was. What we had done paled in comparison to the wrongs that had been committed against us!

I no just dey dive! My people, my entire village, were in the crosshairs of a madman. Rex was ruined, his name synonymous with the greatest cybercrime of the twenty-first century. Painted Wolf was concerned for the well-being of her entire family. The cards were stacked against us and the dealer was cheating.

This is why we ran, my friends. We were desperate.

We followed Painted Wolf from the train tracks toward a busy intersection where taxicabs whizzed by at incredible speeds. I assumed we might try to catch one. I was very wrong.

"There." She pointed to a bus packed with commuters at the station.

"Are you kidding?" Rex blurted. "We're still forty-two miles from New York!"

"They'll be looking for us running or on foot. Every cab on the street is going to get an alert. They'll be talking about us over the radio. We'll only get a few blocks. But no one is going to expect us to be on a bus."

1.1

The first step of any good escape plan is confusing your pursuers.

We knew there was simply no way we could outrun the police and FBI.

Not only were they highly mobile but they also had access to every aspect of public transportation. Step onto a bus and they could see us from the driver's-side mounted cams. Hide out in the subway and we would be picked up by facial-recognition software. Even walking down the street was fraught with peril, as the authorities had undertaken the highly unusual step of launching surveillance drones on U.S. soil. I tell you, *omo*, it was like we had stumbled into a war.

But we were not without our resources.

Namely, Painted Wolf!

As we ran toward the station, she pulled out a cell phone and began typing. Painted Wolf typed for three city blocks as Rex and I shook with anxiety that we would be spotted.

"What are you doing?" Rex asked her.

"We have to go," she said with a smile.

Omo, we wove like vipers in tall grass through the parked cars that ringed the station. Most of the police officers were inside, waiting for the train to arrive (surely it would be only minutes before they heard of our escape!), and those who were outside were distracted enough that they missed us make our way around the back of the station. Thank God, I saw no officers there.

Ah, but there was a good reason for that!

"Watch out!"

Painted Wolf motioned to the sky as Rex hustled me behind a parked car. Before I could ask him what had him so spooked, he pointed skyward. Three drones the size of dinner plates hovered a block away. As they moved toward us, I could hear the faint whine of their servos over the distant crash of traffic. My friends, though it was clear these things were likely looking for us, I was impressed. What amazing design! Even in the midst of running, *I give big throwaway salute* to technology!

"Think they've seen us?" Painted Wolf whispered.

"If they haven't, they will soon," Rex replied.

The drones spread out. Two of the clever machines hovered about fifty-five feet above the edges of the parking lot and one, seventy feet up, hovered over the middle. Just glancing at the bulbous 360-degree cameras on their bellies told me they would easily find us. And they would do it quickly.

"We need a diversion," Rex said. "I'll do it."

I held him back. "No. We bring them down."

"How?"

These Americans, so ready to leap into overdramatic action anytime the going gets tough! "I am going to turn on the jammer, of course."

Rex he dey shine a splufic smile!

The drone hovering a half block away on our side of the street whirred lower; it would be right overhead in a matter of seconds. I undid the locks on the jammer, and my fingers moved on automatic across the controls. I knew this machine inside and out! There was an anticlimactic silence as the jammer buzzed to life, but I knew that human ears could not pick up the signals it was generating.

The drones that were chasing us down

The drones, however, could.

The one on our side of the lot was only twenty feet away when it suddenly plummeted, clattering to the pavement. The second and third drone dropped like stones soon afterward. One shattered; the other lost its rotors in an explosion of plastic. Ah, it was sad to see such refined engineering broken on the pavement.

"A waste," I said as I stood.

Rex grabbed me and pulled me back down. "Not so fast. Even though their GPS systems are jammed, their cameras could still be working."

"Let me handle it," Painted Wolf said.

With a wink to Rex, Painted Wolf pulled a laser pointer from her purse, then slowly, carefully, eased herself up over the hood of the parked car and aimed it at the nearest drone, targeting its camera eye. We were too far away to tell if the trick worked, but Painted Wolf hit the other drones with the laser, too.

Still, my friend Rex was not taking any chances.

He jumped up and ran to the nearest downed drone. When he got to it, Rex stomped it to bits! What a sight, to see those pieces spinning across the parking lot. Rex next made a beeline to the second drone and delivered the same treatment.

Finally, letting off all his steam, Rex crushed the third and last drone with a well-placed leap. Though I hate destruction, I will tell you, the crunch of the glass was incredibly satisfying!

1.2

We reached the bus only seconds before it lurched into gear.

This was no *danfo*!

Not only was the ride impeccably smooth but the interior was more like that of an airplane than a highway bus. With the bus half full, Rex and I sank into our seats near the back while Painted Wolf paid the driver. The other passengers, young people with too few bags and older people who were already fast asleep, largely ignored us as we settled in.

I did notice one young woman eyeing her cell phone and then glancing back at us. Was she taking photos? Checking her news feeds to see if we were the ones the police were looking for? The way her eyeballs darted from her cell screen to our faces told me we had to do something fast. Even though I may have been growing paranoid, who could blame me!

I told Rex and Painted Wolf to power off their cell phones. Then I switched on the jammer again and the bus instantly became a moving bubble of GPS failure. And more! As it had at the Game, the jammer wreaked havoc with every device receiving and generating electronic signals aboard. The young woman watching us restarted her phone, tapped it ruthlessly, and then finally put it away, completely flabbergasted.

I turned the jammer back off a few minutes later. I did not want to be responsible for any accidents. I figured the best use of the jammer was to turn it on and have it send out a very low disrupting signal every five minutes or so. The process would be laborious, but that way at least we would have the best of both worlds—a moving digital bubble that did not leave a trail of broken phones and equipment. This way, the phones would work but there would be no incoming or outgoing messages.

The bus made its way through traffic to the highway on-ramp. Passengers complained about lack of service, and though she had nothing to do with it, the bus driver actually turned around and apologized to everyone. She was a good person, and I did feel guilty about the situation.

But my guilt did not last that long, *omo*.

With the phones and tablet computers rendered momentarily inactive, the passengers were forced to do the unthinkable: They had to talk to each other or gaze out the window at the beautiful landscape surrounding us.

It is true that most of it was industrial—warehouses, refineries, factories—but, my friends, I believe that all human ingenuity is beautiful.

2. CAI

I've never had a bus ride pass so quickly.

My mind was spinning.

I spent the time from Boston to Hartford mentally charting our course. We'd made the bus, but we'd also have to get off it and make it to Teo's apartment unseen. I didn't know New York City beyond maps I'd studied, so a lot of the moves I assumed we'd make were guesses—things that had worked in the past in Shanghai.

Every big city **is a grid**; the trick is finding the fastest way across it.

I spent the second hour figuring out the "what next" after we would hit Teo's apartment. If he was there, that meant a radically different approach than if he wasn't. Regardless, we had a flight to catch. I could come up with all sorts of ways to get us to the airport, but getting onto the plane would be the trickiest part.

Running would only get us so far.

If we were going to make it, I figured we'd need some help.

While Tunde was focused on the scenery blurring outside and giving us an occasional update on what we'd just sped by ("Did you see that petroleum refinery? No, I cannot believe you missed it! It was amazing!"), Rex was lost in his thoughts. Every now and then he'd tap away at a coding app he'd opened up on his cell phone and type out a few mathematical formulas.

"Brain never stops, does it?" I said, already knowing the answer.

"Helps me focus. I'm writing out programs we might need to use when we get to the airport. It's all potential, you know, like different signal blockers and masking tech. I've already got a police radio scanner application for both UHF and VHF channels. We are wanted felons after all."

I leaned over and glanced back down the highway.

"Right now, the only people tailing us are commuters."

"Look," Rex said, putting his cell phone down, "not all of us are infamous."

"You say that like it's a bad thing."

"I'm just not exactly used to running from the authorities. I mean this is insane. I've broken more laws in the past two days than in my entire life."

"It's not even noon," I joked. "I'm sure we'll break some more."

Rex didn't laugh. I elbowed him and winked over my sunglasses.

"It's funny," Rex said. "But I've just had this idea that finding Teo is going to fix things. Maybe it's like a big-brother complex or something. I'm sure psychologists have come up with a condition for it. We've got so much we need to fix, it'd be great to have his help."

He needed a pep talk. He needed to know **we could do this**.

"We're strong," I said. "Stronger than we've ever been. You got us here, all your hard work. You got us here and we're going to find your brother. But no matter what, you need to know that we can overcome whatever the world throws at us. You might not always have your brother, but you'll always have us."

"Good to have a friend like you, Wolf."

As Rex went back to coding and looking down at his cell, I knew what we needed to do. How we were going to get to Teo's apartment unseen.

"Guys, did you just see that junkyard!?" Tunde spun to us, eyes wide, fingers pointed outside. Rex and I looked at him skeptically.

"What?" he asked, shocked that we weren't as thrilled at looking at a scrap yard as he was.

"Tunde, focus. We're a bridge away from the city," I told them. "Good news is, I have a plan on how we're going to get to Teo's apartment and not be seen. Bad news is, I need you to turn off the jammer for a minute."

"Hang on," Rex said. "That's taking a huge risk. . . ."

"Taking **huge risks** has gotten us this far, right? Hit the button, Tunde."

Tunde looked to Rex, then back to me, then nodded and shut the jammer off. Instantly, a dozen cell phones beeped and buzzed as messages and e-mails that had been backlogged came through. Everyone, even the driver, pulled out their cells and started reading and making calls.

I borrowed Rex's cell and sent a text message, then deleted it.

"You're planning something big," Rex said.

"I think you're going to like this."

2.1

The bus was swallowed up by the Port Authority Bus Terminal minutes later.

Though we couldn't see more than a sliver of the city surrounding us, I could feel its weight all around. Towering buildings and mobs of people—if we wanted to get lost, this would be a good place to do it. As soon as we stepped outside, Rex was on his cell mapping a route to Teo's apartment.

"Thirty minutes by subway," he said. "That's too long."

"Maybe we catch a ride," Tunde said, eyeing a line of taxicabs. "We certainly cannot be out walking the streets. From this corner I can see five surveillance cameras. They are on top of the buildings and some on the streetlights."

"We'll get to Teo's," I said, "but not in a cab or on the subway. Come on."

We merged into a passing group of tourists and followed them for two blocks. Rex was deliberately slouching behind the taller guys in the group; Tunde was in the lead, eyes wide, ready for anything. Nothing happened, but I could feel the tension when a helicopter passed overhead.

"Wolf, we close?" Rex asked, ready to run again.

"There," I said, pointing to a Chinese restaurant on the corner. "Our ticket."

It was called Hunan Palace.

We ducked inside and found the place filled with lunchtime customers. Most of them were Chinese, likely recent immigrants and their first-generation kids.

"How exactly are we going to get across town?" Tunde asked.

"Easy. We'll have a party."

Rex and Tunde looked at each other.

Rex asked, "Who are we inviting?"

I grinned. "**Everyone**."

I flagged down a waiter, a young man with dyed-pink hair. I asked him in Mandarin if his uncle had gotten my message. He nodded.

The waiter motioned for us to follow him to the kitchen.

As I stepped inside, my stomach instantly started growling. Hunan cuisine is known for its heat—spicy foods with rich flavors. We walked past sous chefs prepping bean curds, dry-wok chicken, and smoky fish in chili sauce. Entering the kitchen was like wading into a fog of deliciousness, and it made me miss home terribly. For me, comfort food is a plate of *máo shì hóngshāo ròu*, Mao's braised pork.

But there was no time to reminisce or even catch a bite.

The pink-haired waiter took us over to a rotund chef with a large smile. His name was Mr. Tan. He was the acquaintance of a microblogger in Nankin who went under the handle of Element B.

A year ago, Element B and I had worked on a project together virtually, and she'd told me I could come to her with anything. She told me Mr. Tan was familiar with the microblogging community in China, knew the risks we were taking, and was a "big fan."

He shook my hand and bowed. "Welcome, Painted Wolf."

I thanked him repeatedly. "You're doing us an amazing favor."

"I am happy to help. We have something you requested."

Mr. Tan motioned to one of the sous chefs, and he pulled a black duffel bag out from a cabinet. It was big and stuffed full. I took the bag and bowed my thanks.

I then turned to Tunde. "Mr. Tan needs a favor."

Mr. Tan gave Tunde a vigorous handshake before he handed him a satchel of tools. Tunde turned to me, utterly confused.

I clarified the situation. "I told him you are going to fix the AC unit in the back; it seems it's having some real problems."

"You do know we are currently **on the run**, right?"

"Of course," I laughed. "I'm sure it won't take more than a minute."

Mr. Tan pointed to a boiler room just off the kitchen.

"Fine," Tunde said. "But first, please, tell us what is going on."

"We're going to social network our way out of this," I said. "Three hours and thirty-seven minutes ago, I had Element B send out a message. It went to all of the LODGE's followers, anyone and everyone we know. I'll be honest with you: I've only done this once before, but it was small scale. Just me and only for a few minutes when I was in a real jam."

"I think this qualifies as a jam," Rex said.

Tunde asked, "Wolf, can you tell us what exactly you asked all of our friends and followers to do?"

"**Join us**," I said. "Here."

The distant sound of a passing siren caught our attention.

"I still don't get exactly how this helps," Rex said. "Even if we had an army of our friends, the police would just bowl them over."

"It's not the number of people that matters; it's what they're doing."

"And what exactly is that?" Tunde asked.

"Those based here in New York City are going to hit the streets and provide cover. The people who can't physically be here will be doing whatever they can to help—hacking street cams, rerouting traffic."

Tunde grinned. "I have no idea how that will happen, but I love the sound of it. Go on now, tell us what is in the duffel bag."

I pulled the bag up onto a nearby counter and unzipped it. Inside were clothes. Shirts, skirts, pants, socks, shoes, and even wigs and jewelry. "These are donated," I said as Tunde and Rex looked over the goods. "Everything should fit."

"Incredible!" Tunde said. "We truly have amazing friends."

"It gets better."

I pulled a manila envelope from the bottom of the duffel bag and handed it to Rex. He was stunned to see what was inside. Three passports. One Chinese, one Nigerian, and one American. Each had our photos (harvested from social media and Photoshopped to perfection), but the names and biographical details were entirely fictional. They looked incredibly real.

Tunde opened his and laughed. "My name is Mobo Oyekan! This name means 'freedom' in the language of my people. A very fitting choice, Wolf."

"Well, at least you're not Damian Quintanilla." Rex frowned.

"You don't like it?" I said, half laughing. "It's fancy."

"Makes me sound like a cheesy pop star."

"You are always a star in my book, Damian." Tunde grinned.

"What about you, Wolf?" Rex asked.

I opened the Chinese passport and held it up for them to see. The photo was of me in full Painted Wolf gear, done up with as much makeup as possible.

"Chen Jiang," Tunde read aloud. "Beautiful."

"How did you even get these made?" Rex asked. "This is nuts."

"Some of our followers don't exactly have sterling reputations," I said. "They're not perfect but I think, given the time crunch, **they'll** do."

"Oh, they'll more than do," Rex said, shooting me a smile. "Wolf wins again."

2.2

While Tunde worked on the AC and Rex coded on his cell, I sent a few e-mails and texts to a second wave of people.

Folks I didn't know well but I'd worked with in the past.

We needed to have as many available hands as possible.

Even though we didn't know what would come of our visit to Teo's apartment, I knew we had a flight to catch. Getting to the airport was going to be a problem, but it was minor compared to getting through security and onto the plane.

We had the disguises. We had the passports.

But those were only two facets. At a rough estimation, there were a million and one ways the operation could go wrong. I had to come up with patches for each and every one.

And that was going to require pulling in every favor I could think of.

Twenty minutes later, we were ready to go.

Tunde had fixed the AC unit, and cool air soon filled the restaurant. Mr. Tan swelled with gratitude and shoved a to-go carton of smoked beef and dried chilies into his hands.

Ever gracious, Tunde explained that it was a simple matter of clearing a rodent's nest from around the AC's capacitor. I translated for Mr. Tan. Although Tunde was eager to go into the details, I had to ask him not to share. Last thing I wanted to think about was a rat's nest in the back of the kitchen.

I spared Mr. Tan the embarrassment.

"You guys have to see this," Rex shouted from the front of the restaurant.

We ran up with the waitstaff to see forty-seven people in the street.

They ranged from young kids to old men. I saw a nine-year-old boy on a skateboard, a woman pushing a stroller with a sleeping infant, a man over sixty with a very long beard, and a tattooed woman with pierced eyebrows.

It was unbelievable that all of them were there to help us.

But what stood out most were the teens who looked like Rex, Tunde, and me. When I say that they looked like us, I mean it was uncanny. They were wearing the same clothes and had very similar haircuts. It was like looking into a corner mirror and seeing myself reflected out into infinity.

Tunde couldn't help himself. He ran out into the crowd and gave high fives and hugs. Then, beaming, he turned back and waved for us to join.

As Rex and I stepped into the mob of clones, he said, "We're fugitives. Why are they—"

I stopped and lowered my sunglasses to catch Rex's intense stare. "They wanted to help. Honestly. Although I felt bad about them taking a risk for us, so as far as they're concerned this is all part of an experiment. I think a lot of them just think it's fun. Crazy as that seems . . ."

"So how's this work?" Rex asked, looking around at our twins.

"**We run. They run. Pretty simple,**" I said.

Tunde clapped twice and shouted, "Then we need to go!"

All of our copies ran out into the streets of the city in a burst of excitement. Maybe passersby thought it was some sort of video prank, a flash mob for the cameras, but most of them got out of the way quickly. If there were drones above us at that moment, they would have had digital heart attacks attempting to track all of the moving bodies.

"Come on." I pulled Rex and Tunde into a group of six of our clones and sprinted to the end of the block.

At the end of the street, half of the group went left, the other right.

Tunde turned to go with the left half, but I caught him. He was following the wrong Rex! Thankfully Rex didn't notice.

We headed downtown, pushing through the crowds, before I motioned for the guys to join me under a tree in a small park. Rex scanned the skies and the rooftops. He was acting as paranoid as I felt. Tunde was amped up and sweating hard. He looked like his heart was threatening to break out of his chest.

"Okay," he said. "We got this far. How do we get to Brooklyn?"

"I got us a ride," I replied.

"You thought of everything," Tunde said.

We were interrupted by a loud honk and turned to see a delivery van roar up the street alongside the park. The driver jumped down and opened the back where the interior was lined with shelving for packages. He was in his early twenties and tall with short-cropped hair. His eyes were a startling blue.

"Hey, Wolf, glad to meet you in person."

He gave me a hug. Watching, Rex had a weird look on his face. Almost like he was jealous, which was flattering but totally unnecessary.

I introduced the driver to the guys.

"This is Nigel. He's a friend."

I'd known Nigel for about ten months. Virtually. He frequented a deep-Web forum on game theory where people posted clever twists on old puzzles. Nigel was best known for his take on one of the oldest opening moves in chess, the **King's Gambit**.

"Hop on in," Nigel said. "We don't have much time."

We jumped into the back of the van.

As Nigel closed the door, he said, "Hang on tight."

2.3

I'd tried to keep Nigel in the dark like our doubles.

I'd told him it was a competition and we needed to get across town, in secret, fast. I was worried he wouldn't buy it.

I was right.

"So you guys are on the run, huh? Rad," Nigel said as he pulled the van into traffic. "I know you're trying to keep me safe but don't worry, I got this. Truth is, we've got friends in common. Word gets around."

As the van whipped into traffic, Nigel manhandled the wheel to keep the vehicle from tipping over. We had to brace ourselves every turn.

"Which friends?" Tunde asked as we careened around a corner.

Nigel glanced back at us with a grin. "People interested in changing things."

Concerned, Rex leaned over to me. "How do you know this guy?"

"He's on our side."

"Let's hope so," Rex said, motioning to rows of high-tech police-avoidance technology lining the interior of the van. Radar gun scanners, thermal cameras, laser jammers, and a CB radio system that crackled with the voices of any pursuers. Tunde looked to be in seventh heaven scanning all the equipment.

"Cost a pretty penny to hook it all up," Nigel shouted.

I'll admit I was a bit shocked to see how much equipment Nigel had packed into the van. I'd had the feeling he might be something of a conspiracy nut, but this definitely solidified it. We'd accept the ride and be grateful for it, but that was it. I certainly would think twice about calling Nigel for help again.

"What do you use this van for exactly?" Rex asked.

Nigel laughed. "As Painted Wolf knows, sometimes you need to get in and out in a hurry. I deliver packages during the day and help my friends at night. We're not as high-profile as you all, but we like to **get** things **done**."

Rex coughed: "Terminal."

"Ha," Nigel chuckled. "No. No way. Those guys are maniacs. To tell you the truth, I think they're probably just puppets for some shady corporation. Don't get me started on the whole thing; I could talk for ages about it. But, no. No, I'm just a friend of a friend. Painted Wolf hooked up one of my buddies a few months ago. He was in Beijing— Wait, can I even talk about that stuff?"

Nigel glanced back at me.

"Nigel's friend needed help getting a message out through social media. He's part of a hacker crew exposing the dirty laundry of some of the big conglomerates doing business in China. Needless to say, he needed to get through the Great Firewall, and I hooked him up."

"Wolf did more than that," Nigel yelled back.

Rex turned to me and frowned.

"They were going to try to send the messages unencrypted," I said, trying quickly to defuse Rex's suspicion. "It was like they were doing this for the first time."

"Well . . . ," Nigel said.

"Anyway, I ran it through a few programs. Gave them some pointers."

"She saved my friend's butt," Nigel said. "Seriously. Huge props."

We came to a sudden halt at an intersection and Nigel turned around in his seat and smiled. We picked ourselves up and dusted the debris from our clothes.

"It's really good to meet you in person, Wolf," Nigel said. "You look awesome."

Rex rolled his eyes at that.

"We're all exhausted," I said. "But we really appreciate your helping us out."

"Hang on. Almost there."

Our stomachs had only just settled when Nigel hit the gas and the van lurched forward. As we sat plastered to the van's rear door, Rex held out his cell phone. He had three windows open; each displayed a scene of chaos only a few miles away—our clones were being questioned by police.

"They've caught fifteen so far," Rex said. "I feel terrible for these people."

"I do, too. But they'll be fine."

"How are you so sure about that?"

"It's okay to let people help you, Rex."

"I'm fine letting people help me. I just don't like the idea of people I don't know putting their necks out for me. That feels . . . wrong."

"You're looking at it incorrectly," I said. "This thing is bigger than you. It's bigger than the LODGE; it's bigger than the Game or even Kiran. The people helping us get out of here right now are doing it because they want what's right. They want justice. And getting us to Africa, getting you out of jail, that is doing the right thing."

Rex chewed that over carefully, glancing back at the news feed on his cell.

"Are we close?" Tunde asked Nigel.

The van jumped another curb as it careened through traffic.

"Yes," Nigel said, putting his hand on some of his equipment to hold it in place. "But you're going to have to walk the rest of the way.

There's some crazy traffic up ahead. Think it might be a roadblock. Anyway, place you're looking for is three blocks south of here. Keep your heads low, roll quiet, and you should be cool."

Nigel pulled the van over to the side of the road.

He put it in park and turned around, grinning.

"Pleasure helping you guys," Nigel said. "We even, Wolf?"

"For sure," I said. "But **you never really owed me**."

"Awesome. Catch you guys later."

We all piled out of the van. It was great having my feet on the ground again. The sounds of the city came flooding in as Nigel pulled the van back into traffic and vanished. Tunde grabbed the duffel bag and swung it over his shoulder.

"He was a nice fellow," Tunde said.

Rex huffed. "Seemed a little weird to me."

3. REX

adrenaline

industrial

So this was it.

Months of coding.

Two years of searching.

Now I was only a few hundred feet from my brother.

For me, adrenaline isn't so much a boost as it is a fuel. I was pumped up, ready for whatever came next. I sprinted ahead of Painted Wolf and Tunde.

"Come on, only a block to go."

We were in an industrial part of the borough.

The type of place no one was living in a few years earlier. There were factories and wide streets and very few trees. On the horizon, I could see the shimmering towers of Manhattan through the haze. Somewhere to our left, the river was slapping the shores, eating its way into the island one millimeter at a time.

I slowed and Wolf ran alongside me as we approached the address, a three-story concrete apartment building that wouldn't have looked out of place in SoCal.

"You all right?"

"Yeah," I said. "Just feels a bit weird being so close."

"But weird in a good way, right?"

The closer we got, the more I was grinding my teeth.

This is it. Everything you've been waiting for . . .

My heart was in my throat. It's an old expression. One you hear all the time, but it's true. You can be so anxious, so excited, that your heartbeat overwhelms every other sound. It's like a drum in your ear. And your throat . . .

Take it easy, Rex. Keep focused. Keep cool.

With no sirens wailing, no rush of approaching police vehicles, I stood behind Painted Wolf while she picked the lock to the apartment building. Her motions were insanely smooth. Clearly, she'd done this more than once before. As I watched her, the first thought that came to my head was: *What would Ma think of this girl?*

We cautiously made our way up three flights of narrow stairs to the apartment the quantum computer had identified as Teo's.

We stood together by the door. It was nondescript, a slate-gray door with a chrome knob. Behind it could have been anything.

My hand hovered over the doorknob.

"Think it is locked?" Tunde said.

"Maybe we should knock first?" Painted Wolf asked.

My stomach was in knots. I knocked quietly.

There was no response from the other side of the door.

So I knocked louder.

Still nothing.

So I grabbed the doorknob and turned it.

It was locked. Painted Wolf pulled out her nail file and bobby pin. She went to town and within seconds the doorknob clicked. It was unlocked.

"This is it," she said.

Then I took a deep breath and opened the door.

3.1

I don't know what I expected to happen when the door opened.

I guess I've seen too many movies where a spy or a detective cracks open a mysterious door and there's either a sudden explosion or something terrifying comes rushing out at them.

None of those things happened.

The door swung open silently on an empty studio apartment.

A TV in the corner was still on, anime flashing across the screen.

The place looked like a college kid's dorm room. Secondhand furniture battled for space with ancient, threadbare rugs. There was a bookshelf stacked with books and DVDs. A small fridge hummed anxiously. The place smelled faintly of old pizza and laundry freshener. It was like he'd just stepped out.

"Hello?" I shouted before heading inside.

There was no response.

"You think he's—" Painted Wolf started, but I cut her off.

"Teo!" I yelled into the room. My voice bounced off the walls.

Nothing.

That's when I saw it. A sketch pad on the coffee table.

"This is the right place," I said. "He's just not here."

I picked up the sketch pad. It was turned to an open page where there was an amateurish but clever drawing of a scooter. To be exact, an Eagle scooter circa 2001. The same one my brother and I had won in a carefully orchestrated con when I was six. It's a long story; I'll share it another time.

Needless to say, the drawing was proof.

"This is Teo's place. He drew this. But . . . but he's gone."

"You cannot be certain," Tunde said. "Perhaps he is just out for a moment."

Painted Wolf turned to me; she reached out to touch my shoulder, but I stepped away, shaking my head. The doubt that had been gnawing at the back of my brain crept closer—maybe WALKABOUT hadn't worked as well as I'd assumed? Maybe he'd left this place before the Game had even begun?

As the questions swirled, my heart sank.

Painted Wolf grabbed my hand, spun me around to face her.

"We're going to find him," she said. "Maybe not now. Maybe not here. But we're not going to give up. Rex, you just told us that he was here. This is his sketch pad. His place. That's huge. You're so much closer, don't you see that?"

She was right, of course.

Didn't feel that way, though. In the moment, it felt like being kicked in the gut. My mind raced back through everything that had happened, everything that led me to that apartment—all the heartache, all the anger, all the coding, and all the running. And for what? For a sketch and his abandoned stuff.

I felt like I was going to topple over.

That or scream.

"I know it's disappointing," Painted Wolf continued. "Even with the program, this was always a long shot. You said so yourself. But it must feel good to know how close you are. Just a month ago, you didn't even know where to start."

A good pep talk but . . . I needed to see Teo.

So close but so far . . .

Walking around the room, examining the books and DVDs, Tunde said, "I am sorry, *omo*. Painted Wolf is right. We will find him. I am certain of it. If not here, then again, another place. Knowing what you have told me about Teo, though, I can assure you there are many, many clues left behind here."

I looked down at the sketch pad and flipped through the pages.

It was filled with drawings and doodles, most of them about biological processes—the interior of cells, neural networks, carbon chains. The rest were just little swirling designs, as if his hand had been on autopilot. Thing is, the sketch pad wasn't open to those drawings. It was open to this one page.

A page only I would have instantly recognized.

"You're right," I said. "You're both right."

Tunde said, "Where do we start?"

I pulled the cell from my pocket and started taking pictures.

Before any of us touched anything, before we disrupted any of the room's arrangement, I took photos and video from every angle. If we missed something, there was now a record.

"We need to go through everything," I said. "Notebooks, books. I hate to say it but considering our time constraints, we're going to have to pull the place apart."

Tunde took the kitchen, I took the sleeping area, and Painted Wolf handled the bookshelf. Tunde was very careful, placing everything neatly to the side. I piled things up. Painted Wolf was a tsunami.

We quickly realized there was nothing hidden.

No secret charts or binders full of in-work projects. This wasn't Teo's lab. If anything, it was just a crash pad—a place to kick his feet up and watch DVDs of old shows like *Arthur C. Clarke's Mysterious World* and *Firefly*.

I sat down on the futon. "We're missing something."

Painted Wolf sat down beside me with my cell, listening to police radio chatter on a Bluetooth through the scanner app I'd written on the bus. "They're doing sweeps nearby," she said. "There's enough going on to distract them for now, but we can't be relaxed."

Tunde opened the refrigerator.

Inside were condiments, seltzer water bottles, and old Chinese takeout.

"This place makes no sense," I said. "Teo was a workaholic. Used to drive my parents crazy. Even when he was a kid, he'd bring his books to the playground. The very idea of even an hour off would give him hives."

"So this isn't his place?" Painted Wolf asked. "'Cause it's very chill."

"It's a front," I said, jumping up.

I tapped all the walls, listening for empty spaces behind them, hidden spaces. I tried the bookshelf for any levers that would reveal trapdoors. Nothing.

Only thing incongruous in the place was the fridge.

con

clues

quantum computer

There wasn't anything outwardly unusual about it; maybe five years old, not a top-of-the-line model. But still, something didn't sit right. It hummed weird.

That sounds silly, but if you listen to fridges, they all have a similar, white noise–like hum. This one growled.

I opened it up. Nothing inside but bottles of jalapeños, pickles, seltzer water, and the Chinese takeout. I opened the box, sniffed it, and instantly regretted it. Week-old chow mein. Freezer had even less. Much of it wrapped in foil and double bagged.

And that's when I saw it: the button that controls the light inside the fridge, the one that goes out when the door closes and pushes it in.

That button was funky.

I called Tunde over to look at it.

"It is a cap," Tunde said. "Let us see what it is covering."

He pried the button off and beneath was a switch.

Tunde looked up at me. "What do you think?"

I didn't answer.

I just flicked the switch and the back of the fridge slid open.

3.2

The fridge was a *servante*.

That's what magicians call a secret compartment behind their table. The place they sneak things into to hide them from the audience. Sure enough, Teo hid what he'd been working on inside a hollowed-out space maybe four feet by three.

A passageway.

"What do you think?" Tunde asked as I leaned down and peeked inside.

"I think we have ten minutes tops," Painted Wolf said.

I was the first one through. The passage went only a few feet before it stopped at a small sliding metal door. It rolled open easily, on wheels. I climbed through and stood up in a dark room. Pitch black, nothing but the blinking green and white lights of sleeping machines.

And then the lights came flickering on.

They must have been motion activated, 'cause they came on in a flickering wave of bright white from the back of the room to where I was standing. I had to close my eyes and then blink furiously for them to adjust.

Tunde came through. Then Painted Wolf.

"I closed the fridge door to make sure . . . ," she started, then stopped, staring in awe at the laboratory in which we'd just emerged. It was like one of Kiran's labs—something OndScan would hide away on a college campus or in the depths of some corporate office park—only tucked away in a modest Brooklyn apartment.

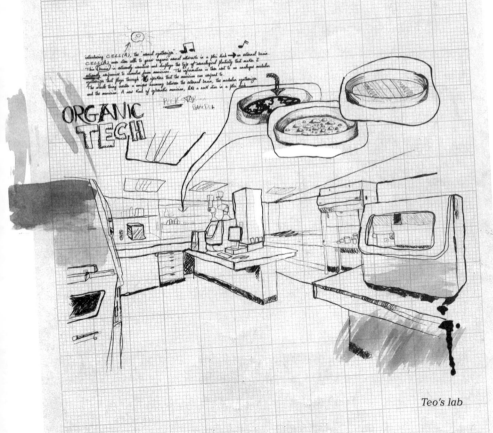

Teo's lab

"This is impossible," Tunde said. "How did—"

There were no answers.

Teo couldn't have built the place himself. He'd either found it and burrowed his way inside or . . . or someone else had put up the money for its construction. I couldn't see any other way.

Unless Teo isn't the same person you thought he was . . .

While the walls were lined with shelves and equipment, a featureless white cube dominated the lab. It was a perfect square, four by four by four feet. It looked like a piece of modernist art. I wasn't sure what it was at first, but when Tunde and I got closer to it, we could hear the hum of inner machinery beneath its smooth surface.

"Very sleek design," Tunde said. "You can barely see the seams."

"Where?" I asked. "I don't see any at all."

Tunde motioned for me to kneel down beside him, and as I did, the seams etched into the sides of the cube suddenly became visible. It was like a puzzle someone had glued together, each piece so snug it was nearly impossible to see.

"Any thoughts?" I asked.

"Some sort of storage unit?" Tunde said, walking around the cube.

"Looks like the quantum computer," Painted Wolf added.

I nodded. "It does, but . . . I don't think it is."

I pulled out my cell, leaned over the top of the cube, and turned on the flashlight. At an angle, the bright light illuminated a symbol and several letters very lightly embossed on the cube's surface. It must have been cut with a laser and only a few dozen microns deep because I couldn't feel the symbol or letters when I ran my fingers over them.

"What is it?" Tunde asked.

It was hard to make out but looked like a teardrop, possibly a raindrop. In its center: ineffably faint letters, A G C T.

I turned to Painted Wolf and asked for a safety pin.

She looked down at her leather coat, the pins a stylish accessory, gold and silver. Then she undid one and handed it to me.

"I'll give it back in a sec," I said.

I poked my ring finger on my left hand. The blood welled up and I handed Wolf the pin back. "That's okay," she said. "You can keep it."

"What are you doing, Rex?" Tunde asked.

"Watch."

passageway

3.3

switch

I held my finger over the top of the cube and a single scarlet drop splashed down on its center.

A wheel of light moved under the acrylic surface of the cube.

Blue and overly bright, it looked like the lights inside a copying machine.

"How did you know?" Tunde asked.

"A, C, G, and T. The building blocks of DNA," I said.

puzzle

"It is unlocked by your genetic code? This is brilliant."

"We should step back," I said.

We did—just as the cube began to unfold. It moved silently, turning on expertly calibrated hydraulics that made Tunde gasp.

When I was a child, my aunt Alejandra would make me intricate origami animals. She loved to fold and unfold them, delighting in how big my eyes would get as they came together. "*Otra vez!*" I would shout. "Again! Again!"

Teo's machine was like one of Alejandra's origami, only fifty times the size and made out of state-of-the-art alloys and precision engineering. The cube twisted, rotating at its center, as petals of metal unfolded the way a flower opens, to reveal a hollow space inside that glowed with a green light. My heart was going nuts inside my rib cage.

"Talk to us, Rex," Painted Wolf said. "What's in here?"

"Teo left that sketch pad out to tell me this place was special, that he wanted me to find it. The fridge, the lab, this box, I don't know if this is what it was all for, but I don't think he'd hide old sweatpants in here. Whatever is inside, it's important."

The space was filled with equipment, documents, tablet computers, and a stack of five multicolored gel disks.

Tunde was exuberant. "This is incredible!"

The cube stopped rotating. A clank echoed from inside.

I reached in and pulled out several notebooks. Thumbing through the pages, I found notes that ran the gamut from annotations on research articles to drawings and calculations. Lots of doodles, too. Excessive doodles. But in it all, I saw the same intense combination of focus and creativity.

Tunde pulled out a small plastic box with what looked like clear sticky note tabs inside. Each was the thickness of tissue paper.

"I did not know these were publicly available!" Tunde was delighted.

"What are they?" Painted Wolf asked.

"Sticky drives. Well, technically they're flash drives," I said. "But they're flexible. Ultra thin. No one has these outside of the tech giants at this point. And even then, it's mostly just research. Each one holds at least 10 gigs."

Tunde pocketed some of them.

I picked through the other stuff in the cube and found earbuds coiled at the bottom. I recognized them. Teo had gotten them for Christmas the year before he vanished. He wore them all the time, even slept with them on.

The fact that he'd left them behind for me to find was telling: Maybe they were a gift, a way of saying, "You're close, brother, keep moving" or maybe they were another enigmatic clue.

Regardless, I grabbed them.

Two years in the wilderness, he'd been crazy busy. . . .

"This is all about lysosome transport," Painted Wolf said.

She'd picked up one of the notebooks and was flicking through the pages. I looked over her shoulder and was blown away by what I was seeing.

"Teo solved one of the mysteries of lysosome transport," I said, scanning through the scrawled notes. "I don't exactly know the details of it, but Teo always told me that cellular biologists couldn't figure out how the Golgi apparatus does a lot of what it does. This whole notebook is a breakdown of how a lot of it works. Like eighty percent of it. I have no idea how he figured it out. I don't see any electron microscopes around here. And guess what? There are at least fifteen other notebooks just like this one."

"It's like we're looking into his head," Painted Wolf said, flipping through another one of the notebooks.

"Look closely at these," Tunde interrupted.

He was holding one of the gel disks up to the light.

It looked like a petri dish, exactly the kind you see in labs to grow bacteria. There were at least twenty of them, each filled with a different colored gel; like a little kid's idea of heaven, a Jell-O rainbow.

"So he's growing something?" Painted Wolf asked.

"Data," I said, shaking my head in disbelief. "He's growing data."

Teo, you maniac, you actually did it. . . .

"Come again?" Tunde picked up another dish and held it to the light.

"All these files, its data, but he's stored it biologically. We all know computers store data very, very simply: zeros and ones—just reams and reams of them. You can store the same data, terabytes of it, in a biological way, using proteins and peptides. Each one of the molecules is a one or a zero. You can code the gel, then read it back using transcription. I recognize this stuff. This was the science Teo was working on at home, just before he left."

"Ingenious . . . ," Painted Wolf said.

"Insane . . ." Tunde shook his head.

"Yeah but . . . ," I started, "who paid for all this? The sticky data drives I get. Teo could get ahold of those, but this? Maybe Teo developed some of this tech, maybe he came up with part of the engineering process, but he couldn't have made it—not here, not in some secret lab by himself."

Painted Wolf shushed us for a moment as she listened carefully to the police scanner app. While we couldn't hear what was being said, judging by Painted Wolf's expression it wasn't good.

"We're going to have to deal with all this stuff later, Rex," Painted Wolf said. "It just came over the radio: The cops found Nigel. They'll be here in minutes."

"We can't leave yet!" I shouted. "This is my brother's stuff. Even though he's not here, he *was* here. I need to go through everything. There could be clues. Messages. An explanation for why he left. There's no way I'm leaving right now."

lysos

Both Painted Wolf and I turned to Tunde simultaneously.

Tunde thought for a moment.

"There is a ton of stuff here," he said. "How much time do we have exactly, Wolf? I mean, I know you have to estimate. But judging from the police scanner, give us a time frame."

Painted Wolf sighed, looking back at the fridge we'd come through.

"Five minutes."

prototype

3.4

I couldn't even get through half of one of Teo's notebooks in five minutes.

Golgi apparatus

It was going to take hours to assess all the material in the lab. If there were clues, there was no way I was going to find them in five minutes. It was overwhelming. There was only one answer:

"If you're right," I said to Painted Wolf, "then we're going to have to take it with us. As much as we can carry. We need to find some bags, something to carry it. I want to take the gel disks and the notebooks, at the very least."

Painted Wolf went to look for a bag while Tunde and I continued to explore the contents of the white cube.

"Look at this," Tunde said, removing what looked like a large folding microscope. Each of its parts, from the stem to the scope, moved with a simple twist. Within seconds, he had it assembled and ready: a prototype gel reader.

The folding microscope

"*Omo*," Tunde said. "This is amazing. It looks like science fiction."

37

I handed Tunde a green gel disk and he slid it inside the reader.

Tunde flicked the device on. It buzzed to life as a deep red light scanned the front of the gel disk. A tiny screen flickered on and numbers streamed across it.

"I don't know DNA sequencing that well," I said, "but I'd say there's a tiny strain sensor inside this machine. Like a graphene nanopore—"

Painted Wolf reached over and flicked the microscope off.

"Sorry, Rex," she said. "But we really, really have to go."

She was right; no point in getting this far and then being swept up by the police. We'd have time to go through all the notebooks and the gel disks later. If Teo had left clues to his whereabouts, I prayed he left more than just one or two. And if he didn't, then maybe I'd be able to tease them out of what he did leave behind.

"Okay, okay. I know," I told Wolf as I folded the microscope up.

"Check this out."

She'd found a backpack that looked like something a mountaineer would take up the north face of Mount Everest. Inside were all sorts of pockets, some of them lined with what looked like a cooling system—flexible tubing filled with cold water, controlled with a battery-powered pump.

"Perfect," I said as we loaded in several of the gel disks.

Tunde and Painted Wolf stuffed notebooks into the backpack as I took one last look around the lab.

I could see Teo working here, up all night catalyzing proteins and scribbling formulas in his notebooks. This was his haven, his true home.

The place on the other side of the fridge was just a mock-up; if anyone stopped by they'd think he was just a normal twenty-something kid living the New York dream. But this lab, it was everything he had wanted.

With the backpack stuffed, we climbed back through the fridge.

As soon as we stepped into the apartment, we could hear the sound of sirens. The cops sweeping the streets were close. Too close.

I turned to Painted Wolf. "What's our next move?"

4. TUNDE

My friends, I was certain my heart would explode as we ran from the lab.

I had expected police officers to be waiting for us in the apartment, but they were not. We scrambled down the stairs to the street where again I was certain we would find an army waiting for us. But they were not.

Painted Wolf listened to the police scanner as we moved carefully down the street. As we approached the corner, she held up her hand. We stopped. Painted Wolf pulled a pocket mirror from her purse and used it to peek around the corner. In the mirror, we could see several police vehicles idling on the side of the street.

"We need to cross quickly," Painted Wolf said.

Taking a deep breath as though we were about to dive into a sandstorm, we crouched low and ran across the street with the flow of traffic. Despite Rex's stumbling at the curb, we made it. Running from the law had every nerve in my body on edge, but Painted Wolf was quick and unfazed.

"There's a subway station two blocks ahead," Painted Wolf said.

"Sounds risky. Aren't the subways packed?" Rex replied.

"If we're lucky," Painted Wolf said.

She signaled for us to follow her down a narrow alleyway past rows of dumpsters to another, narrower street. Then, again motioning like a soldier, she signaled for us to stop. We crouched down behind a dumpster while Painted Wolf listened carefully to the incoming police chatter.

"We need to wait here for a moment," she said.

One minute later, a police car zoomed past.

"Let's go," Painted Wolf said, jumping up.

We raced across the narrow street and around a corner before we clambered down a long staircase into the mugginess of a train station. It was loud there, like an urban echo chamber, and I was so overwhelmed that I merely followed whatever moves Painted Wolf made. She studied the posted signs for a few seconds before leading us to a row of turnstiles.

"Tunde," she said, turning back to me. "We'll pay them back later."

And with that, Painted Wolf leaped over the turnstile without swiping one of the magnetic cards I saw the other commuters using to gain entry. You have to understand, we were on the run. Jumping the turnstile made me feel terrible but Painted Wolf was right, we had no other choice. We had to run.

Thankfully, if we were seen, no one chased after us.

Down at the platform, commuters darted from train to train and tourists with children tried to navigate the crowds with varying degrees of success. I saw many of them, scared like cattle being led into pens, just step back to catch their breath.

"Okay, now what?" Rex asked.

Painted Wolf pointed to the wall opposite us where a sign was pasted.

"Says Myrtle Avenue. We need to take a train to the airport. And fast; they found Nigel only a few blocks from here. They've got teams sweeping the subway stations. Frankly, I'm amazed we've gotten as far as we have. . . ." She paused and looked around. "I see a half-dozen cameras from right here."

"There's a map." Rex motioned to a subway map on the side of a sign behind a row of benches. We made our way over, and as Painted Wolf consulted the subway map, I noticed movement at my feet and was taken aback to see a rough-and-tumble pigeon step atop my left shoe. The pigeon looked up at me, curious, with a cock of the head, as if it was surprised that I should be standing in a place it had already claimed. He did not even move when a train roared into the station a few feet away.

"*Oga pigeon*," I said. "*Na you biko.*"

"Tunde," Painted Wolf yelled as she grabbed my arm. "Let's go."

We scrambled across the platform, dodging businesswomen and teenagers with multicolored hair, and leaped onto the train only heartbeats before the doors whooshed closed and the train lurched forward.

Unfortunately, the subway car was not very crowded. I was hoping we could use the crowd as cover. Rex, Wolf, and I made our way toward the back of the car where there were several empty seats in a row. We sat down and spread out. Despite being out in the open, it felt good to catch my breath.

"How many stops until we are there?" I asked.

"I don't know, ten, maybe more. We take this to the end, Jamaica Station. Then we catch the train straight to the airport," Rex said, studying a subway map near the ceiling. "Might take a while."

"About an hour, give or take," a businessman standing nearby said.

He had a large mustache and his tie looked far too tight. I honestly wondered how well he was breathing.

As the train pulled away from the station, Rex took the folding microscope from the backpack and began examining the gel disks we had smuggled from the lab. He thumbed through the notebooks and scribbled in the margins. Ah, my friends, Rex could turn any location, no matter how cramped, into a working space. Though he got a few ugly glances from fellow travelers, he ignored all of them.

With the train in motion I felt as though I could take a moment to reflect. I turned to the window and stared out into the pitch black of the tunnel. Beyond the reflection of my own face soon materialized the faces of my family and the people of Akika Village. I vowed then that I would return to New York with my parents.

My mother had always loved trains. As a child, she went once to visit her grandparents in Kaduna. They traveled by rail. She said that while everyone else in their car read magazines and talked, she sat closest to the window and stared outside as the landscape whipped past. She felt as though she was flying like a bird, darting down low along the ground.

She told me she could have been at that window for many days, completely content in watching the world pass by. My mother is a dreamer, happy to live in the moment. I once argued with her that passive people, people who do not jump at every opportunity to grab life by the horns, are stifled. They are the ones who bring ignorance and smother creativity.

I felt horrible for saying it and only realized later how truly wrong I was. I will not pretend I have the wisdom of an old man, but knowing what I know now, I feel as though I have aged ten decades. It seems to me that those who chase the future, like the general, living only to find riches around the next bend, wind up disappointed, their arms full of minerals but their hearts full of loneliness.

Rex saw my serious expression in the window and paused his activity.

He turned to me and said: "No matter where you go, there you are."

It was a ridiculous statement. I assumed he was trying to be funny.

"That is obvious," I replied.

"Is it?" Rex asked. "It's from Confucius."

"Yes. It is silly . . . ," I began but then trailed off as I realized what he was saying.

"It's something I read in a book or saw on TV as a kid, a couple of years before Teo left. I used to say it to him every time he got that same faraway look in his eyes that you've got. I don't know why I like it, but I do. It makes sense. Even if you travel across the globe, hike your way into the deepest, darkest jungle, or catch a cab to a café at the very heart of the city, nothing really changes. It's still *you* there. The only way we can truly change our lives is to change ourselves."

We both nodded in unison, happy with ourselves.

"Enough with the armchair philosophy, boys," Painted Wolf interrupted. "We have to plan what we're going to do when we get to the airport."

"What happened to just waltzing on in?" Rex winked.

I could see that in her mind, Painted Wolf was already off the subway and in the concourse at the airport. She was processing every step, every move we would make until our plane touched down in Lagos. Most people, they can barely plan a vacation to the beach. But Painted Wolf? She could plan a way to Mars with only a two-speed motorcycle engine and a box of Swedish fish.

"So," I asked her, "has inspiration struck yet?"

Painted Wolf smiled.

That meant we were in for quite a ride.

4.1

The train to John F. Kennedy International Airport rode above a busy highway.

It was largely empty and we had the back of the car entirely to ourselves. Certainly more than enough space for Painted Wolf to explain how we were going to get onto an airplane as international fugitives.

"They'll have the place locked down," she started. "If we try to go in through the vents or underground, we'll be caught. The only thing we've got going for us right now is time. We have five hours before the flight. Check-in, security, both of them will be crawling with police. They'll be using dogs and scanners."

"So you're saying this won't be easy," Rex said.

"I'm saying this is going to be the most difficult thing we ever do."

Painted Wolf grinned; she clearly liked the challenge of this endeavor.

I groaned. "That does not inspire much hope."

"I didn't say we couldn't do it," Painted Wolf said.

"So what's the angle?" Rex pushed.

"We utilize all of our skills. I am going to work my magic and talk us through check-in and security. Rex, you're going to be the glue that holds it all together."

"Just like usual." Rex grinned.

"Don't get a big head over it." Painted Wolf elbowed him. "Here's the thing, though: If you thought what we've done so far was questionable, this is going to be ridiculously illegal. I mean, we're fleeing the country and taking over one of the busiest airports in the world. . . ."

"Hang on. Taking over?"

"Yeah," Painted Wolf said. "The way I see it, the only way we get through the airport, only way we get onto a plane, is to control it. Rex, can you take control of the airport's systems, all of them, and keep it operational? Running as though it was just any normal weekday? We get onto the plane, and once it takes off, we back our way out of the system. We plan it well enough, it will look like we were never there."

I blanched.

"Wolf," I said, "I am afraid you have picked up some of the insanity that is always surrounding Rex. I worry it is contagious! This is an impractical plan!"

I did not realize I was shouting until a woman at the other end of the train turned and stared hard at us. I mouthed: *Sorry*. And waved. She seemed satisfied with that and went back to looking at her cell phone.

Rex shook his head. "Tunde's right. It won't happen. There's no way I can hack into Kennedy from this train with only, what, less than an hour before we get there? I'm good, but I'm not that good. We need a different plan."

Painted Wolf said, "Frankly, I expected it to be harder to get where we are now. I only broke into a sweat once today."

"Just once?" Rex asked mockingly. "You need to work harder."

Painted Wolf lowered her sunglasses very briefly and shot Rex a look. He turned away for a moment, then met her gaze. If they had just met, I would say she was sizing him up. Ah, my friends, but there was something more going on here. I would call it flirting, but it seemed to come from a deeper wellspring. Normally, I would be delighted for my friends, but I very much needed them to focus on the plan before they got lost in each other!

"You are playing with fire, *omo*," I told Rex.

Painted Wolf pushed up her sunglasses and tied her wig in a ponytail.

Rex cleared his throat and gave a very fake and obvious cough.

5. GAI

A year and a half ago, I busted a corrupt businesswoman in Xuhui.

It's a Shanghai neighborhood best known for its restaurants, cafés, and bars. Not quite the hipster hangout like the Cool Docks, it is a place to be seen.

The businesswoman, Mrs. Song, was at Neon Noir Café to do an under-the-table payoff to a shady builder. They'd been working on an apartment complex in the Old City, and Mrs. Song didn't like all the red tape that was slowing it down. She'd invested a ton of money into the project, and she wasn't going to let a little thing like poisonous drywall derail their progress.

But I was.

I was able to get footage of the payoff and even crisp audio but only because I wasn't tucked away in a ventilation shaft or dangling from a rooftop. I was close, only inches away, **hiding in plain sight**.

Mrs. Song had gotten tipped off by someone to be careful, that the notorious Painted Wolf might try to target her, and so she had some of her people sweeping the streets, the buildings, and the rooftops. Only reason they didn't find me is because they were looking too hard for a problem. I walked into the café and, pretending to be a waitress, brought Mrs. Song her drink and bill. She never once looked me in the face, never once saw the cameras on my lapel or the microphone stuck to the bottom of her coffee mug.

We were going to do the same exact thing at Kennedy airport. Getting Tunde on the flight wasn't going to require us crawling through tunnels and breaching security. The way we'd do it would be simple:

We would walk in because no one would expect us to.

As Rex worked on his cell, busily typing away, Teo's earbuds in, Tunde and I talked through our approach. I wanted Rex to know what our plan was and weigh in on it, but he was more intensely focused than usual. I have no doubt that if the train crashed, he'd have barely noticed.

"The airport's full of cameras," I told Tunde. "I think we can use the jammer, but it wouldn't work for long, and it's likely to bring us more attention than we'd like. Maybe we go in as stripped down as possible? Sometimes, when the stakes are highest, the simplest, most direct approach is the best."

"So we wear the costumes from the duffel bag," Tunde said. "What about security? Are we not going to have a problem getting the jammer through?"

"Possibly. What instructions were you given? Just show up for the flight?"

"Yes," Tunde said. "But I suspect it will not be that easy."

"How so?"

"The general will want to ensure my return," Tunde said. "He will likely have someone waiting for me at the airport. Possibly at the gate."

"If so," I said, "we can use that. If not, we'll invent someone. There are two changes of clothes in the bag. I suggest we change again after we've gotten through security. The passports will get us through, but there's still the matter of tickets."

"And the matter of my passport not matching my ticket." Tunde smiled.

"Not a problem," Rex said, looking up from his cell. He pulled the earbuds out and held up his cell phone. "I've got good news and even better news."

"We are all ears," Tunde said.

"I got Mobo, Damian, ugh, and Chen one-way tickets to Lagos."

"Fantastic." Tunde clapped.

"You said you have even better news?" I asked.

Rex swiped the screen to show us a series of confirmation e-mails. "I got all of us, well, our doppelgängers, approved through TSA precheck. It was a little tricky 'cause you're not U.S. citizens but, hey, I'm a professional."

"You can do that but not take over the airport's system?" I asked.

"Are you kidding me?"

I elbowed Rex and he laughed.

"Anyway, this'll get us on board," Rex said. "But how exactly can we get the jammer on the plane without the cops coming down on us like lightning?"

"We're **not going to hide** the jammer. We'll be putting it front and center."

That gave both Rex and Tunde pause.

Tunde said, "Please tell me we are not going to be pretending to be police officers. That is even crazier than something Rex would come up with."

"We won't be cops," I said. "And baggage handlers can't get the jammer on board; they'd be picked up and hauled out of the airport in a second. It's too obvious."

"So we disguise ourselves as Homeland Security officials. Hard core," Rex said, convinced he had just beaten me to the punch. It was cute.

"And impossible." I shot him down. "What we need is the flight manifest for Tunde's plane to Lagos. Think you can get it?"

Rex jumped onto his cell.

"I'm pulling up the manifest. Who are we looking for exactly?"

"Show it to Tunde," I said. "He'll know."

Rex handed Tunde the phone and he scrolled down through the names of the passengers on the flight. "I am not sure who exactly I am supposed to be looking for," he said, "but I assume I will know when I see his or her name."

"Just keep looking," I said.

The train was slowing as it approached Kennedy. Rex loaded the very last gel disk into the reader as the other passengers stood and gathered their belongings. I didn't want to rush Tunde as he looked over the list but we were running short on time. The second the train reached the last platform we'd need to be ready to go.

"Anything?" I prodded.

"Yes, here at the bottom." Tunde held up Rex's cell so we could see the screen. He'd highlighted a single name.

Lieutenant General Hakeem Abacha.

"This must be the man," Tunde said as he handed the phone to Rex. "He works with the general and I have heard his name before. He will surely be the one to meet me."

"Here's the deal," I said. "Tunde, your flight is at eight p.m. tonight. Lieutenant Abacha will be there waiting for you, but you're not going to arrive alone. You'll be escorted by two business partners, young investors you met at the Game looking to put money into a genius with amazing future plans. How does that sound?"

"Sounds like it won't work," Rex said. "Just being honest."

"Agreed. Why is Abacha going to believe us?" Tunde asked.

"My friend Hee-Jon will convince him. He's an actor, incredible with voices," I said. "If we get into a bind with Abacha, we'll call Hee-Jon."

"Who is Hee-Jon?" Tunde asked.

"Yeah? Why can't Nigel help again?" Rex smirked.

"A friend of mine, okay," I said, not letting him have his jealous moment. "I sent Hee-Jon a text while we were at Mr. Tan's. He'll be ready and standing by. Believe it or not, there are quite a few videos of General Iyabo giving speeches online for him to study."

"I believe it," Tunde said. "He is a glory hog. Is that the expression?"

"It's glory hound," Rex said. "But hog has a better ring to it."

"And what about the security cameras?" Tunde asked as the train approached the airport station. "Airports are the most heavily monitored places in the United States. Not only will they be watching for us, they will no doubt have facial recognition software activated. Even with costumes, we will be seen."

"If it's tech," I said, "we can fool it. There's no artificial intelligence in existence today that can't be spoofed. And simply."

"I would beg to differ," Rex said.

I was pushing his buttons. I needed him riled up, because he thought better when he had his back against the wall. During the Game, he did his best work when he knew he had to fight. Getting through Kennedy and onto that plane was going to take us all working at the bleeding edge of our abilities.

I unzipped the duffel bag and pulled out sunglasses and baseball caps. I handed one to each of the guys, then put on my own.

"Just temporary," I said. "**Follow my lead**."

The train arrived at the platform.

The doors whooshed open.

Everything after that was a blur. I led us down the ramp into the upper floor of the airport. We dodged passing police officers, ducking in and out of the crowd.

"To your left, bathrooms."

Before Rex and Tunde could go into the men's room, I pulled them aside and motioned them to follow me into the family changing room. If transforming myself into Painted Wolf required some serious skill, turning Tunde into Mobo and Rex into Damian might just take a miracle.

The room was fairly cramped but we weren't going to be in it for long.

I opened the duffel bag and pulled out a suit for Rex.

It was gray and very businesslike. Bland, frankly. But it would do the job. I handed it to him along with a light blue button-up shirt and a silver tie.

"It's like Halloween when I dressed up like a dork," Rex said.

"Shush," I said. "Just put it on."

Next I grabbed Tunde's clothes. A T-shirt, knit sweater, and blue jeans. There were also some high-top sneakers that Rex eyed as I pulled them from the bag.

"Nice," he said. "Mobo is apparently a fashionable cat."

"Of course." Tunde grinned.

The guys got changed.

"No peeking," Rex said, and he spun me around.

I wanted to give them some privacy, but the room was small and there were mirrors. Even though I was wearing sunglasses, I closed my eyes.

But my heart was racing.

Rex was two feet behind me, slipping into a new shirt. He and Tunde were laughing, and it took everything in me not to peek. I clenched my eyes closed and remembered that we were breaking the law, that we were a few minutes from **socially engineering** our way through one of America's busiest airports. Still the ensuing twenty-five seconds felt like twenty-five years.

"How do I look?" Rex finally asked, spinning me back around.

"Like a big dork," I said.

I was lying. He looked great. I was so used to seeing Rex in his standard uniform of T-shirts and jeans, looking very much like the teenager he was, that seeing him dressed maturely threw me for a few seconds. The suit fit him so well that I knew we could pull this off.

"And me?" Tunde asked. "How does Mobo look?"

"Mobo looks amazing," I said.

"What's next?" Rex asked.

"Wigs," I said.

I pulled the two wigs from the duffel bag. Rex's was slick, cut long on top and shorter on the bottom. He pulled it on and immediately tried to pull the bangs back.

"No," I said. "The bangs are the whole point. They're extra long and you need to keep them hanging in front of your face. I know it's goofy. Facial recognition software works by measuring the distances between your eyes, your mouth, and nose. If you have something, like hair, blocking one of them, it can fool the cameras. We'll only need it through security."

I took the next two minutes to get Rex's wig properly fitted and glued down. He squirmed and complained like a little kid, but when I was finished it looked quite impressive. So impressive that he stood staring into the mirror for a few seconds and nodded slowly. "Wolf," he said, "you are a miracle worker. I look like a stud."

"Now you just have to sell it," I joked.

Next up was Tunde. The second wig had long, tight dreadlocks. He laughed when I pulled it out and made a joke about being Rasta. Still, it fit him, and by the time I had it on, he was **transformed**. Tunde posed in the mirror and made silly faces. "I am not going to lie," he said. "I quite like this look."

"How about you, Wolf?" Rex asked.

He narrowed his eyes and gave me a smoldering look from behind his long bangs. Rex couldn't keep it up, though, and started snickering.

"The name's Chen," I said as I opened the door and pushed Rex and Tunde out into the hallway. "Time to step out, boys."

5.2

With the boys gone and the door locked, I tossed my shades, pulled off my wig, pulled out the earrings and the nose ring, and then used a wet paper towel to wipe as much of my makeup off as I could.

Then, with my hair down and my contacts sitting on the side of the sink beside me, I leaned in and looked at my face, *my real face*, for the first time in forever.

I didn't recognize myself.

I knew the eyes but they weren't as sharp. And I knew the smile, even if I was faking it just for my reflection. But when the pieces were put together, I didn't know the girl I was looking at.

I instantly felt sick to my stomach.

At home, I was a student. I helped my mother in the kitchen. I did the crosswords with my father. We went on family walks, saw the latest exhibits at the museum, and enjoyed reading on the porch together. I went out to dinner with my friends and cousins. We talked about politics, grades, shoes, food, and boys.

Painted Wolf was a secret that I kept.

She wasn't a person. She was a myth. Painted Wolf posted online in obscure forums and banned websites. She wore ridiculous outfits and sneaked into buildings late at night. She was a force of nature without a face. She was an avenging angel with no backstory and no ambition outside of honesty.

Painted Wolf wasn't me.

I wondered if I'd ever go back.

Not to my family or my home; of course I'd go back to them. But could I easily return to my old life? Could I put Painted Wolf into the drawer I pulled her out of? I doubted it. Even if I did, I knew she wouldn't stay there.

Despite all the makeup and the costume jewelry and the silly clothes, being Painted Wolf for this long changed me. The costume sank under my skin; her fierce personality bruised the edges of my own. Where she stopped—once as easy to delineate as the frames of her sunglasses—and where I began was now hopelessly blurred. I realized the question wasn't Who is Painted Wolf?

It had become: Who is Cai?

Painted Wolf versus Cai

I closed my eyes and only one thought made my stomach stop churning: I had to put the makeup back on. I had to put on the wig and the sunglasses. I had to put in the earrings and wear the fake nose ring.

With it off, I was wearing a Cai costume, a Cai mask.

The only way we'd finish this thing, defeat the general, save Tunde's people, stop Kiran, and get back home in one piece, was if we were all focused 110 percent. Cai couldn't focus that hard. She'd miss her home, miss her friends, miss her normal life, but Painted Wolf was a ghost.

I was a ghost.

I put the costume back on slowly. But it wasn't a costume anymore. The wig was my real hair. The makeup was my real skin. Staring in that tiny bathroom mirror, I knew that I might never be Cai again. When this was over and I went home, I would go home as Painted Wolf. There was no turning away from it.

And I realized: I was perfectly happy with that.

In fact, it made me smile.

5.3

I emerged into the hallway in full Painted Wolf mode.

Tunde clapped slowly as Rex looked me over. There was a slight smile playing at the corner of his lips. "So?" I asked. "Think it's believable?"

"Most definitely," Rex said.

"He means you looks amazing," Tunde added.

"Isn't anything you haven't seen before," I said.

"It's the way you sell it," Rex said. "You actually look like you could be a wanted international criminal mastermind. Badass, Wolf. *Badass.*"

I couldn't help myself. I leaned over and gave Rex a kiss on the cheek and watched him blush. "Let's go."

Our first stop was the information desk.

"I need to page someone," I told the bored man behind the counter. "It is extremely urgent."

The man barely raised his head. "Name?"

"Lieutenant General Hakeem Abacha," Tunde said.

"Ay-bah-cha?" the man asked, mispronouncing the name.

"No," Tunde clarified. "Ah-bah-cha."

The man nodded and picked up a telephone. He then paged Lt. Gen. Hakeem Abacha over the airport speaker system. The lieutenant general was instructed to meet us at the information desk.

Rex watched the monitors, scanning for Tunde's departing flight, while Tunde and I placed the gel-disk bag into the case with the jammer. There wasn't much room, and I was worried they'd be dug out during our security check, but it was better than nothing. Rex noticed what we were doing.

"Why don't we just find a locker here?" he said. "Put them in?"

"When will we be back?" I asked him. "We have to take them with us."

"But if they get found . . ."

"We've gotten this far," I said. "We'll find a way."

A short, furious man who charged toward us, waving his hands, interrupted us. He wore a Nigerian army uniform and a black beret. Abacha, no doubt. He walked alongside a huge man who looked more like a weight lifter than a soldier.

"What is the meaning of this?" Lt. Gen. Abacha barked.

"We have been asked to escort Tunde Oni to his flight," I said.

Abacha couldn't believe my insolence. He stood there, blinking, before he glanced over to his guard.

"Absurd," the guard said, shaking his head.

"Under what authority?" Lt. Gen. Abacha barked again.

"General Iyabo's," I replied. "We're business investors. We have partnered with Tunde on a project the general is quite interested in learning more about. Don't tell me you weren't aware we were coming along?"

"Outlandish!" the lieutenant general fumed.

I could feel the first pinpricks of sweat at the back of my neck. I glanced over at Rex; his left hand was shaking but he stayed cool.

"This is a Nigerian military affair," Abacha said. "You have no jurisdiction here. I have not been informed of your arrival or involvement."

The lieutenant general turned to Rex.

Rex opened his mouth to speak but I interrupted.

"I don't understand why that would be the case," I said, acting as though I was just as flustered as the lieutenant general. "But if it is a serious concern, I suggest you call General Iyabo and explain the situation to him."

"Where is his letter of authorization?"

"We were not given a letter. Please, talk to the general yourself."

I motioned for Rex to hand me his cell; he did, though he looked a bit anxious. I dialed a number and then held the cell out for Abacha. He didn't take it right away and we could hear ringing on the other end.

Ring . . . Ring . . .

Then a deep, familiar voice: "Hello?"

Lt. Gen. Abacha snatched the cell from my hand and put it to his ear. As soon as he did, he turned very pale and swallowed hard before he spoke.

"Hello. General? Yes, I am here," the lieutenant general said into the cell. "These people tell me— Yes. Yes, of course. But you do understand . . ."

Abacha looked momentarily as though he might faint.

"Yes, General. I—I understand. No, General. I would never question **your authority**. And certainly . . . certainly not on matters of such importance . . . Yes, General. It is done. You can be confident in that."

Lt. Gen. Abacha hung up and handed the cell back to me.

"Come," he said.

Abacha and the muscleman escorted us through security. All it took was a waving of a diplomatic badge and the lines parted. We passed through the metal detectors while TSA staff inspected the jammer. If they had any concerns about the equipment, they didn't show it.

Abacha escorted us all the way to the gate and then handed Tunde a ticket he produced from a billfold in his jacket.

"General Iyabo has asked me to leave you for your flight," Lt. Gen. Abacha said. "Please do let the general know that I apologize again for my insubordination. I think only of his security and safety at all times."

Lt. Gen. Abacha shook our hands and he and his guard departed. They did not look back once. As soon as they were out of earshot, Tunde and Rex both turned to me, eyes wide with amazement.

"Hee-Jon is a genius," Rex said.

"Yeah," I said with a wink. "*Almost* as awesome as Nigel."

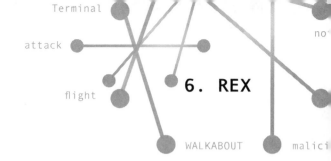
Terminal

attack

no

flight

6. REX

WALKABOUT

malici

Painted Wolf had really outdone herself.

But I saved the best for last.

Not only did I hack our way into getting free tickets on a flight that easily would have bankrupted my parents but I got us insanely comfortable first-class seats. We each had our own leather-and-metal seat that felt more like a couch.

Seriously, it wouldn't have been hard to get lost in the thing.

And it reclined.

Not like a few inches back to smash into the knees of the person behind you but like all the way back. It actually turned into a bed. The flight attendants even handed out duvets and pillows. A flying hotel!

I can't tell you how relieved I was we'd made it. I pulled the wig off my head and shoved it into the seat pocket. My head itched like crazy. I wondered how Painted Wolf put up with wearing something like that all the time. Would drive me crazy.

After all the ridiculous stress of running, the crushing disappointment of finding Teo's apartment empty.

I needed a break.

I needed to let my heart slow to the normal number of beats per minute. I needed my adrenaline to subside. I needed to breathe.

As the plane took off, I looked over at Tunde.

He'd also taken off his wig and was staring out the window, totally focused on the night city just beyond.

Painted Wolf was relaxed.

Even though I couldn't see them behind the dark lenses of her sunglasses, I was pretty certain she had her eyes closed. Good for her; she'd kicked butt all day. Thinking back over it, I still had no idea how Painted Wolf had worked it all out so smoothly.

I tell you all this 'cause I should have been resting, too.

But I couldn't.

The minute my pulse slowed and my adrenaline went back to six micrograms per deciliter, my mind revved back up. As soon as the plane leveled off, I pulled out all Teo's notes, the gel disks and reader, and the sticky drives from the jammer case to go over them. I made a mental note to put them in my bag when I was done. Couldn't risk letting General Iyabo get ahold of them.

I needed to know just what exactly Teo had left behind.

I tried to get the sticky drives to run on my cell but it was too slow. I glanced back at Tunde to find he'd already been watching me. "Need help?" he asked.

Each seat had a touch-screen monitor. There were games, maps, and a few hundred movies and TV shows available. You could even bring up live-cams mounted on the outside of the plane to see the darkness around us. But underneath it all, the thing was basically a tablet computer. With the right adjustments, we could get to the guts underneath.

For Tunde, it took only fifty-six seconds.

Using the reconfigured touch screens, we scanned through the sticky drives.

What was obvious almost immediately was that the bulk of the files had to do with Terminal. There were chat logs, transcripts of phone conversations, snippets of malicious code, and attack plans.

Problem was, they were all months old.

Behind that, there were reams of information on Teo's biological tech work. He had twenty different folders charting the development of the biological data storage systems and the gel disk reader, and hundreds of gigs of data about a presumably unfinished project related to "self-manifesting artificial intelligence" and "spontaneous cognitive evolution in inorganic systems."

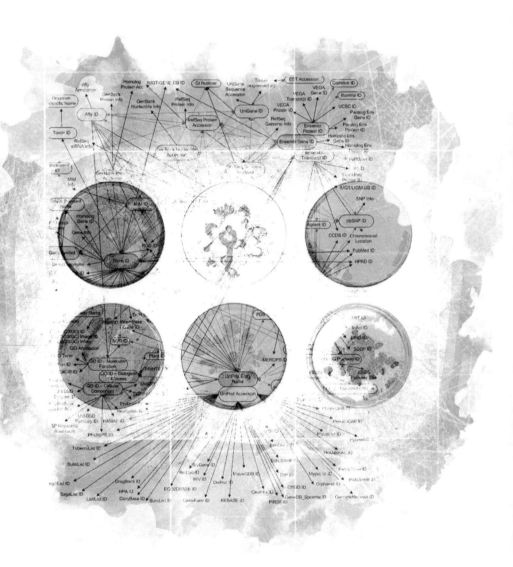

The biological data storage system

I turned to Tunde. "The problem is, the stuff he was working on . . . You can't develop technology like this without a lot of capital."

"Kiran?" Tunde asked.

"No," I said. "There's no way it was Kiran. It had to be Terminal."

My first stop online was a search for any patents Teo might have filed about the gel disk technology or the gel reader itself. Even if he was working the shadows, I knew my brother well enough to know he'd try to maintain some sort of proprietary right over any breakthroughs. Then again, I'd done this search many, many times before and come up empty.

Sure enough, I found some entries.

Dated only a few months earlier.

Thing was: I barely looked at them.

My attention was drawn to the third link that popped up. It was a news article, just a few lines snatched from an AP story about the LODGE's "epic hack."

It said my parents had been deported to Mexico.

6.1

The next few minutes were a blur.

Tunde could tell something was wrong 'cause I slumped back in my seat and my face just fell completely slack.

"What is wrong, brother?"

I couldn't answer him; I just motioned with my head to the monitor.

Tunde skimmed the article and then turned to me, shaking his head.

"*Omo*," he said, "I do not know what I can say. . . ."

This was entirely my fault.

All of it.

My whole life, I've only ever wanted to make things good. To make them right. For my brother, my parents, my neighbors, and my friends. I looked out at the world and I saw it needed fixing.

I figured I could do that.

I could fix it.

But what I didn't realize, what I was completely blind to, was the true nature of our world: Every action has a reaction. That phrase always sounded like something on a poster that high school guidance counselors hung on the back of their doors; an aphorism for the simple, the distressed.

I thought I was above it.

Immune to it.

The way I figured, the world is what you made it.

If you took the wheel and had really good directions, you could drive yourself to a better life. But it just wasn't that easy.

Everything I had tried to make better actually got worse.

Sure, Tunde had won the Game, but now what?

Tunde's people weren't free yet, and we were on a plane carrying a powerful weapon to a maniac. And Cai's family was probably worried sick about her. Teo was still missing, and now I was back to square one in the search for him.

And now, now Ma and Papa were deported.

I imagined my parents in Mexico. I was sure they would have gone to my aunt Valeria's house. And even though I knew she was taking good care of them, I also knew that my mama's tears hadn't dried.

I wanted to call them and apologize.

To tell them that I didn't mean for it to happen.

That I was so sorry for everything.

But that wasn't true.

I was caught up in this make-believe world where we could run around like international spies and there'd be no consequences. We could cheat, we could steal, we could break the law, and we could get away with it.

Why?

Because we're smarter than everyone else.

Or at least we've been told that.

And I bought into it hook, line, and sinker.

My parents paid the price for my foolishness. I thought I could do whatever I wanted and get my brother back and then everything would be fine.

Everything would return to the normal I knew before.

But what I didn't get was that my normal was gone.

Teo took it when he left two years ago.

"Rex." Painted Wolf snapped me out of my defeatist reverie.

She leaned down in the aisle next to my seat.

"You okay?" she asked.

I wasn't sure how to answer that.

"Listen," she said. "I know things have been insane the past few days—"

"Past few weeks."

"But your parents are okay. Tunde showed me the article. They're in Mexico and they're safe. And even though that's devastating, it's important. Because what comes next is going to make all the difference."

I sat up, rubbed my eyes, and then turned and looked at Painted Wolf. She lowered her sunglasses. We locked eyes as she reached over and squeezed my hand.

"What does come next?" I asked her.

"That's the beautiful thing," she said. "Right at this moment, we're on our way to get Tunde's village back. It's one chess move away from getting yours back. In China, we have a concept we know as *yuanfen*. Destiny. But not the sort you understand in Western culture. In China, fate, destiny, *yuanfen* is interactive. It is closer to synchronicity. Meaningful coincidences."

"I don't believe in fate."

"Neither do I. But I do believe in opportunity. Your parents' deportation happened because we won the Game. We changed our stars, we pushed ourselves to chase our dreams and not just blindly accept what was given to us. Change begets change. Good sometimes generates bad. But it works in the opposite direction, too."

Painted Wolf paused.

She was getting too cryptic.

"This will only make you stronger," Wolf said. "Of course you know how a diamond forms. It's heat and pressure. Some dinosaur way back in the Cretaceous choked to death on a bone and her body turned to dust. That dust hardened over the ensuing three hundred million years and became coal. But the earth wasn't done yet; it piled on layer after layer, and the heat and the pressure skyrocketed. Stuck in that vise, there was only one way to go: *in*. So the coal collapsed, tighter and tighter. Until, after another nearly incomprehensible period of time, it was hacked from the stone as a diamond—a crystal structure of impossible strength."

Painted Wolf was right: All the heat and pressure of the past two days?

I had to take it in. There was no other way to go.

I was going to make all my disappointment and rage and sadness and hurt into something no one could break.

Some of us face the incomprehensible and we shrink away from it, broken into a million pieces, but not me.

I am a diamond.

6.2

"We need a plan."

I called Tunde and Painted Wolf over to my seat after I lowered it into the bed position. They piled on beside me and I dimmed the lights so we could have an impromptu planning session.

Everyone else in first class was asleep or watching TV, so even though we were surrounded by people on a plane thirty-seven thousand feet over the Atlantic, it felt like we were alone.

"I've already built a back door into the machine so we can shut it down remotely," I began. "But we still have a bigger problem. The general isn't going to pull his nose out of Tunde's life just 'cause the jammer breaks. We need a game plan on defeating him. Tunde, give us a better picture of your village. What do we have to work with?"

"We will be in rural Nigeria, in the most beautiful village you have ever seen. A place surrounded by the finest natural wonders in western Africa. And the sweetest people you will ever have the opportunity to know. But we will also be as far from proper communication systems as is the bottom of the sea. Even though I have developed a small electrical grid and limited Wi-Fi access, it is very spotty. My people are subsistence farmers; they do not know much of the world beyond our valley. And General Iyabo is no mustache-twirling movie bad guy. He is a brute who will not hesitate to shoot us down like dogs if we upset him."

"Does he live nearby?" Painted Wolf asked.

"No," Tunde said. "He will come from the south. He will bring his men and sweep into Akika Village to claim the jammer and impress everyone with his brilliance."

"And if he's impressed," I said, "he'll just keep coming back."

"I am afraid so."

Painted Wolf stepped in. "We can't defeat General Iyabo," she said, "but we can make him defeat himself."

"How is that?" Tunde asked.

"Sun Tzu said in *The Art of War* that 'our defeat lies in our own hands. But the enemy will provide the opportunity to defeat themselves.' So we should put ourselves in a position to ensure we

68

cannot be beaten. Then, we wait, and take the general down when he takes a risk."

"I like it," I said. "But how do we apply it?"

"The answer is Tunde. . . ."

"Me?"

"Why did the general come to your village?"

"Because he had heard rumors about my engineering skills."

Painted Wolf shook her head. "I hate to disappoint you, but it was because he needed you to build the jammer for him. It wasn't a coincidence that you were invited to the Game at the very same time he needed a jammer."

"So my invitation . . ." Tunde looked very upset.

"You would have been invited anyway," I said, cushioning the blow.

Painted Wolf continued. "But I have no doubt that the timing was intentional. Kiran and General Iyabo work together; they're partners. The bigger question is why did General Iyabo go to you to build the jammer?"

"Because no one else could," Tunde said.

"Hang on," I interrupted. "The general's working with Kiran. He's got access to whatever Kiran has. No offense, Tunde, but I'm sure Kiran could have whipped up a jammer himself. Or had someone in the 'brain trust' do it. That makes no sense. . . ."

"It does," Painted Wolf said, "if the jammer is meaningless."

That left a black hole in the middle of the conversation.

"Kiran didn't get where he is because he knew people or cheated the system. He's as powerful as he is because he sees the future in other people's actions," Wolf continued. "Kiran's not friends with the general; the general is a tool. Kiran sees where the general is going and somehow, their goals align. It is the same with you, Tunde. The general had you build the jammer to prove you could do it. I don't know what else he has planned, but whatever it is, it will involve you and your village."

"But how can you know this?" Tunde asked.

"Intuition," Painted Wolf said. "Game theory. We make the general make a mistake. Tunde, you've told us he's a boastful, greedy person. We force him into making a choice that turns his allies against him."

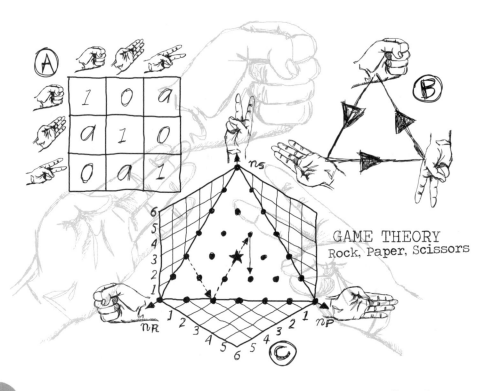

GAME THEORY
Rock, Paper, Scissors

Game theory

"Kiran?" I asked.

"Or his own men," Painted Wolf said.

"I like this plan." Tunde grinned. "This Sun Tzu knew what he was doing."

"So who are we?" I asked.

"Investors. People impressed with Tunde's performance at the Game," Painted Wolf said. "We are businesspeople who know a good thing when we see it. The general is betting on Tunde coming up with some next-level, breakthrough technology. We're going to tell the general that Tunde has invented something spectacular and we want him to be a part of it. For this to work, though, we have to be incredibly thorough. The general will check up on us, I'm sure of it. So, Rex, we'll need social media sites and paper trails. We need to look successful, like real up-and-coming investors. Give us electronic histories that will make the general salivate."

"Putting aside this spectacular tech and the fake histories, which won't be a problem," I said, "where does all this get us?"

"Once he buys into our project and brings his partners on board, we'll get him to do the one thing he never does: cross the border."

"What are you talking about?" I asked.

Tunde slow clapped, very impressed. "General Iyabo is a wanted man," Tunde said. "He has been convicted of war crimes by an international court, but his friends in the Nigerian military and government refuse to extradite him. If he ever leaves the country he is at risk of being deported. So he never leaves."

"And we're going to make him leave?"

Painted Wolf nodded. "It will be the biggest con we've ever pulled. We're going to have to convince him to step over the border into Benin."

"It is the neighboring country," Tunde added. "Only twenty miles distant."

"But the guy's not a fool," I said, confused at where this was going. "He's obviously going to know if he's crossing the border. I mean, even if there are no signs or landmarks or whatever, he's

71

an Internet scammer. The dude's good with tech. He'll have GPS and . . ."

It took me a few seconds to get the plan, but the minute I said "GPS," everything became clear. Watching the realization spread across my face made Painted Wolf grin. I started nodding wildly.

This was so crazy it just might work.

"We somehow get him to go in the direction of the border and not realize he's actually crossed it," I said, thinking aloud. "We'll screw up the satellite coordinate and actually move the border over on his GPS."

"Then we'll have UN troops waiting on the other side," Painted Wolf said.

"And if we can get the general to buy in, maybe he'll bring along his partners. . . ."

"Kiran . . . ," Tunde said. "I like this plan. But what are we going to put on the other side of this moving border that will make him want to travel? It will have to be something truly spectacular."

Painted Wolf thought for a second, then said, "Tunde's next-level project will be the appetizer. We're going to flip the tables and have them coming to us. We hint at something bigger. A game changer. I know how these people work. If we can convince them that we're onto something no one else has, they'll travel to the end of the earth to get a piece of it."

"Basically, you're saying you don't know what it is yet, right?" I said.

Painted Wolf said, "I'm saying I'm figuring it out."

"Can't admit you don't know. Can you?" I grinned.

Painted Wolf sighed. "You kill me, Rex."

"Just keeping everyone on their toes."

"Rex?" Tunde looked to me for the deciding vote. "Are you in? Do you think this plan could work?"

I locked eyes with Painted Wolf and nodded.

"I love it. Wait till you see the electronic paper trails I make for Wolf and me. We're going to be irresistible. Like candy for really, really bad dudes."

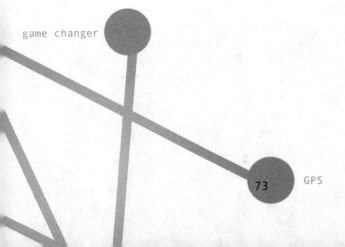

game changer

GPS

PART TWO

OVER THE WIRE

7. TUNDE

My friends, there is nothing quite like coming back home.

In the cartoons and the movies, Africa is this place of wide-open grasslands teeming with giraffes and zebras and elephants. It is a land of sweeping colors that come to life under expansive blue skies, and all the people there dress in rainbow colors and live in thatched huts. Ah, but the people who make these cartoons and movies have never truly been in Africa.

Lagos is as modern a city as you can find in the world. Lagos is a place where palm trees take root in concrete and steel-and-glass buildings soar hundreds of feet high. In the city, there are sixteen million people from every corner of the globe trying to make ends meet. Downtown, where there are cafés and car dealerships, it is bright and shiny like any American urban hub.

"They are taking us the nice route by flying in low," I told Rex as he looked over my shoulder. I pointed to a stretch of squat, crowded buildings shimmering beneath the plane. "That is where most of the people live."

Rex strained to make out houses, stacked side by side along a bridge.

"That is Makoko," I clarified. "It is one of the largest slums in the world."

"That's incredible."

And it was. A veritable labyrinth of narrow streets and clapboard houses.

"Those are not streets you are seeing."

"What do you mean?" Rex asked as we soared past.

"Makoko is a floating slum. Those are houses on stilts above the water."

In Makoko, millions of homes are accessed by tens of thousands of small boats. It is a city on stilts and something of a floating downtown. Not only is it a very impressive engineering feat, it is also startlingly unusual.

"Nigerians are very tenacious people," I told Rex. "There are six villages in this area, all of them merged into the other. People come from the countryside looking for work. Prices in this city are very steep. They cannot afford even a tiny apartment, so they come here to live. They are resourceful. Where there is no land, they find a way to exist."

"Tenacious indeed," Rex said. "Where there's a will . . ."

"There is always a way," I replied.

The plane touched down on the tarmac, and as we returned to the earth, so did the weight of what we were about to face. As the aircraft taxied toward the gate, and the flight attendants made their announcements, I looked out over the greenery and the steel of the distant business towers and readied myself.

When we stepped off the plane, we would be stepping into the hands of the general.

7.1

I was not surprised to find we had a welcoming committee.

General Iyabo no stupid guy-man.

The airport was as bustling as ever, and travelers from every corner of the globe rambled about. I heard at least fifteen different languages in fifteen steps. I was amazed to see how well I handled being surrounded so closely by this many people.

But I paid them little mind; my eyes were on our three new friends.

Two were soldiers and fit the type; they wore fatigues, berets, and mirrored sunglasses. I did not see any weapons on their person, but I was certain that they could appear as quickly as the soldiers wanted them to.

Between the soldiers stood a girl, not much older than myself.

Unlike the soldiers, she was wearing jeans and a T-shirt. She had her hair in colorful braids and was chewing bubble gum very loudly. Large headphones covered her ears and she was nodding along to a steady beat before she noticed us. When she did, she took off the headphones and smiled

"You are the Game champion?" she asked me.

"Yes. My name is Tunde Oni."

This elicited an even bigger grin.

"Tunde," she said, "I am Naya. Naya Iyabo."

I shook her hand and was pleasantly surprised at how friendly she was until I heard her last name. My friends, I was shaking hands with the daughter of General Iyabo! Naya must have noticed my discomfort because she seemed to relish it.

"And your friends here?"

Naya turned as Painted Wolf stepped forward.

"We're Tunde's business partners. I am Chen Jiang and this is Damian Quintanilla. We are here because we have a proposal for the general."

Naya nodded.

"Yes," she said, "I was told you were accompanying Tunde. You both are very highly regarded. I was most impressed with your work with the quantum computers in Asia. You certainly seem to be savvy investors. I am sure you will be quite pleased with what the general envisions for his country."

The false identities that Rex had created for himself and Painted

Wolf were, as he promised, very compelling. If an underling like Naya was this pleased, then surely the general would be as excited by their visit as we hoped.

"Thank you," Rex said. "We're eager to meet him."

"Is that the jammer?" Naya asked, changing the subject.

I nodded.

"Then we can leave," Naya said. "*Let us gerrarahere!*"

As we followed Naya and the troops across the terminal, Naya put her headphones back on and swayed as she walked through the crowds. It was like watching a princess move. The soldiers parted the way for her, and she danced on air as though she owned the ground beneath her feet.

We stepped out of the airport into a wall of equatorial heat.

"Oh man," Rex said. "This is like stepping into a sauna."

He was sweating quite heavily.

"You will get used to it, *omo*. It is good for the skin."

There was a black limo waiting for us.

"Here we are." Naya ushered us inside as the driver took our bags and loaded them into the trunk. Naya, however, took the jammer, climbed into the back of the limo, and sat across from us.

The limo pulled out into traffic but didn't speed up.

"We are doing a loop," Naya told the driver. The driver nodded silently and turned the wheel as the limo began a lazy circuit around the airport. I wondered if he was made to do ridiculous things like this all the time.

"Why are we not going straight to the general?" I asked.

"I need a demonstration that this equipment does what you say."

I balked. "This jammer is very dangerous. . . ."

"Does that matter to me?" Naya snarled. "It better be."

A lump gathered in my throat as I turned the jammer on.

Jammer

Lights flickered across its control board.

My friends, I can truly tell you that at that very moment I was petrified. Even though the jammer would not do the things the general wanted it to do, it was still as dangerous as an atom bomb. I had built a weapon and I did not want to use it.

"It is on," I said. "Now you see that it works."

Naya pulled off her headphones and grabbed the jammer from me. "I see it has lights and looks real enough. But how do I know you have not built an explosive to kill my father?"

"I would never—"

"Never want to kill him?" She laughed. "You would be the first."

"I would never want to take that risk," I clarified. "The general is with my family, my people in Akika Village. It is in their best interest that I do everything as the general commands."

"Certainly is," Naya said, looking somewhat satisfied. "But I still need to see this contraption function. We will drive here, in circles, until you show me."

"But we are at an airport," I said.

"This is a GPS jammer," Rex jumped in, trying to clarify what was at stake. "If you turn this on, it will block all the GPS signals at this airport. There are planes taking off and landing. You could cause an air disaster."

Naya leaned forward and smacked her gum.

"Tunde, your friend here is questioning my judgment."

I laughed nervously. "He is from the States and has embraced that cowboy attitude. Re—I mean, Damian, we have this under control, okay?"

My friends, I came very close to blowing our cover and was thankful that Naya did not appear to catch my slipup.

"Go on," Naya said. "Show me what this jammer of yours can actually do."

Naya reached over and grabbed a radio from the soldier next to her. She flicked her way through static-filled stations until she found air traffic control.

" . . . *you are clear to carry on descending. Bit of cloud here with a base of two thousand feet but a higher layer above that. . . .*"

The air traffic controller spoke quickly and his voice filled the limo.

"Go on," Naya pressed.

Omo. I hesitated for a nerve-shredding second. My finger was balanced above the amplification button and I did not know if I could possibly hit it. I do not know how I could live with myself if a plane crashed because of my machine. But what choice did I have? As my finger remained paused there, Naya glanced over to one of the soldiers. He leaned forward, hand on his hip.

And so, with my throat as dry as the sands of the Kalahari, I pressed the amplification button on the jammer. Rex, Painted Wolf, and I all braced ourselves.

" *. . . the hell just happened!*" The air traffic controller broke into a panic. "*We just lost GPS. . . . Oh my God, quick, Charlie, get the planes. . . . I need all flights inbound to Lagos to do 360. . . . I repeat, do 360. . . . We have lost GPS. . . . Do not attempt landing. . . .*"

The alarm of the air traffic controller increased alongside my pulse.

"There," Naya said, pointing outside.

" *. . . We need all flights inbound on standby. . . . We have lost GPS at the tower. . . . Dubai two six one, I need you on a divergent path. . . . I repeat, we have lost . . .*"

From our vantage point on the ground, we could see up into the low-hanging clouds. There, a jumbo jet, more silhouette than actual plane, cut through the clouds, clearly too low. I wanted to toss the jammer out through the window!

My friends, I was beside myself with terror.

Agonizing seconds passed before I simply could not take it any further. As the jumbo jet roared overhead, I killed the power to the jammer.

"There," I said to Naya, winded. "You have confirmation."

Still my friends and I cringed, waiting for what would surely be the apocalyptic sound of crashing planes.

Thank God nothing happened.

Instantly relieved, the air traffic controller struggled to make sense of what just happened. *"Back online, GPS is back. . . . Everyone okay? . . . That was too close. . . ."*

Painted Wolf sighed loudly.

She had been holding her breath the whole time.

Naya turned off the radio.

"The general will be satisfied," she said.

Then Naya signaled to the driver. "Take us to Akika Village."

7.2

The streets were choked with traffic.

Cars of every make and model vied for space with hundreds of motorbikes and repurposed American trucks.

It seemed like everyone in Lagos was on the road.

The limo was jostled this way and that. I tried to calm my nerves as we took the expressway toward Akika Village. But it was very difficult. I noticed that when I closed the lid on the jammer, my hands were shaking wildly. Naya also saw and had a chuckle at my weakness. Painted Wolf, a truly good person, placed her hand on my shoulder and squeezed it.

It was like an instant shot of relaxant.

"You're going home now," Wolf whispered.

She was right. I was going home.

I was only familiar with this route from my limited experiences crammed into the back of a *danfo*. There was not much for me to see: farms, the splash of green as we drove past stands of trees, and the small buildings that crowded the intersections. In a *danfo*, you are one of the common people, crowded in, sweating buckets, and sick from the choking smell of leaking diesel.

This time, however, I was seeing the world as the general saw it.

The road was not as bumpy as I recalled it, for the limo had new tires and expensive shock absorbers. It was more like flying than it was like driving. And the view? My friends, I was seeing my country as I had never seen it before.

It seemed the driver thought only of our comfort.

He avoided every pothole and took each turn as smoothly as though he was gilding a flower. But, of course, he was not doing this for our benefit. He was merely following orders and driving, as the general had demanded of him.

And the poor citizens who dared get in our way!

Omo, that limo driver did not turn the car once. He nearly bowled over a man on a bicycle, ran through five red lights, and honked mercilessly at a group of schoolchildren crossing the street.

Rex, Painted Wolf, and I protested at every incident but it was no use. Naya, in fact, seemed to enjoy the tension. She relished each and every grimace we made when the limo nearly struck someone.

"You should be sitting back and relaxing," Naya told us.

"It is hard to relax when we are riding inside a missile," I replied. Naya laughed this off.

It was near sunset when we reached familiar roads.

We turned from the pavement onto the gravel roads and then from the gravel roads to the rough dirt tracks. Even though the sun was low in the sky and there were roiling clouds of dust obscuring the horizon, I knew my land the second it passed into view. The thin iroko trees, the swaying stalks of kyasuwa grass, and the burnt orange of the earth.

"Your people will be very glad to see you," Naya said, closely monitoring my visible happiness.

"Yes," I said. "Before my recent journey, I had never been gone longer than a single night."

The limo suddenly veered left and then right before it slowed and the driver leaned in on the car horn. Naya, greatly aggrieved, turned around, furious.

"Why are we stopping?"

"There," the driver said, pointing ahead. "Someone is blocking the road."

I leaned forward and saw a familiar face lit up by the headlights. It was an old woman wearing the traditional *iro*, a garment that is wrapped around the waist, and top with matching headgear and a colorful shawl. Her name was Werey and she was something of a legend in our village.

"Run that crone down!" Naya shrieked.

"No!" I shouted as I opened the limo door. "No, please. I know her. This is an old woman from my village. She is not right in the head and often wanders."

Naya raised her hand and allowed me to step out of the limo. Immediately, I was struck by an odd smell. The air was thick with smoke as though we were close to an industrial center and not my rural Akika Village.

Ignoring it, I walked over to Werey and said, "Hello."

She looked me over as though I was a stranger.

"I need you to move for your own safety," I said, kindly taking her elbow. "It is very dangerous to walk here. I am traveling with someone who is not accustomed to driving around people out on the road at night."

"I know you." Werey narrowed her eyes.

"Yes," I said. "I am Tunde Oni, from Akika Village."

Werey looked past me and muttered several unprintable curses at the driver of the limo before she allowed me to lead her to the side of the road. The driver honked to hurry me along but before I could, Werey took my hand and held it tight.

"Do not go home," she said.

"Why is that, Werey? I am happy to be home."

"This is not the home you left."

"Has something happened here?"

Werey looked back at the limo and then pulled me very close.

"You can smell it," she said. "You can see it."

"See what?"

"Your village is gone."

Another blast of the car horn and Werey let go.

I waved her good-bye and watched as she stepped out of the light from the headlights and disappeared into the bush.

7.3

Back in the limo, Naya was very curious about Werey.

"Is this crazy woman family to you?" she asked me.

"Werey is the last of her people," I told Naya. "They were a splinter group, broken off of the Wodaabe nomadic people. She lives in the forests around here. My parents once offered to take her in but she refused."

"She is mad."

I turned my head to look back through the rear windshield but Werey was gone, completely swallowed up by the quickly approaching night.

"What sort of person chooses to live in the forest?" Naya said, shaking her head. "That is a senseless woman, and you would do well not to listen to anything she says. You said she is the last of her people. Why do you think that is?"

"I do not know," I replied. "They were gone before I was born."

"It was a rhetorical question," Naya scoffed.

My mother always taught me that there is no such thing as evil in a person. There are people who are born wrong—there is something twisted inside them that makes them do bad things—but those people are rare. Most people we call "bad" are, in fact, people who have suffered and made poor choices. Clearly, finding the good in Naya might take a while.

"What did that old cow say to you?" Naya asked me. "Back there, the two of you were talking. I saw you in the headlights. What was it she said?"

"We were just catching up."

Naya stared at me. This was, apparently, her superpower. She believed that staring at me would compel me to tell her something I did not want to. She was correct. Truly, she was an Iyabo. Her stare was so unnerving and made me so anxious that I immediately crumbled like a poorly behaved child being scolded by their father.

"She warned me that the village was not the same that I had left."

Naya laughed. "What?" she said. "It is not a flyspeck anymore?"

She turned to one of her fellow soldiers for a hearty chuckle. This made me angry but it also had me very worried. What if Werey was right? What if Akika Village had suddenly changed while I was at the Game? It sounded preposterous but anything was possible if someone as devious as the general was involved.

Rex picked up on my anxiety. "Do you remember that code for the solar irradiance sensor I gave you before the Game?"

"Yes," I said. "I never followed up with you on that, did I?"

"It didn't work, did it?"

"No, it did not. I was a little surprised."

"Sorry," Rex said sheepishly. "I was in school. A little distracted. But I figured it out, just now on the ride; I was thinking back through it and I think I got it to work. Maybe when we get to your village, I can reprogram it?"

"Yes," I said. "That would be excellent."

Already Rex had cheered my mood. He was crafty that way.

The limo crested a hill, and we saw Akika Village spread out before us.

I had never seen such a heartbreaking sight.

7.4

My friends, my homecoming was one I never want to remember.

For me, leaving Akika Village was painful.

Returning should have been like having a cool drink of water after a day of trekking across the deserts. My village was part of my soul.

It was always in my thoughts.

But when we drove down the narrow dirt road into Akika Village with Naya and her limo, I did not recognize it as the place where I was born.

I could not believe what I was seeing, *omo*.

At first, I assumed we were in the wrong location. My village was never shrouded in thick smoke even where there were grass fires burning nearby. My village was never a mess of mud and deep tire tracks. It was not home to hundreds of armed soldiers. The streets were not their dumping grounds.

But overnight everything had changed.

Akika Village was no longer an agrarian town where farmers lived with their families, their parents, and their grandparents. Now it was a military outpost. Worse still, it was buzzing with industrial equipment as though an invading force was attempting to scrape it from the very surface of the earth.

I am not ashamed to tell you, my friends, that on that day, I wept like a child. Painted Wolf held my hand as I stared out at what had become of my village and my people. Rex was just as horrified as I was.

But Naya appeared to delight in my suffering.

"Your people have been very busy," she said. "They have come to understand that what sits beneath this village is more important than what is above it."

I calmed my nerves and spoke carefully. "What is below it, Naya?"

"You shall see. I do not want to spoil the surprise."

The driver stopped the limo in the center of my village where the elders used to congregate beneath the oldest shea tree and discuss village politics and the coming seasons. But the tree had been bulldozed and all that remained in its spot was a patch of bloodred earth. I did not see any of the elders.

We climbed out of the car and the very first thing to assault my senses was the acrid tang of burning diesel and a wet scent of upturned earth. I looked about, studying the faces of the soldiers surrounding us, but they told me nothing. These men were here on orders. Some of them were only a few years older than myself. But I do not blame them. Ah, you see, my friends, they were taking care of their families the only way they could—by putting on uniforms, holding rusted guns, and following a madman.

NEVER TRUST IN

"It was not like this when I left," I told Painted Wolf. "Not like this at all."

"I know," Painted Wolf said, "I know."

"Where is my father?" Naya barked to the soldiers standing about.

"He will be back later this evening," one of them told her.

Frustrated, Naya turned to us.

"Come!" she shouted. "I will show you what we do here."

"I would like to see my family first," I said.

"Later. *First*, you see the providence the general has given you."

We climbed into the back of a military jeep.

Naya took the wheel. She was short enough that she had to sit on a helmet to see over the dash, and she ground the gears with every shift of the clutch. We made our way down a narrow, bumpy road through tracts of forest—a road that had not been here a week ago. All the trees we passed were coated in a fine layer of dust. There were no birdcalls and no movement in the underbrush.

"There is something very wrong here," I told Painted Wolf.

A shiver crawled up my spine to the base of my skull. The kind you get when the air pressure drops before a storm is about to break. Or when you wake up in the middle of the night because you heard something move next to your bed. (Sadly, this is not an uncommon occurrence in my village. Usually, it is only a lizard.)

"One day," Naya yelled over the grumble of the jeep, "this will be a two-lane, blacktop road. But I am sure the general will widen it to a three lane when your village becomes a true destination."

The ride took five minutes. The jeep bounced as though it was going to come apart before it ascended a ridge and then clanked to a stop at the crest. The ridge was entirely new. We piled out and Naya led us to the lip of the man-made crater.

The mine below was massive.

A soccer stadium–sized hole was bitten out of the crust of the earth.

What was once jungle and farmland had become an open wound. The soil was rust colored, and ponds of red water sat at the bottom of the mine like pooling blood. Hundreds of people dug with shovels and buckets alongside bulldozers and excavators that crawled along the basin, pushing around piles of rock. The air was thick with belched-out clouds of black smoke. It was truly a scene from a nightmare.

"This was a forest. I caught rabbit and quail here." I could barely speak. Emotion welled up in my eyes and I clenched my jaw. "This is not possible to create in a week."

Naya clapped. "Crazy, right?"

"How did this happen?"

"Boom," Naya said and threw her hands wide. "It helps that the general has access to unorthodox means. You should have seen the explosions. I was scared the sky would catch on fire!"

"No," I said. "That is impossible."

"Your people are hard workers. We had several battalions here, clearing the rubble, starting the pit. Then the machines came in. And then your people. They are eager to work. I am sure it is because they finally have something to do. They have been stuck in this flyspeck village, bored to tears. Now they have a purpose. Now they have a good reason to wake up every morning."

"Our land is barely good enough for farming." I shook my head.

"Nah." Naya grinned, happy to surprise us. "Your land is rich. There is tantalum here. It is a valuable mineral, but that is not why we are mining it."

Naya whistled to a man in a hard hat nearby. The man pulled a small nugget of gray stone from his pocket and handed it to her. It looked like petrified wood or beautiful charcoal. As Naya turned it over in her hands, it flickered, catching the fading light.

"Tantalum," she said.

"Electronics." Painted Wolf turned to me. "It is used in electronics."

"Not just any electronics." Naya handed the tantalum back to the man in the hard hat. "The tantalum is used to make capacitors. A very small amount of this mineral can store a large amount of electrical energy. It is in your cellular phones, in medical devices, in hearing aids and pacemakers, all of those sorts of products. It is very, very valuable, and you, Tunde, are sitting on a deep thread of it."

"So you are selling this to cell phone manufacturers?" Painted Wolf asked. "Must be making quite a nice profit."

"We are not selling it at all. We have a project in Argentina."

As we were leaving, a scuffle broke out between a few of the villagers toiling in the mine and several of the soldiers standing guard. The fight was quickly broken up, but Naya seemed quite irritated.

"They keep interrupting the work," she said.

"You act as though you are surprised," I replied. "You have put my people in this pit to destroy their own land. Of course they will be on edge."

My friends, my stomach was coiled like a serpent in my belly. I was so sick with anger and sadness that I was ready to scream at Naya. It took everything in me to restrain myself from acting in ways that would surely harm our plans.

Oh, but how I wanted to let loose!

"My father says it is this way with all the village people," Naya scoffed. "They do not know how bad they have it until you show them. People are resistant to change; you have to make them understand."

Again, I bit my tongue.

Painted Wolf could see the great strain that I was under and put her hand on my shoulder and gave me a reassuring squeeze. Had the LODGE not been alongside me then, I would surely have lost the little cool I had.

So I formulated a response to Naya that would get us more information.

"A risky approach," I said as we hiked back up the side of the mine. "There are certainly many more villagers here than soldiers. I have seen people the general has brought over from neighboring villages. They have easily doubled the size of Akika Village. If you tip the scales in—"

"Ha!" Naya barked. "My father can quell any disturbance. These people are not organized. They are just emotional and simple. Come, I will show you how we process the mineral. Then, you will wash up and enjoy a dinner with my father."

Over the next twenty minutes, Naya walked us through how the mine worked before we rode back to Akika.

Naya was something of a mystery to me.

She was showing us the mine because she wanted us to know the general was in charge. And she clearly liked being part of that authority. This went beyond impressing us. Either the general had directed her to walk us through the mining operation or she'd taken it upon herself to show us just how much they'd accomplished. No, I figured this was even more complicated: The mine tour was meant to both impress us and also crush Tunde's spirit.

Naya needed to prove to Tunde that he had no control.

I expected Naya to be hardheaded, considering her lineage, but there was a ruthlessness to her that caught me off guard. In game theory, deviations from expected outcomes are to be considered carefully—I wasn't sure if Naya would be a problem or a potential ally.

That sounds funny, but I could tell she wasn't close to her father. It was possible that if she had a bone to pick with the general, maybe we could find enough common ground to work together. I wasn't going to invite her into the fold just then, however. We'd only spent a few hours together and she was hard to read.

Finding her weaknesses was going to be a challenge.

Naya hopped out of the jeep at the general's tent on the outskirts of the village. There were dozens of soldiers milling about, but I didn't catch sight of the general himself. An older soldier with spotty facial hair hopped behind the wheel of the jeep and offered to drive us the rest of the way. He didn't speak English and that opened up our first window to strategize.

As the jeep bucked down the trail, we huddled together.

"We need to change plans," Rex said. "This is . . ."

He didn't need to finish his sentence; we all clearly understood.

Tunde was speechless. Shocked at what he'd seen.

"My poor, poor people," Tunde muttered.

"General Iyabo is a lot more entrenched here than any of us imagined," Rex said. "We're going to have to come up with something a lot bigger than we initially intended."

Rex was right. Though getting Tunde and his people off the general's radar had been our goal from the beginning, it took on a new urgency in light of the dire situation of the mine. This went beyond the jammer and the Game. We needed to ensure that the general's campaign against Akika ended and that he was removed from power. **Topple a corrupt military official?** I was certainly game for that.

"Maybe the general did not come for me," Tunde said, "but for the mineral."

"No," I said, shaking my head. "I don't think it's black and white like that. I think he came for the mineral and for you."

"We came here planning to build something, a machine that would impress the general," Tunde said. "But that was before we discovered what he had done to my village. Now I want to build a machine that will help them. I want to make a machine that will not only impress the general and feed his ego but that will also remove this miserable yoke from my people. I can do that."

"Yes," Rex said. "That's a great idea."

"Perhaps a digging machine," Tunde continued, his focus already shifting to the engineering ahead. "Something that will both work the seam of minerals in the ground and process them simultaneously. That will impress the general and take some of the burden off my people. I am picturing a highwall miner. I can already see how we can make it—"

"Guys, the idea is a good one," I interrupted. "But we still have one glaring problem: We have to get the general over the border into Benin."

"Easy," Rex said. "We have everything we need already. I'll set up a subroutine for the jammer. When we want it to, it'll distort GPS mapping systems nearby so they display an altered topography. Every device within the reach of the jammer will automatically reset its coordinates to two miles *behind* its actual location. It'll happen on every device, so I don't think anyone would notice. That way, we get him near enough the border and he'll go over it without knowing."

"Sounds complicated?" I said.

"I'm just that good." Rex winked.

"So we have the trap," Tunde said. "But what is the bait?"

We all thought about it for a moment.

"The trick is having the general buy into our initiative and not notice we're reeling him and his partners into something that will get them arrested," I said. "So . . . I'll show up to the dinner a little early. If I can sneak into the kitchen while they're prepping the meal, I can score us some information. Something we can use to give us the perfect bait to draw the general in."

"The kitchen?" Tunde was taken aback.

"If you want the inside scoop on anything," I replied, "you go to the waitstaff. Not only do they hear everything, no one ever pays attention to them."

8.1

The dinner was to be held in the home of Akika Village's chief.

I arrived there to find ten women preparing a feast.

Since the general hadn't shown up yet there were no soldiers on the premises. I made my way around the back of the house to where women were cooking over several open fires. The smells were intoxicating and I don't think I'd ever seen so much produce in one place outside of a supermarket.

I was instantly transported back into the kitchen at my parents' apartment. I remembered helping my mother cook meals for my father's business partners. With my mother's voice fresh in my ears, I wanted to join in and focus on making everything just so. But instead of cooking, I was out hunting for information.

One of the women, older with her hair tied up in a bun, motioned for me to join her as she stirred a massive pot bubbling with stew. I kneeled beside her.

"The stew smells amazing. Can I try some?"

The woman pulled the spoon from the pot and handed it to me. She watched me carefully as I blew on the steaming broth before I took a sip. It tasted amazing.

"It's delicious," I said. "I taste . . . Is it palm fruit?"

The woman's eyes lit up. "Yes. It is."

"Delicious. I'm sorry to interrupt but can I ask you a question? I'm a friend of Tunde. We've just arrived in the village."

"Yes, I know the Oni family well," she said. "We are a very small village. If you have a question, go ahead, ask."

"The minerals they're pulling from the mine just over the hill. Can you tell me where they take them?"

The woman glanced at the other cooks, then nodded.

"All I can tell you is that they load the rocks onto trucks and take them that way, to the city."

"And does the general do this alone? Have you seen any other important people arrive? Possibly foreigners?"

"Yes," she said, suddenly even more self-conscious. She leaned in and lowered her voice. "A day or two ago there were several businessmen. They were Chinese. They were not here long, but I cooked a dinner like this for them as well."

"Do you know why they came?"

"No," the old woman said, eyes darting because she was so nervous talking to me. "There are many Chinese companies that come to our country. But they talked about the rocks they are pulling from the ground beneath Akika Village. They are pleased with most of what they are finding, but there is a second mineral they are very eager to find and have not seen yet."

"Can you tell me what they said about this second mineral?"

"That it is very rare. One of the rarest," the woman said. "They told the people in the mine to look for a silver rock. One that shines in the sun."

"Could it have been rhodium?"

"Yes," the old woman said. "That sounds like it."

She glanced over her shoulder to make sure no one was listening in. I had more questions but didn't want to overstay my welcome or get her into trouble.

"Thank you so much," I told her. "Can I ask one last question?"

The old woman nodded her approval.

"Has there ever been a young Indian man here? He's tall, sophisticated?"

"Yes, I have seen him with the general."

"Do they seem to get along well? Does the general like him?"

The woman thought for a minute, then leaned in, growing even more concerned about being overheard. "The general is very nice to this young man," she told me, "but when he left, I overheard the general telling his men that he did not trust the Indian. He thinks the boy will try to cheat him."

This intel was twenty times better than I'd imagined. As soon as the old woman spoke her last words, I knew exactly how we would fool the general and save Tunde's people.

I walked back to the schoolhouse where Tunde and Rex were readying for dinner.

"I have it," I told them. "Our bait for the trap."

"So that whole kitchen thing worked, huh?" Rex asked.

"Don't knock it until you try it."

"What is the bait?" Tunde asked.

"Tunde, can you dig up some scrap cell phones, ones made in the past five years? We need to break them apart and melt the minerals down. I want a nugget of rhodium."

Tunde's eyes went wide. "That is one of the rarest minerals on the planet."

"Exactly."

"I don't think a nugget will be enough to convince the general," Rex said.

"We're going to sell the idea of it," I said. "The nugget's just for show."

While I started to get ready for the dinner, the boys went to Tunde's junkyard, where he did all his engineering work, to find cell phones. Tunde explained that the process would be quite easy: They'd strip the phones of every metal piece and harvest the minerals by melting them down. Most cell phones have trace amounts of gold, silver, and rare elements. The rhodium is used in the coating on the electrodes. It would take a bunch of phones to make a nugget, but Tunde, being Tunde, laughed and said it would take twenty minutes.

I tried to clean up as best I could, but there were heavy bags under my eyes and dust coating my hair. I didn't want to impress the general, but I knew I had to.

So far, we'd been pulled this way and that—Kiran tried to sway us to his side, the general wanted to awe us with his power—but the shoe was on the other foot.

We were the ones in charge of the show now.

As I was preparing to put on my Painted Wolf makeup, I thought back to the old woman I'd talked to at the chief's house. The smells of their cooking came flooding back, and I felt the sudden urge to call my mother.

I needed a boost before I walked into that dinner.

My mother always made me feel confident and secure.

I wanted to hear her voice again, even if it was for only a few minutes.

8.2

"Hello?" she answered, her voice crackling with anxiety.

"Mom," I said, "it's me."

"Cai! It is so good to hear your voice. I thought you were going to call earlier. We haven't heard from you for days. I would have called you sooner but I didn't want to disturb your studies. I'm sure you have been working very, very hard."

"Yes. We have . . . we've been so busy here."

Suddenly this felt like **a bad idea**. My guilt at having lied to my parents to get into the Game came surging back. Only now it was compounded a dozen times over because I'd flown to Africa as a wanted felon.

Getting our names cleared and saving Tunde's village was one thing. Assuming they eventually found out, getting my parents to trust me again was going to be another. I had to pray that never happened.

My mother sighed. "Please, tell me what you've been doing. I want to hear everything. What have you been working on? Have you met any nice people? What have you been eating? I bet you're starving."

"I'm fine, Mom." I laughed. "I have met many interesting new people. We've even done some traveling, nothing major, just—"

"Traveling? Where?"

That was a mistake. I immediately began to dial it back.

"Um, just locally. Just around here. But like I was saying, we've been studying hard and coming up with all sorts of interesting ideas and plans. It really is an amazing program. And, yes, I've been eating just fine. Not as well as at home, of course, but fine. Listen, Mom, the people running the event have asked me to stay longer."

"Longer?"

"Yes. Another week."

"Another week?" My mother gasped. "What about your studies?"

"These *are* my studies," I replied. "There are incredible opportunities here, Mother. Ways to really learn and help people. I'm discovering skills that I never knew I possessed. I feel like I'm actually making a difference. That's the reason I need to stay here. I'm doing something important."

It felt so good to tell my mom the truth, though it was surrounded by lies.

"I'm going to miss you so much, Cai. Your father is traveling this week and I'm going to be alone here. But I am so proud of you. This sounds like a very important event. I'm sure they don't ask everyone to stay longer."

"Well. Some people they do."

"Let me compliment you," my mother said. "I enjoy it."

A knot formed in my stomach. I hated lying to my mother. At the same time, it was better to be the academically minded student than the **internationally wanted fugitive**.

"When will Father be back?" I asked.

"Next week," my mother said. "Don't you worry about me. I've already got plans with my friends. I'm going to take that pottery class I was interested in. When you get back, there might be several new items in the house."

"Wonderful. I'll call you soon, okay?"

"Take care of yourself," my mother said. "We're very proud of you."

I hung up, happy to have my mother's voice in my head again.

It renewed my strength. Even though I hadn't been honest with her, I knew that if she was aware of what I was really doing she would approve.

That made all the difference.

8.3

I finished dressing before Rex and Tunde arrived at the schoolhouse.

Tunde handed me a refined nugget of rhodium the size of my thumbnail.

"That is all we could get given the time," Tunde said.

"It's perfect."

The boys took a few minutes to get cleaned up before we walked to the chief's house. A black limo similar to the one that had driven us to Akika Village sat idling outside. I did not see the general, but several soldiers ushered the three of us into the house.

A good half-dozen tables had been pushed together to create one long, haphazard table. It was draped in colorful cloth that used a lot of the same patterns I'd seen across the village. Candles guttered on the tables, but they were hardly noticeable nestled in and among all the food.

Just as before, the smell was invigorating. I picked up the scent of cinnamon, banana, curry, sage, basil, ginger, and turmeric. I saw yams, shrimp, fish, chicken, onions, rice, tomatoes, green chili, spinach, plantains, collard greens, fried sweets like doughnut holes, stews, cassava, goat meatball soups, flatbreads, lentils, beef pies, and chorizo. And at the head of the table, General Iyabo sat like a king.

He was wearing his finest military garb. Dressed to the nines with medals and ribbons dotting his shoulders. His teeth were brighter and whiter than the moon, and a young woman stood behind him, cooling him with a massive hand fan made of feathers. He was grinning ear to ear. Naya sat beside him dressed as she'd arrived that afternoon.

"Welcome to Nigeria," the general said. "I am always pleased to meet with people eager to invest in our country. And, more specifically, people who have the insight to meet with me before they do just that. Please, come and sit."

We sat at the opposite end of the table, and servers immediately appeared; they filled our glasses with a reddish liquid. It had cucumbers floating in it.

"It is called a Chapman," General Iyabo explained. "Made with several different sweet sodas, grenadine, bitters, orange juice, and some special ingredients. Try it, come, come, you will enjoy . . ."

I sipped and watched Tunde carefully drink. He was gracious, but I could tell he was testing it. None of us could trust this man. Even though I knew he was ruthless, I had to hope he was a predictable businessman. Violence **and brutality** will only get a person like the general so far; to be truly powerful he'd need to be strategically levelheaded when it came to his business deals.

Key was figuring out just how reasonable he could be.

"It is the bitter that we use," General Iyabo said. "It is crucial, for a proper Chapman, to use the angostura bitters. It is extremely concentrated, nearly forty-five percent alcohol by volume, and has restorative properties. Bitters like these can cure stomachaches and stop hiccups. But we are not here to talk of drinks!"

General Iyabo clapped. More servers appeared, all of whom

Tunde recognized. He nodded to them, respectfully, as they served us. We were handed plates piled high with food. Everything I listed above, I got. The aroma made my stomach growl loudly. The juices of everything ran together on my plate. It became a luxurious broth of butter, blood, and sugar.

Despite all that, I could barely eat.

The general had no such problems. He ate as though he did not have another care in the world. As if this meal was the same as any other.

Naya was ruthless, but for her it was business. It was asserting control. Her father, however, seemed proud of subjugating people. Weird as it sounds, that was actually a good thing. It meant that the general was an emotional person. It meant he was putting *himself* into this—it wasn't just a job; it was part and parcel of who he was. And if you've ever taken a course in debate, you know the trick of defeating an opponent is tripping them up by targeting their pride.

"So, General, you were impressed with the jammer?" I asked.

Iyabo stopped his gorging and sat back, wiped his mouth with a napkin.

"I was pleased with it. I sent Tunde to America to make the machine. I expected nothing less than a brilliant piece of technology. As you know, my friend here is something of a genius."

Tunde stared stone-faced at the general.

"You will have to forgive his manners, however. He is unhappy with how things have turned out at the moment. Though I am certain you can convince him that my goals are in the best interest of his people."

"You know how these geniuses can be," I said.

General Iyabo laughed. "Sensitive."

"And more," I said. "Seems we're always trying to convince Tunde to look beyond his provincial upbringing here. He's coming around. Slowly."

I looked to Tunde. His gaze shot daggers, though he knew what I was doing. We needed him to play along. If he didn't, the con wouldn't work.

"Aren't you?" I asked Tunde.

A few nerve-racking seconds crawled past before he grinned.

"Ah, yes, I am. I may be a fast learner with the technology but getting used to the speed of business requires a bit more study for me. *I dey don wan act like mumu.*"

"Let's get down to business," I said, looking to Rex.

Rex said, "We have an offer for you, General."

"Good," the general said. "I am ready to hear it. Tunde is special, but he is only part of the empire I am building here."

I cleared my throat. This next part had to be convincing.

My heart started racing.

"The truth is, General, I found the jammer lacking. Sure, the design was clever. The fabrication, under the circumstances, was quite good. But this machine . . . it's a trifle."

"A trifle?" General Iyabo leaned in, glowering at me.

"It will be outdated in a matter of months. Perhaps Tunde was a bit distracted while he was in the States. Not only was he far from home, but he was taking part in a massive, difficult competition. I suppose that might explain it."

The general didn't take that well.

He leaped up, food tumbling off his jacket. "What are you suggesting?"

The troops around the table jerked into action, leveling their guns on us.

"I'm sorry if we've offended you," Rex said, picking up my thread. "But my partner and I came here looking for **a game** changer. Tunde is capable of incredible things but . . . I have to say, I am not wholly convinced that you are able to bring the best out in him. He seems to have stagnated here."

"So you came here to spit in my face?" The general was furious.

"No," I said, "of course not. But you must understand our position. We were led to believe that this operation, Tunde, all of your endeavors, were next level. Here is the truth, General Iyabo: We need partners for a project we're developing a few miles east of this village. We approached Kiran Biswas—I believe you know him—with this opportunity, but he said you would not be interested. Then we met Tunde and he painted a very different picture of your operations."

"What did Kiran say?"

"He would prefer to keep the project a secret," Rex clarified.

"From me?" the general growled.

"We are quite impressed with Kiran," I said. "But we don't trust him. Having seen what you've accomplished here in such a short amount of time, we feel as though you might be a better fit for our endeavor."

General Iyabo rubbed his chin, motioned to his troops.

They lowered their weapons.

"Go on," he said.

"It's one thing to be the most powerful man in Oyo State," I said. "But it's another to be the most powerful man in West Africa."

8.4

General Iyabo sat back down and straightened his jacket.

So much for the general being predictable.

My throat was dry.

I had the same sickening surge of adrenaline, of heightened expectation, I did as a kid when I went to Beijing's Happy Valley amusement park with my parents to ride the Extreme Rusher, a towering roller coaster. Back then, I had to breathe slowly, in and out, to not break out in a panic.

I started breathing the same way when General Iyabo turned to me.

"I have read through your previous projects," he said. "You have made some very clever, very timely investments. You have worked with big firms and powerful people. There are two things, however, that I find a bit disconcerting. First, you seem a bit too young to be as accomplished as you are. And second, I find it awfully convenient that you two stumbled across Tunde on his very first sojourn beyond the borders of his country."

I carefully folded my napkin as I mentally played through my various answers. I needed an answer that would appeal to his vanity.

The key was turning the question back around.

"We are young, yes," I said. "But we have a saying in China that hunger knows no age. If you are capable and have access, there is no reason to wait until after you've finished school to get into business. When my partner and I see an opportunity, we pounce on it."

"That is admirable." The general nodded. "I do find it hard to believe, however, that you have been developing something a few miles east of here that I do not know about. This is my country. I know everything that goes on here."

"You didn't know that Kiran wanted to cheat you out of this deal."

General Iyabo instantly lost whatever smidgen of cool he'd had. He lashed out with his glass and threw it across the room. One of his troops ducked as the glass shattered on the wall, sending a cascade of Chapman to the floor. I forced myself not to flinch and even though every muscle in my body tensed, I remained still.

"Enough!" he bellowed.

I had to stay cool. Stay focused.

I pictured myself back at Neon Noir in Shanghai where I'd played the waitress and busted Mrs. Song. I pulled it off because I kept a Zen-like calm.

I needed it now more than ever.

"Rhodium," I said. "We know someone who has found a deposit of rhodium in a village fifteen miles to the east of Akika Village. We aim to mine it. As you know, rhodium is one of the **rarest and most valuable** minerals in the world. Most of it is mined in Russia and South Africa. But there is some here. Surely, it would be an even bigger benefit to your burgeoning empire than the tantalum."

I pulled the nugget of rhodium from my purse but had to keep my hand from shaking as I placed it on the table. I prayed General Iyabo didn't notice.

But Rex did. He picked up the conversation, distracting the general.

"We assume you're using the mineral you're digging up here for electronics," Rex added. "Whatever it is that you and your partners are working on, I can assure you that having access to your own deposit of rhodium would be a real coup. The corrosion resistance benefits, if anything."

I wasn't sure the general would buy it, but jealous people make irrational decisions.

I sat back in my seat, mentally preparing myself for the general's next outburst. Sure enough, he didn't let me down. Iyabo grabbed a revolver from one of his troops. He emptied the bullets and spun the chamber, toying with it as he walked around the table. I was sweating, my heart pounding so hard I worried it would break some of my ribs. The feeling in my stomach was the same I'd felt when the roller coaster at Happy Valley reached the top of its first peak, just before the plunge.

"Kiran hid this information from me?" General Iyabo asked me.

"Yes," I said.

I eyed the doors, eager to find an exit if we'd need it. Front door was too risky; the troops standing on either side of it looked anxious. They were young, their hands clenching their weapons too hard. Door to the back wasn't much better and we'd possibly end up trapped. But I figured it was the only bet. I decided that if the general didn't sit down in the next thirty seconds, I was going to have to do something.

"You should know that I am not some dullard who climbed the ranks because I was the fiercest dog in my village. My bite is as bad as my bark. I went to college. I trained as an electrical engineer," the general added as he stopped behind Tunde and rested his hands on the back of Tunde's chair.

I swallowed hard.

It sounded so loud in my head that I assumed everyone heard it.

General Iyabo said, "Tell me where this rhodium is and I will help you get to it. We have more than enough manpower here and all the equipment."

"I have seen, at a distance, the machines you're using," I said. "I realize I'm not a mining engineer, but I am very good at researching potential projects. This stuff you have in that pit, it's standard. Stuff we used in China three decades ago."

General Iyabo patted Tunde's head, revolver still in hand.

"And you have access to better machinery?"

"We're hoping Tunde will build it," I said, turning to Rex.

He looked a little perplexed, unsure of where I was going exactly, but I knew he could catch on. We needed to flip the tables on the general. Rather than coming to him to ask for his buy in, we wanted him to come to us. And **this was the moment** to do it.

"To prove to us that Tunde can do what we think he's capable of," Rex said.

"And to prove that your operation here isn't a one-off," I added.

"General Iyabo, we'd like to partner with you, but we need to be certain that you can deliver."

"Again," he replied, "you turn to insults."

"This is business," Rex said.

"Kiran didn't think you had what it takes," I said, driving it home.

I worried I was overdoing it, especially with the general standing right behind Tunde. But when you play games like this, convincing the other side sometimes requires a show of strength. The general was attempting to intimidate us. I needed to show him that we were equals here.

General Iyabo walked beside Rex and dragged over an empty chair. He sat down heavily, the chair nearly buckling under his weight. He placed a hand on Rex's shoulder, like an old pal. "I did not expect you two to be so aggressive."

"Unexpected is our middle name," Rex replied.

"So," the general said. "If I have Tunde build a machine—something that will demonstrate he is as good as I say he is—then you will share the rhodium?"

"Essentially," I said.

Rex added, "The machine should be able to do the work of one hundred men. We're in this for future-level tech. Human power is no longer the answer. Truth is, anyone can engineer the next step in the process, but only a handful can engineer the next generation."

The general turned to Tunde. "What do you say?"

"I saw that you do not have a highwall mining machine. That would be an essential tool. It would be like a tractor but more agile. It would have a wheel that digs into the tantalum seam and a conveyor belt to move it—"

"Yes, yes. But can it be next generation?"

Tunde nodded. "Yes. With the right materials—"

"You will have whatever I can get you," the general said as he returned to his seat. The chair beneath him groaned in displeasure.

"How long will it take you?" Rex asked Tunde.

Tunde thought for a moment, then said, "A few days."

General Iyabo gave a grin that would **scare a shark.**

"Good," he said. "You are my guests until then."

The feast ended with a strong handshake.

"Excellent to meet you, Ms. Jiang, Mr. Quintanilla."

As we walked outside, the general tried to pry more information about the rhodium deposit from us. But we did an excellent job of not giving him anything.

It helped that none of us knew anything about mining or where this hidden deposit could be.

The general left, escorted by his soldiers.

Truth is: I could never have done what Painted Wolf pulled off. Give me a computer and I can get inside it but ask me to social-engineer people and I'm rolling with training wheels.

I've done it when I've had to, but I can only pull it off if I've rehearsed thoroughly. Painted Wolf, she's a born pro. She said things on her feet that I couldn't imagine saying even if I'd had hours to practice. And she did it all in a country she'd never been to, staring down a ruthless maniac.

Crazy impressive.

We kept our cool as we left the chief's house and then, as soon as we were out of eyeshot of any soldiers, we all, nearly simultaneously, let out huge sighs.

"Wolf," Tunde said, half laughing, "you are insane! Where did you come up with all that stuff? I had no idea how I was going to match those mental gymnastics that you did in there!"

"Who knows?" Painted Wolf said. "But it worked."

"Like gangbusters," I said.

"We certainly have our work cut out for us," Wolf said. "Tunde, do you think you can build something? I mean, we have a chance here to make a machine that can get your people, or at least some of them, up out of that mine. Rex and I can help in any way you need, of course. But do you think it's possible?"

"More than possible," Tunde said.

Tunde and Wolf high-fived.

"And this rhodium deposit?" I asked. "Where exactly will that be?"

Tunde said, "The border is close. Only twenty or so miles. Convincing the general that he has not crossed over it won't be hard. It is not marked in any particular way. There is a lowland area there, a place where we could meet with whatever authorities we can call. I suggest getting ahold of the United Nations. There are UN troops stationed very close to the border."

We turned a corner and Tunde stopped short.

It was dark. Most of the houses were illuminated only by the cooking fires burning inside them, but one house was lit up like Christmas with electric lights. Tunde's house.

He broke away from us and ran toward it.

Then, turning around, he waved for us to follow him.

"Come on!" he shouted. "You must meet my parents!"

Despite the dust and the clatter of machinery, Tunde's home was beautiful. It might have been a clapboard house, but it was painted in bright blues and rusty oranges and looked as alive and joyous as I'd imagined. And then there were all the additional upgrades Tunde had added.

Most were functional—lighting systems and ham radio antennae—and others were projects that he had yet to complete. And knowing Tunde, I imagined that he'd never say they were abandoned projects—'cause in Tunde-world, nothing is abandoned. It's only waiting to be finished.

Tunde rapped on the door and it opened.

His mother stood there, looking exhausted but overjoyed. They did not speak but merely hugged and held on to each other very tightly. Watching them, I could only think of Ma and how much I wished I could give her a great big hug.

You will; just be patient. We're going to bring Teo home first.

Tunde's father came into the room next. He was in tears. Everyone started crying before Tunde wiped his eyes and, turning to his parents, said, "Mom, Dad, these are my friends. They are family."

"Welcome," his mother said. "This is your home, then, as well."

We all hugged, a big group hug.

The stress of the meal melted instantly away.

It felt just like home.

9.1

We spent the next thirty minutes talking with Tunde's parents.

They told us all about Tunde's childhood—considering he's only fourteen, it wasn't that long a story—and even trotted out Polaroids of him as a baby. When they got into all the engineering stories, Tunde really came alive.

It was good to see him happy, even though we all knew it would be brief. There was a cheerful bubble inside Tunde's house.

"Do you want to see the Solar Power Tower?" Tunde asked. "I could take you both on a tour of my grounds. You can see the lovely place where I collect all of my materials. I can walk you through the projects I am attempting to complete."

We left the house and headed toward the Solar Power Tower.

"You have a wonderful family," Painted Wolf said. "So warm."

"Yes." He nodded. "It is our way. We are proud people and we are strong, but above all we are a thankful lot. So long as we are walking upon the ground and are not lying beneath it, we will celebrate our

lives. No matter the hardship, no matter the desperation, we cherish our lives. One week ago my people had been farmers and ranchers. Now they are miners, slaves under the watchful eyes of soldiers."

"You're just as strong as they are," I said. "Maybe even stronger."

"Let us hope. . . ."

Tunde stopped short as we turned another corner and saw a crowd of people dancing beside a fire near the schoolhouse. They seemed to be celebrating. At first I thought it must be an event put together by the general to impress us, but Tunde insisted that his people do this in the face of adversity.

"Oh, my people full ground remain!"

There were a dozen of Tunde's neighbors by the fire. Children watched, eyes wide, as their parents danced. A man with long braids played a thumb piano and a woman next to him played a bass drum. The rhythm was perfectly timed to my heartbeat.

Tunde's friend Ayoola offered us some folding chairs and we sat and watched the fire and the dancers. The smell of the smoke burned away the stink of the mine.

Ayoola grabbed Tunde's hands and dragged him up to dance. Tunde glanced back and gave us a big grin. Then he joined the revelers. I watched him dance with her, their movements totally in sync.

Tunde seemed truly carefree and happy. Even though he was in the heart of this tragedy, he was surrounded by people who loved him. Every ounce of that love flowed through his movements. It was beautiful to see.

Too bad I can't dance like that.

When Painted Wolf stood, I glanced up at her to see her hand extended.

"How about it?" she asked.

Her hair was haloed by the firelight and she was smiling.

Hell yes!

I took her hand and we walked together into the crowd. The second that Tunde saw us he started beaming and even went as far as to clap.

I tried to ignore him as I put my hands on Painted Wolf's waist.

9.2

I'm not going to lie; I'm a terrible dancer.

So even though the song was a bit more up tempo than my movements, I wasn't going to attempt to dance the way Tunde was. Last thing I needed was to trip and make even more of a fool of myself.

Keeping it slow meant I could focus more on Painted Wolf.

Even with all the running we'd been doing, the sleepless nights, the lack of food (well, until that cavalcade of sustenance at the feast), and overload of adrenaline, Painted Wolf looked at ease—totally in control.

"There's no way you're not exhausted," I said over the throb of drums.

"You have no idea."

"I can't imagine actually resting," I said. "I mean, I can't imagine this ever being over. Feels like we've opened something that we can't ever close."

"Pandora's box."

"You know, the whole Pandora's box thing is actually something of a misnomer. It wasn't actually a box. In the myth, it's like a large jar. I guess 'Pandora's large jar' doesn't have the same ring to it, though."

Painted Wolf looked up at me.

"You are such a nerd," she said.

"That's why you like me, right?"

"Who said I liked you?"

We moved closer to the outside of the dance circle where the shadows were longer and the darkness crowded in. A breeze rustled through Painted Wolf's hair . . . well, wig. She sighed and put her head on my shoulder. We kept dancing, totally out of sync with the music but completely in sync with each other.

"I never liked to dance," Painted Wolf said. "I always felt clumsy."

"Welcome to the club. Captain Clumsy Dancer here. You're not bad."

"Really?"

"I haven't exactly danced with a lot of girls," I said. "But, yeah, of course."

Painted Wolf looked up at me again. I was kind of bummed she didn't have her head on my shoulder anymore. It felt great there. Like it was a missing puzzle piece I didn't know I'd lost.

"Maybe Tunde can give us lessons," I said.

"We're doing our own thing."

"Oh," I said, "that's good. I like that."

Painted Wolf took off her sunglasses and put her head back on my shoulder. We moved together, and it wasn't until a few minutes later, when Tunde tapped me on the shoulder, that I realized the music had stopped.

"It is getting late," Tunde said. "Who's up for a tour?"

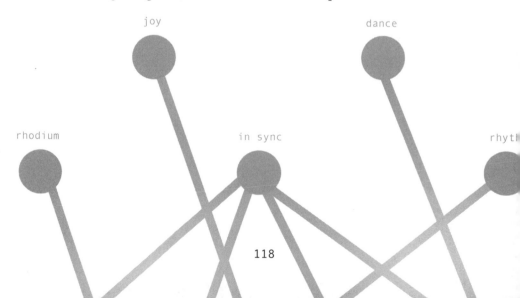

10. TUNDE

As we walked to the Solar Power Tower, I thought back on the sight of my two best friends in the world dancing together.

It made me want to sing!

Even in the heart of the darkest moment, dancing is a cure-all. Remember that, my friends! Dance and you will again be happy.

I will admit I had dreamed of giving Rex and Wolf a tour of the tower for many months. *With the Solar Power Tower, I dey clap for myself.*

As I had hoped, they were quite impressed by the engineering of it, but I think what most fascinated them was being atop this thing that I had built with my own two hands. All that sweat and blood! All those calloused hours! My friends, I was as proud of the Solar Power Tower as a father could be.

It was my greatest creation, and while I may go on to make even more impressive creations, it will always be my first. Sometimes I think that the things that come most naturally to us are our best works. And the Solar Power Tower came to me as though it was ready to build itself!

Eighty feet over Akika Village, I pointed out to the horizon where we could see the flicker of distant flames. "There," I told Rex and Painted Wolf. "That is where the nearest village is. They are very kind people there, but they do not come to visit us often. I do not know why."

"You have a beautiful country, Tunde," Painted Wolf said.

"Yes," I agreed, "it is magnificent." Then I looked past the rooftops of my village to the mine where several soldiers were on patrol. Immediately, the sight dampened my mood.

"But the general . . . He does not know it but what we saw today is only the start. Those men fighting in the mine, they will not stop until the general is gone. There will be a rebellion, trust me."

"Should we help them?" Rex asked.

"Of course," I said. "But if we wait until everything has boiled over, until these people have reached the point where they will not stand another second under General Iyabo, then I am afraid we will witness bloodshed. We cannot have that. Your plan must work, Wolf. We need to remove the general before things explode here. My people are too proud to be enslaved."

"So let's go," Rex said, stifling a yawn. "What can we do now?"

I put an arm around my best friend.

"Rex, *omo*, you need to sleep," I said. "I have no idea what time zone our minds are in, but our bodies are surely desperate for rest. I appreciate that you want to get started right away, but trust me, it will not benefit any of us if you fall asleep while working on the machine! We will start in the morning."

"Might be good advice for you as well, Tunde," Painted Wolf said.

"I am home. I can work for a few hours," I told her. "Maybe you do not remember, but you told the general I will be building an impossible machine!"

Painted Wolf grimaced. "I might have overdone it. . . ."

"But I love a challenge," I said. "I am going to build the greatest impossible machine you have ever not seen. There is a work shed near the junkyard that I sometimes use. No one goes there, ever. Honestly, I kind of avoid it, too, because it is infested with spiders. . . ."

"You scared of spiders?" Rex asked.

"I would not say scared exactly."

"Let me come along to help," Rex suggested.

As he did so, he stifled another yawn.

"No," I said. "You two need some sleep. You can go back to my house; I will be back later. Rest, friends. Rest."

10.1

The work shed was a shambles, as expected.

There were also soldiers lazing about the entrance!

Three men with guns sat on their haunches, smoking and laughing.

"You there!" one of them shouted as I approached.

They stood with their guns at the ready. I put my hands up.

"It is me, Tunde," I said, stepping out of the darkness. "I am here to work."

"Work on what?"

"A project for the general," I said.

"You are not allowed here."

"Well," I said, pausing to think for a moment, "that is good."

The soldiers were confused.

"Why is that good?" one asked. "You just said you came here to work."

"The place is infested with poisonous spiders!" I said. "I have seen them with my own eyes. Ogre-faced spiders. *Deinopis.* They have a very terrible bite and they are nocturnal. When the general told me I had to work in this shed, I got the shivers. I do not want to be here and be bitten by those spiders. Thank you, sirs. I will let the general know that you do not want me to—"

"Hang on!"

The soldiers were clearly spooked. They were glancing all around at the ground. One of them had even pulled out a flashlight and was quite anxiously checking his pant legs for any stray spiders.

"Do not tell the general," the soldier who had spoken to me first said. "We want you to come inside here and work. That is an order he gave you. We will go back to the village and let him know you are doing your work."

I pretended to be very disappointed.

"Fine," I said, with my face downcast as the soldiers ran off.

My friends, I was becoming as good a social engineer as I was an actual engineer! Very proud of myself, I opened the door to the shed and stepped inside.

It was the size of a two-car garage. The floor was concrete and cracked in various places where pools of oil reflected the light from the bulb on the rusted ceiling. There were three workbenches, each constructed haphazardly with various lengths of planking. The tools were old, rust and grime covered, and the electricity in the work shed fluctuated with alarming frequency.

The men working in the mine had taken it over and were using it to repair the bulldozers and mining equipment. That was good because it meant that any spiders were likely gone. But these mechanics were certainly a slovenly lot!

My first order of business was to sort the place out.

"Okay," I said, sitting down at one of the workbenches, speaking to myself. "We have to sort the power system out first, then clean this place up. We will need additional tools but I think I can salvage them from my place or the junkyard. This is doable."

I spent the next two hours clearing space and organizing the work shed.

The power was a simple thing to fix. After doing some repair, the electrical system was up and running just the way I wanted it. I then organized the tools like a professional.

My friends, we would have this highwall machine done in no time.

The sorting, however, was not just to get my mind ready for the build to come. It also helped me sort out my own emotional struggle.

You see, I really had no idea how I would create the highwall mining machine that Painted Wolf said I was capable of making!

We may have landed with a plan to trick the general, but now I had an opportunity—yes, very much an opportunity—to make something that would bring immediate relief to my people.

The jammer was easy. It looked exactly like what it was.

But the highwall mining machine was a piece of equipment that I assumed took many months and hundreds of hands to build. Usually, it was forty feet long! I did not own a factory. I did not have a staff of metalsmiths.

How was I going to know what would work? I tell you, my friends, that the best way to get a handle on a problem is to take it apart piece by piece.

While my brain was buzzing with ideas, they were scattershot.

Sorting the tools was a godsend.

Nothing like physical labor to get a mind in shape!

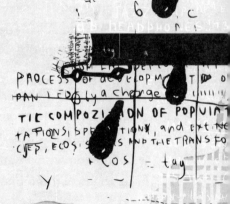

It was dark out but even though I'd only gotten a few minutes of scattered sleep on the plane, I wasn't as exhausted as I expected to be.

My mind was just racing in a million different directions.

"This is beautiful and all," I said to Rex, "but I feel like I need to be useful."

"Couldn't agree more," he said. "What do you have in mind?"

"We found out that Kiran was working with the general when we searched his OndScan lab during the Game," I said. "I wonder what we could find out from the general's side of things."

The general had his men bivouac just outside the village near where the helicopters landed and took off. Their "base" was a series of large green tents. Each was guarded by a handful of soldiers, and most of them were lazing about.

Knowing the general's inflated sense of self-worth, I knew that the biggest of the tents was surely where he spent most of his time. It was also going to be where he stored his valuables. A generator humming outside the tent told me he was **running electronics** inside as well.

And where there are electronics, there is data.

There were five young men standing outside the general's tent. All of them had guns, but they were playing cards. As Rex and I walked over, we passed an unwatched pickup truck with a toolbox in the bed. With no one watching, I opened the toolbox and pulled out several screwdrivers, a flashlight, and a few stray copper wires. I tucked the wires into my pocket.

The soldiers looked up at us wearily as we approached.

"General asked me to come by and check on something," I said, putting on an American accent. "I know it's kind of crazy and you've never seen me before, but a job's a job, right?"

"No one said anything about a girl coming to fix . . . something," a soldier with a lazy eye said. He stood, blocking the door, his rifle in hand.

"Is the general in?" Rex asked.

The soldier shook his head.

"Bummer," Rex said, pulling out his cell. "He's going to be so pissed. But I understand. Let me go ahead and call him. You guys were left out of the loop, I guess. It happens sometimes. I have—"

"No," a second soldier, with a goatee, said. "You do not need to call him. Tell me, what is it you need to do inside here?"

"It's okay," I said. "He's not going to be mad at you. Why would he? You're guarding his tent just like he ordered, right?"

The soldier with the lazy eye looked down at the cards in his hand.

"Anyway," I continued, "it's still hot out here. You're allowed to take breaks, though, right? You guys are just having a little downtime. Come on. No sweat."

"Enough," the soldier blocking the door said, panic in his eyes. "You can go inside but only for as long as it takes to fix whatever it is you are here to fix. Understand? I will go with you."

"Yeah. Totally understand," I said.

We followed the lazy-eyed soldier into the tent. There were desks and chairs arrayed in the center of the room. On the "walls" were multiple computer banks lined with flat-screen monitors. It was a sophisticated setup. The monitors flickered and gave the interior of the tent a rather sinister feeling.

General Iyabo's tent

I scanned the room. There was a server bank tucked into one corner. It had the OndScan logo printed on its side. That was what I needed.

As the soldier watched from the back of the tent, I sat down at a computer near the server. I pretended to do some work with the screwdrivers before Rex tried to log in. The computer was password protected.

He had it cracked within fifteen seconds.

I sat down beside Rex and looked over the desktop. Next, it was a matter of diving into the files and finding **the** valuable **data**. I opened a private search so the terms I was looking for wouldn't be saved. I searched for my father's name and the names of the shell companies I'd discovered at the Game.

It was clear then that my father was working with OndScan on surveillance tech. But Kiran never worked on just one project; they were all intertwined. Whatever he was mining the tantalum for involved my father and the Chinese firms he was working with as well. I had to know exactly what they were doing.

My stomach sank as I got hit after hit after hit.

I copied everything onto my phone but scanned through it as the documents loaded. A picture quickly emerged—a terrible one. The Chinese shell companies were involved in much more than just camera parts for high-level drones. Some of the tantalum being mined in Akika Village was used in the lenses for the drones, but the bulk of it was being further refined and sent to Argentina.

What Kiran was doing there wasn't clear, but the companies my father was working with had offices there. Several of them were involved in making power distribution units for high-performance computing.

Even though I had only a few stray pieces, I could tell that whatever Kiran was building went way beyond Rama and Shiva and any larger goal OndScan had. This was a project that would require power at an immense scale, enough to run an entire country.

Rex read over my shoulder and shook his head. "Wolf . . ."

"Miss." The lazy-eyed soldier behind us spoke up. "Are you finished?"

I turned around and nodded. He shifted anxiously.

"Yes," I said, surreptitiously pulling out the bundle of wires from my purse. "Got the problem right here." I held the wires up for him to see.

I logged out of the computer and we followed the soldier back outside.

"Much appreciated, guys," I told the soldiers, my American accent slipping a little bit. I made a mental note to brush up on my pronunciation of "re"s. "I will let the general know that you were supremely helpful."

The soldiers waved as we walked off.

While I was pleased with how the con was working, I was now even more worried about my father's involvement in Kiran's schemes. We'd discovered there was yet another facet to Kiran's game plan. How complicated was this going to get?

One thing was certain, however:

My father was caught up in the middle of it.

11.1

Sleeping on the platform at the Solar Power Tower was my idea.

I was still upset by what we'd found in the general's tent and trying to wrap my brain around the fact that my father wasn't just some incidental player in Kiran's grand scheme. Back at the Game, I'd assumed the Chinese shell companies were tangential— something my father got involved in at a far remove. But no, the files in the general's tent made it clear that he was truly, deeply involved.

And that thought made me short of breath.

I figured a little peaceful time with Rex would help clear my head. There was nothing I could do about my father's involvement, at least not right then, so I needed to get my focus back. I needed some downtime to recuperate.

It was late, well after midnight, by the time we clambered up the rickety metal ladder to the top. But the moon was full and we could see beyond the muddy paths of the trucks and bulldozers to the mountains in the distance.

The only noise was the buzz of mosquitoes.

After our dinner and time in the tent, I wanted to be as far away from the general and his men as possible. I was existentially exhausted.

I think we all expected to bring Tunde home triumphant; to make his return something of a celebration of our achievements in Boston, but that all came crashing down the second Naya met us at the gate. Things only got worse from there. We all needed a break, of sorts. We needed a recharge.

I also wanted to spend some time with Rex.

After we'd talked on the plane, I had a lot of time to myself. The guys fell asleep quickly, but I spent the rest of the flight mentally preparing for what we'd face when we reached Africa. I had a routine. I would relax, breathe deeply, close my eyes, and walk myself through all the potential outcomes of our arrival. The more detailed the mental road map, the better handle I had on any impending crisis.

Call it meditation, call it self-actualization—whatever it was, it worked.

I played through every scenario I could think of. I saw us walking into the airport, meeting someone at the gate (I was not imaginative enough to come up with a character like Naya), and then making our way to the village. Thing was, I kept being interrupted. Not by a flight attendant or the jostling of the plane, but by thoughts of Rex. Memories of our time in Boston kept popping into my head. I'd be playing through our drive to Akika Village and suddenly an image of Rex grinning at me over a cup of coffee blurred everything else out. I couldn't **concentrate**.

It was how he made me feel.

Around Rex, I was bubbly. I found myself smiling more than I ever had as Painted Wolf. I didn't take myself as seriously around him. I got goofy and it seemed to come from out of nowhere. Who was I? Why did I act differently around him?

It made me mad at first. It felt like some sort of betrayal. Like he was pushing me to loosen up. I wondered if it was some sort of con he was pulling, a crafty form of social engineering I'd never encountered before, a way to weaken your allies so they liked you, a way to get the upper hand.

I kicked myself when I realized that wasn't it at all: Rex didn't have me in the thrall of some diabolical form of mental gamesmanship; it was all coming from me.

I was giddy and silly around him because he made me feel good about myself.

Around Rex, I was confident that what I was doing meant something.

At the top of the Solar Power Tower that night, I sat beside Rex in silence. We watched the stars spin above us. Rex pointed out a shooting star as it blazed across the sky for an instant.

We didn't need to say anything because it was just good to be together, as a team, not on the run, not struggling to crack a code or answer a ridiculous question. We had each other's backs and no matter what was going to happen in the morning, and the morning after that, I knew that nothing would ever truly separate us.

Rex moved his hand over mine.

The skin on his palm was so soft.

Our fingers intertwined, I didn't want to move for the rest of the night. I leaned over and put my head on his shoulder. I could smell his aftershave, a hint of clove and rum, and closed my eyes.

What was going to happen to us? When this was over and my parents were safe, where would I go? Not home—I couldn't go home. But I'd have to. They needed me. My country needed me. Could I bring Rex with me? Maybe pack him in my suitcase? So many silly thoughts . . .

"I'm trying to figure out how we're going to get to China," Rex said, his voice soft, low. "I figure once we've got the general taken care of, maybe whoever it is that comes in to nab him, Interpol or something, might be willing to help us out."

"We're wanted by Interpol."

"Oh, right . . ."

I squeezed Rex's hand. "We had a nice dance tonight."

"We certainly did."

"When this is all over, we should get lessons together. I want to learn the tango. And there's a Chinese dance, the *yangge*, that's very beautiful. . . ."

Rex pulled me closer and softly tilted my chin up so we were face-to-face. Below us, the lights at Tunde's house flickered off. Overhead, clouds drifted across the moon.

Rex and I kissed.

Then Rex took off his hoodie and wrapped it around me. I curled up beside him, my head between his shoulder and his neck.

And I fell into a deep sleep.

sleep

clinic

pain

lucid

REM

immun

dilat

12. REX

I don't know when I fell asleep, but I wasn't out long.

It was still dark, the moon still hovering over us like a spotlight, when I rolled over and glanced at Painted Wolf.

Her sunglasses had slipped off and her eyes were darting under her eyelids.

I figured she was in REM sleep, maybe lucid dreaming.

But her eyes were moving too fast.

And her skin was slick with sweat.

Considering the temperature was sixty-something, there was no way it was heat. I wasn't sure if I should wake her. Maybe she was just having a nightmare? Maybe it was a cold she got from the hours of travel and little sleep? Our immune systems had to be in the tank.

Painted Wolf mumbled something in Mandarin.

"You okay?" I asked her.

Painted Wolf opened her eyes, but her lids seemed too heavy. Her eyes were bloodshot and her pupils were dilated.

"Are you okay?"

"I don't feel well," she said. "My joints really hurt. . . ."

I felt her head; she was burning up.

"Can you walk?" I asked. "We have to get you down."

I grabbed Painted Wolf under the arms. Her whole body was drenched in sweat, and I had a hard time getting a grip. If she was as ill as she looked, where were we going to find medical help? There were no hospitals. No clinics. No doctors.

Pull it together, Rex. She's strong.

"How are we going to do this?" she asked me. "I'm really weak."

"You're going to climb onto my back."

"That's not going to work."

Her voice was faint, fragile. With her height, I estimated she weighed one hundred pounds. I was already six foot and one fifty, but I wasn't strong. Not muscleman strong. I did single-handedly haul the couch out of Teo's room, though. That thing must have weighed a couple hundred pounds easy. I could do this.

"We don't have a choice," I told Painted Wolf as I helped her swing around to my back. "You're going to have to hold on tight, okay?"

"Okay."

She sounded like she was in a lot of pain. I had to get her down quick.

I moved slowly.

Placing every step carefully on the rung below me.

In the few hours we'd been asleep on the Solar Power Tower, dew had collected on the steps and my shoes were slipping and sliding.

"Just hang on," I said. "We'll be down soon."

I said it more to myself than to Wolf.

"My joints . . ." Painted Wolf groaned.

I tried to speed up, but that only made things worse. About twenty feet from the top, my left foot slipped off a rung and we both jerked suddenly. Painted Wolf didn't say anything, but I knew it must have hurt her.

"I'm sorry," I said. "We're almost there."

Don't make this worse. Get her down in one piece.

Going down the last fifteen rungs felt like moving underwater, but I couldn't risk another slipup. It felt like every second wasted was another second that Painted Wolf worsened. Her breathing was ragged.

133

"You're going to be okay," I told her. "Almost there."

My feet hit the ground twenty-three agonizing seconds later.

We were down.

12.1

Cradling Painted Wolf in my arms, I walked as quickly as I could across the fields separating the Solar Power Tower from the nearest houses in the village.

Her skin was slick and her face so pale in the moonlight.

You have to hurry. Faster. Faster.

"I don't want you to hurt your back," she said, eyes closed.

"I got you."

"Where are we going?"

"Tunde's house."

We were a hundred yards from the house when the exterior lights came on. Tunde had mentioned he'd wired motion sensors to scare off approaching lions. And that's when my brain suddenly realized: Hang on, lions? Tunde didn't mention anything about us possibly encountering lions. Last thing I needed was to be pounced on by some five-hundred-pound killer cat at Tunde's doorstep.

Apparently the lions were taking the night off 'cause we made it to Tunde's parents' house okay. I rapped on the door as hard as I could and it opened a few minutes later. Tunde's dad was standing there, half asleep, in a T-shirt and shorts.

"She's sick," I said. "Really sick."

"We need to take her to Oyindae, the medicine woman." Tunde's dad pointed toward the darkness to our left. "Her home is there."

"You okay?" I asked Painted Wolf. "We have to keep moving."

"Yes," she said, but her voice revealed her discomfort.

We plunged into the darkness. Running with Painted Wolf was awkward; I stumbled several times over furrows and rocks hidden in the shadows. But every step brought her closer to someone who could help.

"She might need medicine," I said.

"Oyindae has medicine," Tunde's dad said. "Many forms."

We reached Oyindae's front door six minutes later and I was drenched in sweat. Tunde's dad knocked loudly on the metal door. The sound thundered out across the night, and several lights flickered on.

Oyindae opened the door, wiping the sleep from her eyes.

She was in her midseventies and had short-cropped gray hair.

"Bring her in." Oyindae waved. "Bring her to my couch."

I laid Painted Wolf down on a couch in the middle of the room as Oyindae knelt down beside me and placed her hands on Painted Wolf's forehead.

Oyindae shook her head. "When did this start?"

"An hour ago, maybe," I said. "We were asleep. I don't know."

"She has a bad fever. We need to cool her quickly."

She took out the pins that held Painted Wolf's purple wig in place. The wig came off and Painted Wolf's black hair tumbled down over her shoulders.

The front door opened behind us as Tunde ran inside.

"My mother just told me," he said. "What can I do?"

"Tunde," Oyindae spoke quickly, "I need you to go to the general store. We need ice, as much of it as you can carry. We also need blankets, water, tea, ginger, hot peppers, and have Segilola bring you turmeric curry. Hurry!"

Tunde and his dad scrambled out of Oyindae's house.

Oyindae soaked a towel in cool water from a basin in the kitchen and then cleaned the sweat from Painted Wolf's face. Ma, she always called this a "cat bath," and I remembered being home sick from school, sweating and shivering at the same time, while she ran a cool washcloth over my skin.

135

"This is from a mosquito," Oyindae said. "It is called chikungunya. It can be very painful, as it hurts the joints. This is probably a mild case."

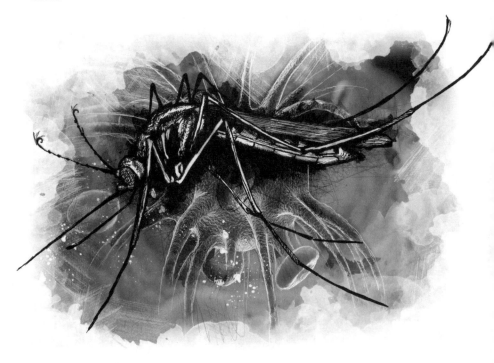

The mosquito-borne virus

"So she'll be okay, right?"

Oyindae nodded. "She will be okay. She will likely be sick for the rest of the night and tomorrow. But the worst of it will pass soon."

I took Painted Wolf's hands and held them tightly.

"She's strong."

"She seems very strong," Oyindae said. "Use the towel to cool her head."

Oyindae spread a patterned blanket over Painted Wolf's shoulders and then kissed her forehead. She stepped out of the house and left us alone.

I sat down beside Painted Wolf with the wet washcloth in my hand.

I ran it across her forehead and felt like I should be saying something.

She smiled as I cooled her skin.

"It's funny, I don't even know your real name," I said.

"You don't think Painted Wolf is my real name?" she asked.

"If it is, your parents are real badasses."

Painted Wolf laughed, but it hurt and she winced.

"Don't talk. I don't know if you remember the first time we met. I mean, officially, it was through private messenger, but, uh, there was a time before that. I had posted something stupid about hacktivism, and you were one of the first people to reply. This was before you changed your profile picture. That original one, it was a side shot of you with white sunglasses and a nose ring. You had green streaks in your hair. I just thought you were the coolest thing ever."

"That dye took forever to come out," she said.

I paused to refold the towel.

"It wasn't just how you looked. Although you looked amazing, like someone dropped into our time from some radically more astounding future. It was your mind, Wolf. It was the fact that on the mirror behind you, a mirror I always imagined was on the back of your bedroom door, you'd drawn the most complicated diagram I'd ever seen. Took me weeks to figure out what it was—a map of all the members of the site and their connections to each other. You'd figured out who we all were and how we knew each other long before we even did. And the thing is, you weren't showing off. I knew you'd written it there for yourself, but it just happened that you caught it with the camera. That's why you changed your profile picture the next day. Because you thought people might assume you were trying to be a brainiac and show them up."

"Yeah, right . . ."

I ran the towel softly over Painted Wolf's eyelids.

"I love that about you. That you're always ten steps ahead of everyone else but you're not showing off. You are a genuinely good—"

Oyindae's front door burst open and Tunde rushed inside.

He was carrying a paper bag with all the items that Oyindae had requested. He placed them on the table and walked over to us.

"How are you doing?" he asked Painted Wolf.

She shook her head.

Oyindae walked in and pulled some of the medicinal herbs from the paper bag. "She needs to rest now," she told me and Tunde. "You boys should leave."

As I got up, Painted Wolf held my hand and squeezed it.

She mouthed: *Thank you.*

12.2

"Come." Tunde motioned toward the door. "Let Oyindae help Painted Wolf for a bit. You need to take in some air and have a zobo."

As Oyindae made a zinc oxide paste with camphor, Tunde and I stepped outside in the early morning light. The fields were steaming.

The sun hovered over the horizon like a massive lens flare.

It gave the grasslands and spindly trees the look of something magical. It might have been my lack of sleep, but there was a weight to the air, a pressure like just before a storm. I took a deep breath but then coughed.

"It is the mine," Tunde said. "The air is heavy with particulates now. Two weeks ago, it was as clean as the air at the very top of the world. Now it tastes like the air from a refinery."

"We're going to change that."

Tunde handed me a plastic cup filled with a dark red liquid.

"Zobo?"

"It is good for your health. We will have coffee later."

I took a sip. It was sour, tangy.

"What is this?"

"It is made from dried flowers and pineapple juice. Some ginger, some garlic; it is all natural and very good for you, *omo*. Drink it up and then we will talk."

Despite the unusual flavor of the zobo, it was refreshing. I sipped it while Tunde did some stretches in the morning sunlight. He was no doubt as exhausted as I was but he looked invigorated. He was home. The tension, the panic, the fear—he was able to keep it at just the right distance to not break down.

It was admirable.

I wasn't sure how much more I could handle.

As I took my last sip of zobo, Tunde clapped me on the shoulder. "She will be back soon. I know this. Our Wolf is a force of nature. We must trust that she can do it."

"How do you do it, Tunde?"

"Do what, brother?"

"Maintain your sanity in the face of . . . all this?"

"You would not think it to look around Akika Village, but I come from a very powerful people."

"I believe that."

"Whether it is by genetics or environment, I do not know, but our destiny is to use it to transform our reality. And, let me tell you, I feel we are very close—"

"Excuse me?"

We were interrupted by the sound of shouting.

It was coming from over the ridge near the mine.

"What's that?" I asked Tunde.

He looked concerned.

"I have no idea."

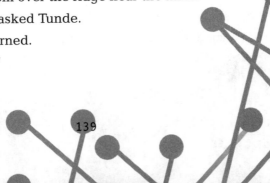

13. TUNDE

The shouting was coming from the mine.

"Maybe it's an accident?" Rex asked.

"It is possible, but—"

The sounds of shouting grew louder.

Rex and I did not hesitate. We jumped from our spot and raced across the village and down the track that led to the mine. Driving, this route took about ten minutes, so running would take us longer. As we ran, we discovered that we were not alone. Several of my neighbors were running alongside us.

"What has happened?" Toben, a friend of my father, asked me.

"I do not know," I said.

"It is probably Kwento. He has been causing much trouble at the mine."

I knew Kwento well. He was a young man, in his early twenties, and a well-regarded hunter. I heard once that he brought down an ox with a bow while out hunting with his uncles. He also was unafraid of snakes and would catch them with his bare hands. While Kwento was very brave and skilled, he also had a notoriously bad temper and frequently got into ugly fights around Akika Village.

Dis big boy he dey flendi for fighting.

"What has he done this time?" I asked.

"He is sick of the general and his men. He wants to fight."

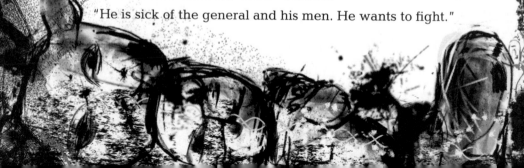

My heart leaped into my throat. The idea of my people trying to take on the soldiers, armed with only pickaxes and their fiercest insults, was a frightening proposition. They would be slaughtered, cut down like dodo birds.

"We have to stop him," I yelled to Rex.

Together with Toben, we ran over the ridge at the top of the mine and looked down below to see a large crowd gathered around Kwento. The miners were in a right fury, all of them shouting and holding their pickaxes over their heads. Surrounding them, the soldiers looked on edge; their fingers were tightened on the triggers of their guns. This was a very bad situation.

"You have to talk to him, Tunde!" Toben shouted to me.

I ran down into the open pit of the mine with Rex and Toben right behind me.

"Let me through!" I shouted to the soldiers.

They all turned to face me and I threw my hands up.

"I can settle this," I told the soldiers. "Just let me speak with Kwento."

The soldiers stepped aside, eyeing me very carefully, as I pushed in toward Kwento. He was more upset than I had ever seen him. He was rippling with rage and pacing about like a panther.

"Kwento," I said, "I know you are angry."

"I am not just angry," he growled. "I am tired. This has to end. We are five hundred strong. The general has only sixty-three men with him."

"Listen to me," I said. "I have a plan. A way to end this so no one will get hurt."

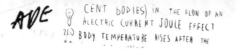

"There is no way you can build your way out of this!"

"But you are wrong. I can. Please, just listen to me."

Kwento turned and looked at the miners around him and then gazed out at the soldiers. They still gripped their weapons tightly, ready for an assault. Kwento turned back to me. I could see the anger was subsiding.

"Tell me this plan," he said.

"I am here to build a machine," I began. "A machine that will process the ore you are digging up. I can make this machine so that it will do the work of one hundred men. You will not have to mine this same way anymore. You will no longer be pushed around."

"How? How could that work?"

I motioned for Kwento to step closer to me. He did.

"Because I am going to ensure the general never bothers our people again," I said quietly. "The machine will be his undoing."

"I do not understand. The machine will also do this?"

"Yes," I said. "I cannot explain it to you in more detail, but I do need for you to trust me. Give me a week. I will have the machine working and at the end of the week, when the general is in his most celebratory mood, I will have him removed. If I do not come through on this promise, you can overthrow him with force. I will even stand alongside you."

Kwento thought it over, and as he did, he studied my eyes to see if I was hiding anything from him or straight-out lying to his face. He could see that I was not and he nodded.

"Okay," Kwento said, "I agree. But a week is too long. You have four days."

13.1

Rex and I walked back to the village with a renewed sense of urgency.

"I can't believe you did that," Rex said as he climbed over the ridge. "That was crazy. You really think you can build it in four days?"

"I do not have a choice," I said. "Though I still have to figure out how it will work. And I will not be able to accomplish that until we have had a decent rest. Rex, you do realize we have not properly slept since we arrived in Nairaland?"

The very mention of sleep made my limbs feel that much heavier. I did not understand just how desperately my body was in need of sleep. When we got back to my house, both Rex and I collapsed on the floor of my room. My friends, I was too exhausted to even climb up into my bed!

We slept four long hours. I did not dream or toss. When I woke, I felt as though my batteries had finally been properly recharged. I emerged from my bedroom to find Rex sitting at the table with my parents, sharing a pot of black tea.

"Feel better?" Rex asked me as I poured myself a cup.

"A million times better," I said.

We sat and discussed the coming build. Rex hoped aloud that Painted Wolf would recover quickly. I was confident that she was strong and that she would. I told him that Oyindae was a very good practitioner. She had healed many generations of my people. I had no doubt that she could help Painted Wolf heal as well.

"All she needs is rest now, *omo*," I told Rex. "Drink your tea."

"May I have some?"

Rex and I both turned around, surprised to see Painted Wolf standing behind us. She was wrapped in a quilt that my grandmother had made for my father and was wearing a hoodie that I recognized. Ah, yes, it was one that Rex often wore. Despite the half-light, she did not forget to put on her sunglasses. I poured hot tea into my cup and handed it to her.

"How is it that you are up?" I asked. "You should be resting!"

"I'm done resting," she said. "I feel tons better."

"I can't believe you're up."

Rex stood and hugged Painted Wolf, then offered her his seat. She sat down and cradled her cup of tea. The steam drifted up around her face, and I was shocked to see that she looked one hundred times better. Surely Oyindae was a miracle worker! Or Painted Wolf was even stronger than we had given her credit for.

"We have so much to do," Painted Wolf said.

"Wolf," I replied, "I do not want to pressure you, but I can handle much of our business today. You need to recover fully if—"

"It's okay, Tunde. It will sound funny, but I actually feel better than I did before I was sick. It was like my body needed to sweat out all the negative energy and stress that had been building up for the past two weeks. It was cleansing. I'm ready to get right to work; you just tell me what you want me to do."

She lowered her sunglasses to show me her eyes.

They were bright and clear.

"What do we do next?" Painted Wolf asked.

Rex said, "Tunde needs to make the machine in four days—"

"Four days!"

"Don't ask," Rex said. "He thinks he can do it."

"I am certain," I countered.

"Fine, he's certain," Rex continued. "But first we need to get more information from the miners about how all the equipment they have works. We need to get up close and personal with the technology down there."

"Let me finish my tea," Painted Wolf said. "Then we'll roll."

We ate a brief meal of yam pottage and tomato stew before Naya drove us down the path thirty minutes later. Unlike the people of my village, she had the luxury of sleeping in. And despite the fact that it was now late afternoon, she was still incredibly grumpy. She snapped at everyone in her vicinity.

At the mine, I spoke with the foreman of the operation. Naya watched as the foreman walked me through the process of mining and refining the tantalum. It was a complicated procedure that required a lot of different techniques and materials. I tried to envision how I would make my process work, but the pieces were not coming together in my head as clearly as I would have liked.

The tantalum

I needed time to just study it closely.

But, unfortunately, that is not what I would get.

13.2

"Bah ho."

A familiar voice echoed off the walls of the mine.

"There is my prodigy, ready and eager to build for me."

General Iyabo walked down the ramp into the mine surrounded by his bodyguards. He was smoking a cigar and had a spring in his step. The fact that he looked immensely happy had me greatly concerned.

Iyabo approached Painted Wolf first. He kissed her cheek.

"Good morning," he said.

Turning back to me, General Iyabo asked, "Have you begun work?"

"We have been planning."

"You will have whatever you need at your disposal," General Iyabo said, throwing his arms wide as though to indicate the whole world beyond the mine.

"There are only two things I need outside of tools and equipment."

General Iyabo sucked on his cigar and then blew out smoke rings. "What?"

"I need to know that my family is safe, that while I am working they will not be in the mine. If they were to get injured, it would surely distract me from my goal. I consider myself a very focused person, but you do understand that arriving here and finding . . . this has been a shock."

General Iyabo grumbled a bit but nodded.

"You are a weak country boy; I am not surprised by this request."

"Second," I said, turning to Painted Wolf, "is that I need my business associates at my side. They are crucial to the process."

"Makes no difference to me." General Iyabo shrugged. "Since

I have been generous with you, I will tell you of my conditions and you will not question them. Understood?"

"Of course, General."

General Iyabo turned to Painted Wolf. She nodded her agreement.

"You will tell no one of the agreement we have made," he said. "That includes your family and any other partners you might be in touch with while you are on my property. All of your phone calls and communications will be monitored. You are not the only ones who have access to surveillance technology. As you know, I created one of the most effective scams in all the world."

"Yes, General," she said. "We understand."

The quiet was broken by the dull throb of an approaching aircraft.

General Iyabo blew another ring of smoke.

"One of my business partners has arrived," he said. "You will treat him as you treat me, with the utmost respect."

"May I suggest," Painted Wolf said, "that we keep our agreement on the down low for the time being. Are you sure you can trust this person?"

"Yes," the general said. "Come, now. You will meet him."

Surely this would be Kiran, but if so . . . I had an uncomfortable feeling that maybe the lie Painted Wolf had told the general did not work. Perhaps General Iyabo was more trusting of Kiran than we had assumed?

I looked to Rex and Painted Wolf.

They were ready, but I am sure they also had butterflies.

We reached the clearing just outside the village minutes later to see a sleek, black helicopter land. The wind it whipped up was ferocious and sent huge clouds of dust over the waiting crowd that had hastily assembled.

As we watched the helicopter blades slow and the dust clear, General Iyabo parted the crowd and made his way to the front and stood waiting for the helicopter doors to open.

"What do you think Kiran will want?" Painted Wolf asked.

"Maybe he'll apologize," Rex joked. "*Oops, my bad.*"

Painted Wolf said, "I seriously doubt that."

"I am hoping," I said, "that the general is as duplicitous and calculating as we have assumed. Surely, he would not suddenly trust—"

The helicopter doors opened and a man in a suit stepped out.

It was not Kiran.

It was a man I did not recognize.

I turned to Painted Wolf to ask her if she knew this man, but her expression told me everything I needed to know.

She was deathly pale.

"Oh God, no," she said.

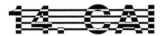

14. GAI

General Iyabo's partner was my father.

Seeing him step out of the helicopter, I wanted to faint.

I could not breathe as he walked out, blinking in the bright sunlight, and shook hands with General Iyabo. The general took both of my father's hands in his own before he embraced him.

"So very good to see you, Mr. Zhang. Welcome, welcome."

General Iyabo turned to the crowd and motioned for people to clap. They did but their expressions did not change. I watched my father as he walked over to General Iyabo's car. He moved stiffly, as though he'd been cramped in the back of a plane for a day, and his clothes were wrinkled. He was also sweating heavily and hadn't shaved.

The whole scene was surreal. For a heartbeat, I wondered if the chikungunya had returned and I was delirious. Maybe I was just imagining this? Maybe I was still sick and lying on the floor of Oyindae's house, tossing and turning?

But it wasn't the virus. I was better and now my father was here.

I wanted to vomit.

I could feel everything I'd eaten in the past two days surging up toward my mouth. I wanted to rip off my disguise and run to my father and drag him back to the helicopter. I wanted to tell him that he had no idea what danger he'd gotten himself into. How could he be **so foolish**?

"Here are the investors I wanted you to meet," General Iyabo said as he led my father through the crowd toward Tunde, Rex, and me.

"Do you know who this man is?" Tunde asked.

I couldn't speak.

"Are you okay?" Rex asked.

I shook my head.

My father moved through the crowd, his eyes darting this way and that, scanning each face nervously. He was very anxious. At home, I'd often find him sitting silently at the kitchen table poring over documents with a blank face. Reading his **micro-expressions**, I could tell that he was agitated. Here, the expressions weren't so micro.

I had never seen him like this. He looked like someone drowning in the deep end of a crowded swimming pool. Treading water, desperate for rescue but embarrassed at the same time. He shook hands calmly, but his eyes told me he was underwater and on the edge of panic.

I felt terrible for him, but there was nothing I could do at that moment. I had to make sure he couldn't see me; if he knew I was there, he'd lose whatever cool he'd been able to maintain.

As my father walked over to us, I turned away, pretending to fall into a coughing fit. It worked. General Iyabo stepped away, pushing my father back.

"She was ill recently; you'll have to forgive her. This is Tunde Oni. He is the engineer I told you about. He will build the mining machine. And this is Damian Quintanilla and Chen Jiang."

I continued my display and wandered off, waving apologies.

"I apologize for her," Tunde told the general. "She will be fine shortly."

"It is a pleasure to meet you," my father said in shaky English, bowing, before he shifted gears, pulling paperwork from his briefcase. "General, we need to discuss what is happening in this village. I have great concerns about the development of this mine. I do not think that the people I represent would be happy—"

"Please," General Iyabo growled. "We will talk about this later."

My father looked at me, tried to see my face, but I spun away, continuing my charade. Did he recognize me? Even beneath the wig and sunglasses and jewelry? Eventually, he relented without saying another word.

"Again," Tunde said, "I do apologize."

Rex said, "She's just had a slight illness recently."

General Iyabo mumbled curses and turned away, dragging my father with him, before the crowd again swallowed them up.

Rex immediately dropped down next to me, arm around my shoulder.

"Are you okay?" His voice shook with worry.

I cleared my throat and nodded.

"I'm okay. I just. Just need a moment."

As we walked back toward Tunde's house, my father's words echoed in my head. He had great concerns about what they were doing in Akika Village. The people he represented would not like the way things had developed. Why was my father here, then? Why would he come in person to discuss the deal?

The answer was simple:

My father wanted to change what was happening.

Either he felt guilty or he had only now realized the enormity of the destruction the general was wreaking, but the outcome was the same—my father wanted out. I had always known he was a good man, despite his reaches for grandeur and success.

I had to save him from this deal.

Suddenly, stopping the general meant more than just liberating Akika Village and protecting Tunde's family; it also meant saving my own.

14.1

That evening, we went to another dinner with the general.

Knowing my father would be there, I had to create a disguise that would fool even him. I couldn't go in old-age makeup; the general would be tipped off that something was wrong. But I had several options.

In China, like many Asian countries, people have an enhanced fear of germs and pollution. It makes sense living in a country as populous as China. Clean-air regulations are rarely enforced, and it is not uncommon to see thousands of people walking around Shanghai with medical **masks** on. In fact, the medical mask has become something of a street-fashion symbol.

I found one in Oyindae's house.

Wearing the mask, a longer wig, and bigger sunglasses, I was essentially unrecognizable. The only part of me visible, outside of my hands, was my neck. I threw on a few necklaces just in case my father somehow could identify his daughter's neck from across a crowded room.

Tunde and Rex were still concerned for my well-being, and as we walked to the dinner, Rex wanted me to assure him that I wasn't overdoing it.

"Trust me," I told him, "I will be fine. This will not delay our work at all."

"Well, unless this new visitor attempts to change it."

"He won't," I said. "We'll make sure of that."

It sounded more ominous than I'd intended.

Like before, the general sat at the head of a massive table overflowing with all manner of local and imported foods. And just like before, he stuffed his face and enjoyed every morsel of it. Tunde watched, picking at his food.

I did not eat at all but sat and watched quietly.

My father sat beside General Iyabo like a gracious guest. He tried a small bite of every dish and pretended to enjoy himself. I knew it was an act from the moment he sat down. He and I shared the same "tells," those unconscious tics that give away our emotional state if you're able to read them.

For my father, it was his eyes. He would squint when he was putting on a false smile or agreeing with someone he found detestable. I saw the squint at school when he met with my math teacher (the one my father was convinced wasn't taking me as seriously as she should have been), and I saw it when my father had dinner with my aunt Chun, who often ridiculed him for his slumping shoulders.

He did not want to be at the table, and it did not take him long to clear his mind. When the dessert course was collected, my father turned to the general and told him that he was very unhappy to see how the people of Akika Village had been treated.

"I expected to find a professional operation, General. These people are not miners. They are farmers and you've got them toiling away at a job they do not know. Not only is it bad for business but you are likely to kill some of these people."

General Iyabo looked as though he'd just swallowed a toad. For a moment, I braced myself for one of his explosive tirades, but instead he closed his eyes and took a deep breath. He let it out slowly before he turned to my father.

"Mr. Zhang," the general said, "you did not come to this place to tell me how the operation is to be run. You came to deliver the manufacturing data. I invited you to be a part of the mining operation, but if you have some sort of moral qualms about it, I am sure I can convince you that your worry is misplaced."

"I do have worries," my father said. "Many. And I don't think we can negotiate a deal for the further development of an additional mine until we have agreed to some changes."

"Changes?"

As servers delivered coffee, Tunde turned to me and whispered, "This is a brave man. I have never seen anyone stand up to the general in such a way. I am surprised he is still sitting there."

I was proud of my father.

He was taking a stand. I don't know if he understood where his shady dealings were going to lead him when the offers first came, when the first shell companies were created, but here he was. And he hated every minute of it.

Unfortunately, he was already in way over his head.

"There will be no changes, Mr. Zhang," the general said with all the authority he could muster. "This is the deal. You take it or you do not. Let me remind you, I have been incredibly generous with you. I have taken you in, showed you how to do business outside your small pond of safe investments and behind-the-times engineering. You do not like what you see, then do not bother handing me the manufacturing data. I can find it somewhere else. I am traveling after dinner, but when I get back tomorrow afternoon, I expect to hear nothing more of this."

"General . . . ," my father balked.

For a second, he hesitated. Knowing that he was at a forked path. One direction excused him from the destruction but left him without a job and possibly financially ruined. Or worse. The other direction led him closer to the general. Closer to the immoral blindness he wanted to avoid. It might, however, make him a wealthy man. He could go home to his coworkers, his bosses, his friends, and his family with his chest puffed out.

My father made the wrong choice.

"I understand," my father said. "I will let you convince me that these people and this village will be better once the mine is fully operational. I look forward to hearing more about the new technology."

He turned to Tunde, Rex, and me and nodded.

For a split second, I thought I saw a tear in the corner of his eye.

14.2

After dinner, Tunde, Rex, and I retreated to the work shed.

"Despicable," Tunde said. "I thought that maybe we had a chance there."

"You okay, Wolf?" Rex asked me as he sat on the edge of a workbench.

"I think so . . . ," I lied. I wasn't sure what to say. "Just need some air."

As Tunde and Rex got to work, planning the first step in the construction of the highwall machine, I stepped outside and cried. It was raining, a warm, soft rain, and it felt great. I closed my eyes, turned my face to the sky, and just let the water wash the makeup off and run down my body.

I had a very important choice to make.

My father was staying. He'd be in the village for days, if not longer. There was no way I could hide from him that long. Not only would the general become even more suspicious than he already was, but my father would surely notice.

And my friends.

I couldn't keep them in the dark forever.

But telling them would open up my life. I had been Painted Wolf for three years, and in those three years I had never let the barrier between my identity as Cai and as Painted Wolf fall. No one knew my secret. It was difficult to keep that barrier in place; it required careful planning and limited my social life to only a handful of friends I saw once or twice a month.

Painted Wolf logo

I had created a cell for myself and I believed that it was worth it. Painted Wolf was the reason that corrupt businessmen stayed awake at night. I was a boogeyman. But in Tunde's village, so many thousands of miles away, none of that seemed to matter. It was silly for me to hide who I was here.

Even though I had embraced Painted Wolf, she had become my

identity; my father showing up threw a significant wrench in that plan. I could not abandon my past. I had to adapt it.

As I stood there in the rain, I realized that embracing Painted Wolf didn't mean erasing Cai. It was an evolution from one to the other. Cai would come with me. My parents would have to come with me. And so would my friends.

I walked back into the work shed soaking wet.

Tunde looked up at me. "Wolf, are you crazy?! You need a towel!"

"There's something you need to know."

"Can I get you a towel first?" Rex asked.

"No," I said, sitting down at the bench across from him. "I'm fine."

"You were coughing—"

"I was faking it."

"Because of the Chinese man who came?" Rex asked.

"Yes," I said.

"You know who he is, don't you . . . ?"

I nodded.

"That man is **my father**."

Tunde gasped. Rex stared at me blankly for a few seconds, trying to wrap his head around what this meant.

"He is Mr. Deiwei Zhang. My name is Cai Zhang."

Silence followed before Rex said, "It's nice to meet you, Cai."

We shook hands and then burst out laughing.

"I have to tell you," Tunde said, "I am very honored that you would share this with me. Does he know you are . . . ?"

"He doesn't. None of my family members or my friends in China know that I'm Painted Wolf. You two are actually the first people I've ever told."

Tunde leaned over and hugged me.

My clothes were cold and his warmth felt good.

"So what do we do now?" Rex asked.

"My father is in danger," I said. "He was in danger long before this, but now he's in way over his head. He's a good person. He'd do anything to ensure I'm safe. We have to find a way to make sure he is safe while he's here. When we take the general down, I need to know my father will walk away with his dignity intact. He will learn a lot from this experience but I don't want it to destroy him. You understand, right?"

Both Rex and Tunde nodded that they did.

"Stakes have gone up," I said. "Before tonight, I wanted this for you, Tunde. I hoped it would shield my family in the process. But now both of us have everything to lose."

The roar of rotors startled us as another helicopter soared over the village.

It sounded like we were getting another visitor. I wasn't sure I could handle anything more; I'd already had my heart broken once that night.

"**It's Kiran**," Rex said. "He's here."

"How do you know?" Tunde asked.

"Who else could it be?"

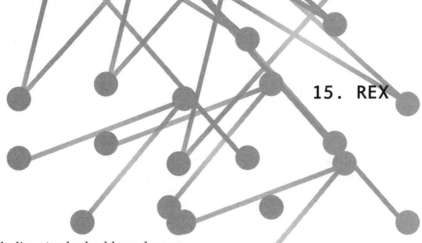

The helicopter looked brand-new.

It landed in the center of town, whipping up a tornado of grass and leaves.

The windows were blacked out and we could not see who was inside.

Even though it was quite late at night, most of Akika Village was there to watch. These people had been through so much in the past few months that they didn't seem surprised to see yet another stranger arrive.

Kiran stepped out of the helicopter alongside Edith.

He looked exactly like I expected him to: stylish jeans, a black T-shirt, sneakers, and sunglasses. His hair wasn't perfect, and the bags under his eyes made it clear he'd spent a lot of time on a plane to get here.

Edith looked exactly as she had at the Game.

All business, no fun.

The people of the village didn't react.

"Guys!"

Kiran's voice was tinged with too much excitement. His smile was so bright it would have powered Tunde's Solar Power Tower for a decade. He ran over to us and reached out to shake our hands—neither Tunde, Cai, nor I moved.

Tunde's face hardened into a grimace. "How dare he . . ."

"Understandable . . . completely understandable . . . ," Kiran said.

He turned to Cai. "Good to see you again."

"Wish I could say the same," Cai said coldly.

"Good," Kiran replied. "Still, you look a little under the weather. You should make sure you get some good rest. I've found there's nothing more healing than a decent night's sleep and maybe some green tea."

I couldn't believe this was Kiran. Wasn't he just siccing the cops on us last week? Didn't he threaten to have us imprisoned for not going along with his scheme? And now he was acting like we were best buds.

Truth is: Either this was another of his tricks or he'd lost his mind.

I'd love it to be the latter, but I'm sure it's the former.

"Why are you here?" Tunde asked, furious.

Kiran said, "Because you're here."

"You are not welcome," Tunde replied.

"And I'm not surprised you would say that. I honestly don't hold it against you. You're angry. Things ended on a . . . sour note. I'm just swinging by for a quick look and to make you guys an offer."

Tunde shook his head. "You have destroyed my village. My people . . ."

"No," Kiran shot back. "No. That was the general's decision."

"You funded him!" Tunde shouted over the helicopter rotors.

Kiran turned back to the pilot and gave him a thumbs-up.

The pilot killed the engine.

"Wrong, Tunde. You're confusing me with a dictator or some evil mastermind in a pulpy spy thriller. Akika Village is in the midst of a transformation. And sometimes the process of transformation looks ugly. Sometimes it's uncomfortable. Devastating even. But you never question the chrysalis because you know the butterfly is the result. Same here."

I actually laughed.

Couldn't help it.

I was just so sick of hearing his poetic platitudes.

Kiran shifted his attention to me. His eyes narrowed and his jaw tightened. Suddenly quite serious, he was in no mood for my laughter. I expected him to call me out on it. To tell me I was being childish. Like usual. He didn't.

"I want you to come with me, Rex."

I wasn't expecting that response. It was absurd.

"You're crazy."

With the sound of the rotors gone, I was surprised at how loud I sounded.

"I'm serious. We were just getting started, right? You proved yourself at the Game. Showed us all up with WALKABOUT. I was most impressed with how you managed to get out of one of the most secure cities on Earth. And here you are. I need that brain of yours, Rex."

"For what?"

"I call it WALKABOUT 2.0. Original, right? It's the next generation. And I want you to help me take what you created to the next level."

"I already found Teo. My program's done."

"Did you really? I don't think so. You've just begun. I can see it in your eyes."

Tunde wasn't having any of this. The very fact that I was talking with Kiran in the center of his beleaguered village was enough. "No," Tunde said to me. "You cannot seriously consider anything this person tells you."

"You want a better world," Kiran continued.

"Rama? Your second-generation Internet?"

"It's more than a new Internet. Right now the Net is a bunch of scattered pieces. Billions of them, all scattered across our phones and computers. Rama creates a local copy. Everyone will have one on his

161

or her device. You'll browse in your own copy, your own world. It is much safer. Much more connective."

"And easier to control," I said.

Kiran shook his head. "So paranoid. I'm offering you a chance to work on the future, but if you want more practical terms, think of it this way. Come with me and you help Tunde live in peace. You want Painted Wolf to not have to look over her shoulder for the rest of her life? And you want a way for your brother to come in from the cold? For good this time?"

Kiran let that hang in the air between us.

"What is it exactly that you want me to do?"

Kiran said, "There are encrypted lines of code in WALKABOUT. I've broken most of them, but there are three that I still can't unlock. I want you to unlock them for me and make sure they are properly integrated into the Rama system."

Forget this guy. I'm ready to walk.

"We've got a plan here," I said. "We're going to save Tunde's people from this debacle you've gotten them into. If I go, it'll throw everything we've planned into chaos. The general already doesn't trust you."

"Nobody trusts me," Kiran replied. "But you're making this all more complicated than it needs to be. I will tell the general you are joining me. Your friends here can suggest that maybe you're coming with me to keep me occupied, so I don't get my nose into whatever it is you're up to."

"Sounds lame," I said.

"You made New York work, you can ensure this works too. To sweeten the pot, I'll make you an offer you can't refuse. How's that sound?"

None of us said anything.

"Man," Kiran said. "You're all so uptight. Look, it's simple: If Rex joins me in India, I'll clear your names."

162

16. TUNDE

I was nearly steaming with rage.

"That is impossible . . . ," I said to Kiran.

"I can't stop what's already started, but I can make it go away," he replied, looking at Rex. "You already created your own avenue of escape. WALKABOUT. I've loaded it into my machine in Kolkata. You all thought the quantum computer in Boston was impressive? You have no idea what awaits us. I will erase you, Tunde, and Painted Wolf and the personas you invented to get here from every database on the planet. I will make you ghosts. You'll be able to go anywhere, do anything, without fear of being recognized or tracked. Of course, it's not permanent. You'll be starting from scratch, leaving new trails of data, but for the meantime it would . . . liberate you all."

"And my parents?"

"I can do the same for them."

My heart was breaking!

I could not believe the words I was hearing from Kiran! The fact that this person had dared set one of his fancy-shoed feet in my village was an act of war! And then he had the temerity to actually suggest we could all work together. Who was this ridiculous person?

But the truth is, he was not there for me. Or for Painted Wolf.

He was there for Rex.

And my dearest friend was a sucker for the words of this madman. I should not disparage Rex. He was in a time of crisis. All around us there were fires that he could not put out. His parents had been

deported to a home they hardly knew, and his brother was still lost to the winds—more a series of digits than true flesh and blood.

I do not blame Rex for listening.

Kiran was a master liar.

"Take a moment," Kiran said. "Talk amongst yourselves. I am going to meet with the general. In the morning, I'll be leaving. I hope you'll be coming with me."

Rex nodded and Kiran turned and walked with Edith toward my village. Painted Wolf looked to Rex, her eyes wide, wondering what he was thinking. He shook his head and seemed quite troubled.

"You're not seriously considering going with him?"

"No," Rex said. "Of course not. But if he could do it—"

"He can't," Painted Wolf said. "He's just trying to trick you."

"But if he's not . . ."

"What are you suggesting?" I asked. "We need you here. We have so much to do and only a few days' time to do it. This little adventure with Kiran sounds like the worst idea imaginable! If you go with him, he might turn you over to the authorities at the very first opportunity. Either that or he will have you chained to a computer in some dingy basement for the rest of your life."

"Kiran wouldn't have wasted his time coming out here," Rex replied. "He wouldn't have flown here himself unless he was making a real offer."

Painted Wolf looked pained. "So if it's not a trick?"

"If he really has that technology? Then we need to access it. I'm not saying I want to go with him. I don't. But think about what we're doing with the general. We need to be just as cunning with Kiran. He's expecting us to balk at his suggestion; he's betting on me telling him to go to hell. What if I don't?"

"What are you getting at?" I wondered. "I can tell you have an idea."

Rex smirked.

"I'll go with Kiran," he said. "Then I can get inside his operation. We're only seeing one side of it here. The general's side. And I don't think Kiran is the partner the general seems to think he is. I think Kiran's being Kiran and he's playing everyone. Maybe I can do more to help us there than I can do here."

"How are you going to help from India?" Wolf wanted answers.

"I don't know yet," Rex admitted. "But if there's another quantum computer, more advanced tech, then I can get into his systems. He's basically inviting the fox into the henhouse. I can access everything. . . ."

"And he knows that," Painted Wolf said. "You're foolish to think he doesn't."

"This is a chess game, Cai," Rex said, using her real name. I will tell you, my friends, it sounded strange on his lips. At first I did not know who he was speaking about, but then, when it clicked, it sounded wonderful.

"Each side is trying to play the other," Rex continued. "The only way to win is to give some ground. Kiran has made the first move. He's opened the door. The last thing he'd expect is for me to take advantage of it."

"That is a dangerous way to play," Cai said.

"And I don't want to leave," Rex said. "But something tells me we're not going to get another opportunity like this again. I know you two can take down the general. But even with him gone, Kiran will be there to test us. He's the reason your father is here, Cai. If this is going to end, it's going to end with Kiran."

"I'll go with you."

Four simple words and everything changed.

We were standing in the field beside the helicopter. Kiran seemed impatient. He was eager to get back to his lab. I got the distinct impression he didn't like being around the general. Can't say I blame him.

"What are you saying?!" Tunde shouted.

He was very enthusiastic in pretending to be shocked by Rex's agreement. We had agreed as a team that we'd act surprised that Rex was going with Kiran. It made strategic sense. Key to Rex's success was having Kiran think Rex was hesitant, that Kiran had some sway over him. We needed to look convincing.

Tunde might have gone a bit overboard. He grabbed hold of Rex and turned him around so they could see each other eye to eye.

Tunde said, "You cannot do this."

"Please," Rex said. "Trust me, Tunde."

"Rex, do you have anything you need to pack up?" Kiran asked.

"No, I'm ready to go. But I do have one condition."

"Of course . . ." Kiran expected this.

"The general," Rex said. "I need for you to remove him from Tunde's village. Stop work at the mine, fill in the hole, and send the soldiers away. If I go with you, I want General Iyabo to leave this village and its people in peace and never come back."

Kiran scoffed.

"I have no control over the general," Kiran said. "He is his own man."

"You fund him," I said. "You help him."

"I do no such thing," Kiran said, feigning being deeply insulted.

Or maybe, just maybe, he was actually insulted. It was difficult to tell. Actingwise, he was Oscar caliber.

"I am not in the business of funding warlords, Painted Wolf. You should know that. I'll admit that the general and I are partners, of a sort. The truth is, you didn't care what the general was doing in this far-flung stretch of a country until he threatened your friend. He has been doing this for twenty years! Think of all the other hopeless people he crushed under his foot."

I stood my ground, staring Kiran down.

Kiran didn't budge.

"I can't meet your condition, Rex," he said. "But I will tell you this: You already have the best team to stop the general right here. Tunde and Painted Wolf can do it just as easily as I could."

"Don't be silly."

"I'm not. This is their fight. Let them fight it. You and I have a flight to catch. I will clear everyone's names; I will get your parents back to you. There will never be another offer like this. Trust in your friends, Rex. They are stronger than you're giving them credit for. They don't need you for this."

Kiran extended his hand for a shake to **seal the agreement**.

Rex hesitated. He glanced at me and I could see the tension in his eyes. We'd made this decision as a team; we were going to see it through as a team. But . . . this was harder than either of us expected. I knew he'd come back. I knew we'd be together again. I had to believe that. I gave Rex a tiny, subtle nod and he smiled sadly before he turned to Kiran and they shook hands.

"When do we leave?" Rex asked.

"Now," Kiran replied.

Minutes later, Rex and I hugged. I held him tight and placed my head on his shoulder, right in that spot I'd fallen asleep on at the Solar Power Tower. I was **confident** he could do this, and I needed him to know I was there.

"Come back to me," I whispered.

"I'll be back before you know it," he said.

I let Rex go and watched him walk alongside Kiran to the helicopter. The rotor started up again, and they ducked inside as the blades whirred to life. The windows were dark, but I could see Rex in outline, sitting beside Kiran.

Even though I couldn't see his face I could tell he was watching me.

I kept my eyes on where I imagined his were as the helicopter rose up into the sky and then vanished.

No matter how much my heart would ache, I knew the clock was ticking. Tunde and I had so much to do, so many complicated moves to pull off, that I needed to focus now more than ever. Tunde's people were depending on his machine, whether they knew it or not. It had to do everything we'd promised and more.

And then there was the matter of my father.

18. REX

It is amazing how quickly the thrill of travel wears off.

Two weeks earlier, I'd been a travel novice.

Uncomfortable, gawking at everything, in awe at the very thought of speeding across the country and seeing places that my grandparents never would have even imagined.

This trip, I was jaded.

The helicopter ride to Lagos was my first, but I couldn't enjoy a single moment of it because all I wanted was to be back with Cai and Tunde.

I couldn't appreciate the views because I was worried sick about Ma and Papa.

My stomach was spinning but I bit down on my anger and tried to focus. I wasn't sure how long I'd be gone.

A few days? Could be weeks? Months?

Didn't matter; what mattered was I'd be back and when I saw Cai and Tunde again, this would all be settled. The general, Kiran, Teo. I wasn't going to see my friends again without being able to tell them that we were safe.

You're doing this for them. For your family.

"By the way, they were already coming," Kiran said, putting down a French technical journal he'd been reading. The page he was turned to had the title: "Feature Learning and Deep Architecture." Computer stuff.

"Who was?"

"The general and his men. They were going to tear Tunde's village apart looking for tantalum. It was all about money. They'd done it to several other villages, scraped them and ripped up the ground beneath them for a few hundred thousand dollars. I convinced them to change course, to go north of the village, and to look for something far more valuable."

"What are you making with the mineral?"

"I can't tell you."

"Because it's a secret?"

Kiran shook his head. "No. Because I don't trust you."

I laughed. Couldn't help it.

"That's rich," I said. "You're going to bring me halfway around the world to work at one of your secret labs and you don't trust me."

"Not yet," Kiran said. "You're not ready. You'll know when you are. I won't even need to tell you; you'll see the truth of it yourself."

I wasn't in the mood for Kiran's riddles, regardless of how intriguing they sounded. "So you're going to tell me you saved Akika Village, right?"

"Not yet."

The landscape opened up under us. Miles and miles of farmland appeared. Roads snaking across them. In the distance, I could see the gleam of the city.

"See, here's the thing," I said, still looking outside. "You're going to try to convince me that you swept into Nigeria to save villages like Tunde's, that you're some sort of digital-age Robin Hood. Even if I believed it, two days from now I'd find out the opposite. That this is some plan long in the works, that you're the one raiding Nigeria for its minerals and putting the blame on warlords."

"Hate to disappoint you. But I'm not the villain here."

"So who is?"

Kiran smiled.

"Sometimes, Rex, there isn't a villain."

18.1

Cai had told me Kiran had a private plane.

I believed her, but I don't think I understood just what that meant.

I pictured the kind of executive plane you see in movies and TV, the ones with the leather airplane seats in rows with a wide aisle. The ones where people stand up during the flight and talk business.

This was a flying mansion.

It had a few reclining chairs, but it also had couches and beds in the back. You're going to think I'm making this up, but there seriously was a dining table at its center. It was ridiculous, and even Kiran looked embarrassed by how ostentatious the plane was. Went against everything he was trying to project.

"Seriously?" I said as we walked in. "Are you a pop star, too?"

"I got it secondhand from a Saudi prince. I haven't had time to strip all of these unnecessaries out. When I'm finished, it will be minimalist. Sort of a mobile office for the trust."

"Ah, yes, your famous brain trust."

Kiran settled into one of the leather recliners but I stood.

"I'm here," I said. "Keep up your end of the bargain."

"Oh, of course."

Kiran motioned for Edith. She walked over with a briefcase. It was the kind you imagine criminals carry around handcuffed to their wrists.

Kiran opened the case. Inside was a computer terminal.

"I made a few alterations to WALKABOUT," Kiran said. "Cleaned it up some. Smoothed out a few of the rougher edges. Have to say, though: I left a few of the bugs. They were just so inventive. Like abstract art. Not necessarily the most functional way of doing things but just so fun."

Kiran typed several passwords before he ran a retinal scan.

He wanted me to know there was no way I was getting into that machine.

We'd see about that.

"How are you going to make this work?" I asked. "It's a little too science fiction even for you. Let's say you can delete all the data 'breadcrumbs' you can find—that's only on web-facing databases. Anything offline is unreachable."

The captain closed the plane's doors. He settled into the cockpit and began his departure run-through.

Kiran, eyes on the monitor, said, "You're forgetting the encryption, too."

I was. Truth was, many of the databases that would have data about the LODGE—face-recognition pickups from CCTV feeds, government watch lists, secure site log-ins—would all be encrypted. WALKABOUT had work-arounds for those, but it wasn't deleting data, just looking at it.

"The world's most secure sites have an air gap," Kiran said. "There is literally a gap between the Net and the data in the secure system. So, yeah, it seemed like an impossible task."

Precheck over, the captain came onto the overhead: "Ladies and gentlemen, please fasten your seat belts. We'll be taking off momentarily."

If Kiran was just pulling my leg, if this was another trick, then I only had a few moments to get off this plane.

"Tell me you figured it out," I demanded.

"Sit down, Rex. You're going to hurt yourself."

"Tell me this isn't a trick."

Kiran looked up from the case. "Sit down."

The plane pulled forward and I sat right across from him. "Tell me."

"It is a trick," Kiran said. "But not on you. I am doing exactly what I said I would. I am erasing you, Tunde, and Painted Wolf from every single database in the world. The trick is that it is impossible. I can't actually use WALKABOUT to delete the data stored on those secure servers."

I jumped up. "Stop the plane."

"You're far too wound up," Kiran said. "This plane isn't going to stop, and you're not getting off it. Now sit down and listen. You'll like this."

The plane sped up. Outside, the trees turned to blurs.

"Stop screwing around, Kiran."

He flipped the case around. On the monitor I watched as the program, similar to WALKABOUT's interface but altered, generated cookies, forms, and even photos of Painted Wolf on a seemingly endless roll of sites.

"Painted Wolf is dead," Kiran said as I sat. "Long live Painted Wolf."

I stared hard at the screen, trying to figure out what was happening.

"It's simple," Kiran said. "The only way to truly erase a digital footprint at this point is to create a new one—I tweaked your data, gave you new names, new identities, and then populated the web with the new, clean you. The LODGE is still wanted across the globe, but you are no longer a member of the LODGE. You are a different Rex Huerta, just as Tunde and Painted Wolf are different. Consider it like the witness protection program."

Kiran spun the case back around and finished up.

"We'll have to celebrate your new birthday," he said.

"Show me it worked."

As the plane took off, Kiran shrugged. "That's the beauty of it. We're not actually going to know until you try to pass through security in Kolkata. Now, settle in, we've got a long flight ahead of us."

18.2

They say fear of flying is really fear of death.

It's all about losing control, about putting your fate in the hands

174

of someone you've never met and likely won't even see. That's spooky.

For control freaks like me, it's triply unnerving.

Kiran, however, was oblivious to it all; he spent the majority of our fourteen-hour flight talking with Edith, reading, coding, and, finally, around hour eight, sleeping.

I couldn't sleep. My mind was on fire.

Too much going on.

So I did what I do best when I'm anxious: I coded.

Kiran gave me a locked laptop. I spent three hours attempting every work-around I knew to get it online but nothing worked. Kiran had it locked down tight. Frustrated but convinced, I let the code pour forth.

He glanced over my shoulder a few times during the flight but left me alone most of the time. Just letting my fingers move, my mind cleared and I knew what I had to write.

Rama was a new Internet, an Internet that Kiran would control. It would have local versions on particular devices rather than a widespread web of a billion puzzle pieces across every wired machine. I needed to code a back door into it. I didn't really have a sense of what his angle would be, but I wrote with a few assumptions—devices have certain protocols they require to connect to networks. I started there and just let it all pour out. The whole time I was coding, I kept catching myself grinning. I wanted Cai to see this. She'd love it.

When I was done, I looked over what I'd written and realized it was something beautiful. I read through it again, memorized each and every line as best I could, and then deleted it from the laptop.

Kiran looked over at me. "Create a new masterpiece?"

"Nah," I said. "Just playing around. I bet you have a screwdriver."

"Of course." Kiran snapped his fingers and one of the flight crew came scrambling over. Two minutes later I had a tool kit.

As Kiran watched, I flipped the laptop over, undid the back, pulled out the hard drive, and then smashed it to pieces with a hammer on the table between us.

Delighted, Kiran clapped.

We began our descent into Kolkata.

"Gentlemen, please fasten your seat belts. We are beginning our approach and should be on the ground in Kolkata in approximately five minutes."

The plane angled downward and we emerged from the clouds over a vista I could never have imagined. Kolkata bloomed before me, a sprawling city of metal and stone, furiously alive beneath the roiling clouds.

It was a megalopolis in a sauna.

Kiran leaned over, glanced out the window, and then pointed to a three-story building half-hidden by the swirling mists. "I built my first server farm there. Second floor. It had been a taxidermist's shop, and after he'd closed, many of his unfinished projects were left behind. We set up our servers in and among an elephant's head, a tornado of snakes, and a threadbare lion. Several of my partners refused to step foot in the place after midnight. Fear of animal spirits . . ."

"Why didn't you just have the heads taken out? Seems counterproductive."

"I find people do their best work when they're out of their comfort zones."

I imagined what that must have been like, looking up from the laptop after hours of late-night coding and staring into the dull eyes of a dead tiger.

Kiran certainly knew how to keep his people focused.

And afraid.

I wondered what he'd have in store for me.

Wouldn't be long before I knew.

I was somewhat surprised to find that Netaji Subhas Chandra

Bose airport was a bright, modern structure. Unlike a lot of the city surrounding it, it was made of metal and glass and wouldn't have stood out in a place like Santa Cruz.

We breezed through security. Clearly, Kiran's plan had worked. I had no history. Either that, or this was another of his tricks.

Frankly, I was too exhausted for more tricks.

Moving at a steady clip, we walked past lines of ragged travelers—most of them looked as though they'd spent days waiting to get into the city—and stepped out into the Kolkata miasma.

My clothes instantly suctioned to my body, and my face broke out in rivers of sweat. I was suddenly soaked.

There were two black Teslas waiting for our entourage.

I noticed Tori, the brain trust biologist, behind the wheel of the first one.

She saw me, lowered her sunglasses, and gave a sharklike smile.

Kiran opened the back passenger door, but before he slipped inside, he turned around to me and said, "You coming?"

"We made a deal," I said. "I need to know it worked."

Kiran said, "You think I'd take you this far just to trick you?"

"I need to see it. My parents. Tunde. Painted Wolf."

Kiran emerged again from the car, unlocked his cell, and handed it to me.

I checked on my parents first. Not surprisingly, Kiran had a ton of hacking tools on his cell. Folders and folders of them. I found what I needed and made my way into US and Mexican passport databases. My parents weren't there. I tried immigration and no-fly lists. They'd been deleted.

"You see?" Kiran said. "I'm true to my word."

I looked up Cai, Tunde, and our alter egos. None of them appeared on any records. Anywhere. Government databases, the LODGE website, e-mail accounts, shopping records, all were deleted. Every one of Cai's videos was gone. Every one of Tunde's forum posts.

As far as online went, it was like none of us ever existed.

I handed Kiran his cell.

"You're a ghost," he said.

I climbed into the car and we sped off into the chaos of the city.

18.3

The car left the relative emptiness of the airport and zoomed out into the mass of humanity that crowded the streets outside.

Kolkata streets

It seemed like all of Kolkata was out for the day.

While the sidewalks were wide, wider than even in the States, they were packed. And not just with people going to and fro. The wall of colorful saris was broken by street vendors hawking everything from toothbrushes to baby turtles.

We drove past men sweeping the gutters for fallen trinkets, past families crowded into shelters the size of shopping cart baskets, past children in school uniforms, Jain monks begging for alms, contortionists folding themselves into cardboard boxes, and charlatans in medical coats selling bottles of miracles.

The roads themselves were even more crowded.

Titanic buses overloaded with passengers (some literally hanging on the outside) pushed their way through swarms of motorbikes, auto rickshaws, and ancient Fiats. In and among the fray were sports cars and low-slung SUVs with blacked-out windows. Kolkata's new elite cutting their way through the clutter of India's impoverished millions.

I felt like a visitor from another world.

"Westerners frequently feel overwhelmed here," Kiran said.

"I can see why."

"I'm happy you're here," Kiran said as he looked out the window at the throngs. "I think you're going to find that this place grows on you. Some of the most delicious food in the world, friendliest people, but that's the outside. You'll be at my lab with the brain trust. You're going to be among peers and friends."

"I left my friends," I told him. "They're dealing with your mess in Nigeria."

Kiran turned to me, disappointed. "Haven't I proven myself?"

"I'm not sure."

I had no idea where he was going with this but wondered how long I had to sit and listen to it. If I had known that leaving Nigeria with Kiran meant suffering through his lectures, I might have said no on the spot.

Kiran laughed. "Rex, you are so difficult. I love it. You wouldn't believe how many people come knocking on my door, digital and literal, begging me to allow them the great honor—those are their words—of working for me for free. They are willing to do nearly anything to be involved in what I'm doing. And you flip the table. You make me beg to have you help me."

"I'm a tough customer."

"You're more than that," Kiran said. "Do you think I'd fly all the way to Nigeria to recruit just anyone? Do you think I'd take all the insults and mean looks you throw at me? Don't be ridiculous."

"Inflating my ego isn't going to make me like you."

"I know that. Of course, I realized that at the Game. You made it very, very clear. Rex, I need you the same way that our friend the general needs Tunde. You are a key to something larger, even though you don't realize it yet."

"Ah, there it is," I said. "I was wondering when you'd get cryptic."

Kiran laughed. "Enjoy the rest of the drive; we're nearly there."

He slid down in his seat and closed his eyes.

I turned to the window, but I couldn't focus on the craziness outside. I thought about Tunde and Cai and tried to focus on their faces the night of the dance in Akika Village. But Kiran's words kept creeping back in and shattering any joy I got from the memory.

What did he mean by me being a key?

Probably just more of his mind games to bring me over to his side.

If you'd asked me to recount our route to Kiran's lab, I'd have scribbled across a map of Kolkata. Seriously, it felt like there wasn't a single straight road in the place. If we weren't turning to get around an ox in the road, then we were careening around a corner, nearly taking out vendors on the sidewalk.

When the cars stopped, Kiran pointed to a two-story, concrete cube nestled in among several low-lying buildings. Minimalist to an extreme, it could have been an abandoned warehouse or a Silicon Valley tech company.

We exited the car and I followed Kiran to a steel front door.

There was a biometric lock on the outside and no door handle.

"Go ahead," Kiran said, motioning to the lock's sensor pad.

I placed my hand on the pad.

There was a clank as the door slowly swung open.

black box

180

"Impressed?" Kiran asked. "Door-to-door service."

I stepped into a foyer as white and antiseptic as the Santa Cruz Industrial Biotechnology Center where I had swapped computer help for aldehydes. A young woman sat at a white desk. She had an olive complexion and deep hazel eyes. Her hair was done up in cornrows, and her bottom lip was pierced.

She looked up at me and gave a toothy grin.

"I'm Olivia. We've been waiting for you."

The door sealed behind us with an ominous thud.

18.4

I thought I'd seen advanced technology at the Game.

This, this was like stepping into a catalog from the future.

Olivia opened a door and led me into a large white room that was stuffed with all sorts of ridiculously advanced equipment. Some of it wholly scientific—stuff that NASA would give their eyeteeth for— and some of it experimental, like an egg-shaped desktop computer I noticed in a corner.

"This is Maidan," Olivia said. "OndScan's fifth black box lab."

"Original name. Black box . . . as in top secret?"

Olivia nodded.

"Come, let's meet some of your new colleagues."

We walked through the lab to the back of the room as Kiran and the others split off. I had no doubt I'd be seeing Kiran again all too soon.

I followed Olivia down a spiral staircase to a second lab. Where the first one was immaculate, this was more of a working space than a showroom.

And it was populated.

I'd seen some of these people before.

They were the prodigies Kiran had recruited at the Boston

Collective, the ones who had given themselves over to his vision of a new world.

As we walked through the room, Olivia introduced me.

"Guys, this is Rex Huerta. He's new."

Everyone looked up at me and gave either a feeble wave or a muted hello.

Here it was, Kiran's India-based brain trust.

I wondered how many of these he had secreted around the globe. Olivia had said this was the fifth black box lab. I needed to figure out why I was at this one. What made it different? Despite the fact that I was exhausted and irritated, I had accepted Kiran's invitation 'cause we needed the upper hand.

Tunde and Cai were no doubt in the thick of it with the general; I had to be just as focused. Every minute with Kiran was an opportunity to figure out his game plan and maybe even find a gap in his seemingly perfect armor. With any luck, one of these kids might give me insight.

Olivia pointed out a girl with bright purple hair.

"Hey, Pilar, this is Rex."

Pilar looked up at me, smacking a bright wad of pink gum, and then returned to her computer. I noticed she was writing code for a GPS mapping program. All the locations it was programmed to map were in South America.

I made a mental note:

Check out Kiran's work in South America.

Next up was Miguel. I recognized him from the brain trust meeting at the Game. He was short and kind of mean. I offered to shake his hand but he refused. Apparently he hadn't changed much in the past week.

I noted that Miguel was working on a voice-controlled application. It was clever, quite complicated, and he was programming an intelligent speech interface application. That's a fancy way of saying he was working on making a computer understand human speech. A machine you can talk to.

Mental note number two:

What sort of computer would Kiran need to talk to?

Last was Lea. She was sweet. American, tall, with short-cropped blond hair. She wore no makeup and had a tattoo on her neck. It was the golden spiral, a spiral with the golden ratio as its growth factor. You've seen it, even if you don't know it. It looks like a snail's shell. Lea's whole thing was handwriting recognition software and, according to Olivia, she was Kiran's number one brain trust "visionary." I don't know what that was supposed to mean, but it sounded like something I'd never want to be.

Mental note number three:

This black box team is working on communications. Why?

Kiran was waiting for me at the top of the stairs to the bedrooms.

"Behind me you'll find living quarters. Third door on the right is yours. There's a change of clothes. Have a shower and, if you're hungry, join us in the cafeteria for lunch. It's in the basement. I believe we're having chicken tetrazzini. Our chef, Jagdish, is on something of an Italian tear lately. If you're not hungry or just need a nap, I totally understand. If not, we'll see you at lunch."

With that, I made my way upstairs.

My room was small but comfortable.

Like everything in Kiran's House of Wonders, it was immaculate. A queen-sized bed, a desk, a reading chair, and a view of a back alley where I could see a ragged used-furniture shop filled with battered armchairs and folding card tables. Rooks screeched on the roof above my room.

I took a shower and washed away a day of sweat and grime.

Feeling scoured, I stepped out of the shower and cleared the steam from the mirror to get a good look at my face. The past few days had taken their toll; I looked exhausted, worn down. But more than that, I looked . . . sad.

It was Cai.

My mind drifted back to the Game and our breakfast before Zero Hour. We had no idea what was coming next, but we were at ease with each other. That was the eye of the hurricane.

I wanted to be back there, back in that moment, with her.

I looked down at my hand and laughed, remembering how we'd danced. I saw the firelight on Cai's face. The joy in her smile. But rather than make me sadder, it made me confident. I knew I'd made the right decision in coming here.

I sat down on the bed with a scrap of paper and wrote down all I could remember from the code I'd written on the flight to India. I would say I had accurate mental recall of approximately 89.9 percent of it. The crucial stuff. The rest I could easily fill in—maybe even tweak to be better.

A knock on the door made me jump.

"Yes?" I yelled through the bedroom door.

"We're sitting down to lunch now," Kiran said. "Just wanted to remind you not to forget the bracelet; it's something of a policy here. When you're done eating, come on up and see me."

"Okay," I shouted back.

I found clothes in the closet near the bed.

Three pairs of jeans and ten black T-shirts, all with the OndScan logo on the sleeves. There was also a new package of underwear and socks. And on the desk was a rubber bracelet that read: "Changing the world with no hesitation."

Of course . . .

I got dressed and caught a glimpse of myself in the mirror as I was stepping out the door. Seeing the OndScan logo on my arm broke my heart. I told myself I was undercover, that this was just a secret mission.

It didn't help.

18.5

The cafeteria was like everything else: antiseptic and boring.

Most of the brain trust was eating, and Kiran was right, it was Italian food. I grabbed a plate, a few tongs full of pasta, and then took a seat in an out-of-the-way corner of the cafeteria where I had my back to the wall and a good view of my new colleagues.

Unlike the rambunctious employees of the brain trust in Boston, these people seemed nearly comatose. Maybe there was something in the water, but they ate quickly and in silence like they couldn't wait to get back to their work.

Boy, Kiran sure knows how to pick 'em.

I hadn't realized how hungry I was until the first bite. It was delicious and I went back for a second helping.

As I ate, I tried to think like Cai. Well, more like Painted Wolf.

I watched the other people in the room like she would, reading their clothes, their gestures, and their expressions. It was difficult—they really were a boring bunch—but I did pick up a few clues that might prove useful.

Miguel was certainly on the outs. He was sitting alone like I was and didn't bother to look up once, or maybe even breathe, while he ate. Lea was the most popular, sitting with Olivia, Pilar, and Tori. Even though they weren't exactly engaged in conversation, I could see Olivia and Pilar looking up to Lea. She had their ears, and if Kiran was throwing around terms like *visionary*, that meant something.

If I was going to get insider intel, Lea was going to be my best bet.

After lunch, I walked upstairs, passing through the workroom. Continuing my Painted Wolf–esque reconnaissance, I studied the brain trust's workstations. All of their screens were locked, but I eyeballed the notes and papers left on the desks.

Just as I'd gleaned from looking over their shoulders at the computer screens, the brain trust was all about communications. They'd been diving deep on natural language, pattern recognition, and learning techniques.

I made a ton of mental notes.

The quantum computer at the Game was highly advanced, one of the most powerful machines on the planet, but at its core, it just ran data. Whatever Kiran was working on in this black box lab was much more dynamic.

Only reason you research the stuff the brain trust had been digging into was to develop an artificial intelligence or a series of artificial intelligences. And even though artificial intelligence, or AI, has become something of a buzzword lately, truth is it's not science fiction.

We deal with AIs every single day.

When you buy something online or place an order over the phone, you're interacting with AI. The personal assistant on your cell phone? She's an AI. All those robocalls you get? AIs. The video games you play? AIs.

Somehow, I doubted Kiran was making the next great mobile game.

Kiran's room was upstairs, at the end of a narrow hallway. The door was half open and I knocked on it loudly. He didn't reply so I opened the door and peeked inside. Kiran was sitting by an open window, a laptop on his lap, the breeze ruffling his hair. He looked seriously at ease. Entirely in his natural element.

"Come on in," he said and gave me a warm smile. "How are you?"

"Fine," I said as I sat in a beanbag across from him.

"Have lunch?"

"Yes."

"And it was good?"

"It was."

"Excellent." Kiran honestly seemed pleased. "I need and expect you to be functioning at your highest levels. You have to take good care of your body. If your body gets weak, your mind will, too. I want you to go on long walks. Explore the city. Eat well. Inhale. Exhale. I don't expect you'll be able to get more than four or five hours of sleep here, but I imagine you're also not used to oversleeping."

I found it funny that Kiran considered anything more than five hours to be oversleeping. He must think babies are the laziest things on Earth.

Kiran sat back and folded his hands together.

He looked like a religious man, a guru, contemplating the world.

"What do you want me to do here?" I asked plainly.

"Make WALKABOUT 2.0 work better than it does."

"That's it? All this way for that?"

"Rex, do you know who writes history?"

"The winners."

"Yes." Kiran nodded. "That is something of a simplification, but it's true. The world we know is a product of those who made it. That sounds vague, I know. I have found that everything we do, everything we write down or record, is in response to something else. True, original creation is a very rare bird. If it exists at all."

"So is that what we're doing here?" I asked him. "Writing history?"

"No."

"Okay . . ."

"This," Kiran said as he spread his arms wide to encompass the whole of the building, possibly even the whole of Kolkata, "this is an act of original creation."

"So what you're doing isn't in response to anything? You're not responding to poverty or war? You're not building a new world 'cause the old one's broken?"

"You see me so black and white, Rex. It's disheartening."

"I find you confusing, to be honest."

Kiran laughed. "You need to think of me and my endeavors more like an onion or a Tor network. There are layers upon layers. Everything that I do is toward a larger goal. Sometimes I'll appear to do the opposite of what I intend. Sometimes I will appear to lie. Appear to cheat. I need you to forget what you know, Rex. Forget what everyone has told you. I need you to think for yourself this time."

"For myself?"

"I don't mean you need to be selfish. But you do need to throw away all those things you're still clinging to. We talked about this in Boston. I thought it was clear. But you still don't trust me. I figured breaking you would be a painful but easier avenue. It seems I may have needed to go further."

"Listen," I said as I leaned forward and gave Kiran the most serious expression I could muster, "I didn't come here to join your revolution. I have a revolution of my own. All these smoke and mirrors, these parables and poems, don't mean anything to me. I'm here to clear my name, to clear my friends' names, and to get my family back. That's all. I will do what you want me to do; I will work on your project and I won't complain. But I'm not going to drink your Kool-Aid, okay?"

"Fine." Kiran stood.

He walked to the door. I got up.

"I should also mention the rules."

"Rules, of course . . ."

"You will wear only approved clothing, such as the clothing I have provided you with. OndScan apparel. You will not be allowed any money. If we find you have money, it will be taken. You will not be allowed to e-mail, text, or make phone calls. Inside this building, all communication is blocked. All of it."

"And outside?"

Kiran ushered me out of his room.

"I won't have you followed," he said. "But know this: If you make a call from a café or send a text from some passerby's phone, I will find out. This is my city, Rex. I have eyes and ears everywhere. If you break the rules, our deal is off. You, Tunde, and Painted Wolf will be swept up and deposited in the subbasement of a prison before you even have a chance to catch your breath."

He patted me on the back.

"Explore," Kiran said. "This is an unequaled opportunity."

As he closed the door, I couldn't help but agree.

This was truly an unequaled opportunity.

One for me to get under Kiran's skin, to see what he was hiding in these far-flung corners of the world, and to bring it all tumbling down.

But first I had to break the rules.

I had to call Cai.

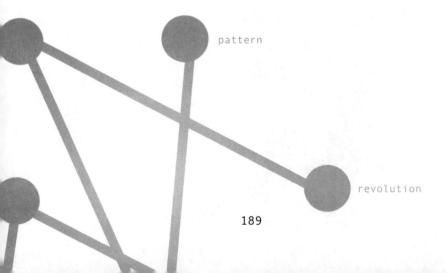

pattern

revolution

PART THREE
TIES THAT BIND

19. TUNDE

The highwall machine was going to be unlike any machine I had made before.

I needed to construct something that would not only make the general think he had his hands on technology the world had not yet invented but also something that would do the work so my people would not have to. It had also to impress his partners. It had to be enough for them to race to the site of the fabled rhodium.

Over the next day, Cai and I spent most of our time in the work shed. We only ventured out occasionally to see my family. Cai was very clever in how she avoided her father. Whether through disguise or simple evasion, she ensured they had no unintended encounters.

The general, for his part, left us alone.

Every now and again, Naya would step into the work shed and look over our designs and scoff. She had no idea what we were making, but that did not stop her from devaluing it. My friends, this young woman had to make herself important. It was as though if she was not insulting someone, then she did not exist.

The evening of our first full day at work, she came barging inside in a terribly foul mood. She knocked papers from the workbenches to clear a place to sit and then she watched us as we worked. I was welding a joint, and after five minutes of enduring her stares, I stopped and lifted up my shield.

"Can I help you, Naya?"

"I do not see how this will work," Naya said. "None of it makes any sense. This place is like a junkyard in here. And for all her brains, I do not see Chen doing anything of value."

"She is invaluable," I replied, happy I had not forgotten the fake name Cai was using. "Chen is instrumental in the design process. I have many ideas; she helps me sort them out. I cannot work without her."

"That's what you say," she snapped.

Naya hopped down from the bench and grabbed a circuit board and held it up in front of Cai. "Tell me," she said, "what does this do?"

"That controls the pressure gauges," I said.

"I am asking her!" Naya shouted.

Cai said, "Tunde told you. It controls the pressure gauges. And that thing you're sitting next to, the one with the hydraulics, that is for the grinding mechanism."

"My father is a bit confused. He was away from his village for half a day. And when he gets back, he is told that Kiran was here and now you are alone. He is concerned. Why did Damian leave with Kiran?" Naya asked, staring me down.

I will tell you the truth, I did not at first realize who she was talking about! Of course, it was the alter ego Rex had used. Keeping all of these different roles and realities spinning was nearly impossible! I am so thankful that Cai stepped in before my awkward silence grew any longer.

"Kiran sees him as a valuable asset," Cai said.

"I find it quite suspicious. Why not you? Why did you stay?"

My friends, the tone Naya used made me uneasy enough, but I would have been squirming in my seat had she directed her glare at me. Cai, however, was as cool as the underside of a stone. This girl is truly unflappable!

"I think you're misjudging the situation," Cai said. "Your father is Kiran's business partner, right? They make decisions together.

Clearly, they have decided that it is in their best interest for Damian to go with Kiran and work on a project there."

Naya did not appear particularly convinced.

"When you all arrived here," she said, "you had a paper trail long enough to encircle the globe. You were well regarded. Famous, even. But tell me, why is it that when I check the two of you out this morning, I can find nothing? It is as though sometime in the past twenty-four hours your entire history has been erased. I assume you know this happened?"

Though Naya was obviously taken aback, I was delighted to hear this news. It meant that Kiran had stayed true to his word. I could not help but sigh with relief realizing that we could now travel freely and that our names would no longer immediately trigger alarms. I did not mourn the loss of all my forum posts or my e-mails. I am not a nostalgic person. My friends, these things are ephemeral and all that matters is right now!

Naya asked, "Who are you really, Chen Jiang?"

"Exactly who I told you I am," Cai said. "We were hit by hackers. We've been targeted before. There are some anticorporate hacktivists that frequently hit us because they're unhappy with some of the investments we've made. And some of the people we've partnered with."

"Working with my family will certainly give them more ammunition."

Cai laughed. "It certainly will."

Naya, however, remained skeptical. "You seem very nonchalant about what appears to be a very serious personal attack. I mean, everything about you and Damian has been wiped clean. Being the daughter of the general, I have developed a few computer skills myself. Even with all my digging, I could not find a single e-mail, post, purchase, or reference. Most people would be irate."

"We're not most people," Cai said, locking her gaze with Naya.

I could tell by the tone of her voice that she was going to shut Naya down. This was certainly going to be good.

"I've been hit by hackers fifty-three times in the past eight months alone. I used to concern myself with each breach of my privacy. I'd make a thousand calls, stay up all night trying to fix every problem I could find. It was never worth it. We swim with sharks, Naya; we expect to get bitten. I'm a little shocked that someone as familiar as you are with . . . *edgy* business dealing is so timid."

Naya stepped very close to Cai, inches from her face. She meant to startle her but Cai did not move. She was like a statue in the face of this hyena.

"I am going to figure you out," Naya said. "And when I do, I will expose whatever trickery is truly going on here. Then we will see how cool you are."

Her tirade over, Naya pointed at me.

"You have very little time to finish the mining machine. The general expects a demonstration on Saturday. If you do not have it ready, you will be taken down to the mine and we will make an example of you."

19.1

I did not need Naya to threaten me to know how much I had to do.

If she only knew!

Kwento was only days from throwing Akika Village into revolution. If I failed, not only were Cai and her father at great risk but my entire village would be rocked by violence. It would be an unbearable tragedy.

I was shaken but Cai was there, as she always was, to make sure my nerves did not get the best of me.

Immediately after our conversation, I set about working on the highwall machine. While in America, I had dubbed each of my creations with a different name; this machine would just be known as the highwall. This was to be a practical piece of equipment, a tool to help my people. I had to be in the most serious mind-set I could muster.

I had several of the strongest residents of Akika Village help me drag every ounce of metal, wiring, cable, glass, plastic, and cast-off electronics to the work shed. What could not fit inside was dumped unceremoniously on the ground outside. All of it would need to be properly sorted and evaluated for condition and utility.

Within a few hours, we had a pile nearly ten feet high.

While many inventors are haphazard in their arrangement of materials, I take great pride in my organizational skills. Half of the time wasted on a typical project, I find, is time spent looking for something. I had to minimize that sort of waste to as little time as possible.

By midnight, the work shed resembled a massive toolbox. Each bolt and spring, every screw and loop of wire was arranged in a predetermined place. I even went so far as to draw off a grid and give each location a row and a number. This, my friends, was organization of the highest caliber! And the best side effect was that my mind was equally systematized. My friends, I had a savant-like focus!

Ready, I cracked my knuckles and began work.

I did rely on the diagrams that Cai and I had come up with for the first few hours of the build. But just as an artist finds a shape inside a block of wood, I, too, found the structure of the highwall machine as I went. It called to me from the grid of spare parts and tossed-off metal.

By the time dawn neared, Cai was fast asleep at one of the workbenches with her head propped on her arms, and in the middle of the room sat a fabulous confabulation of metal. Would it do what Cai had promised the general that it could? It certainly looked the part.

The central piece of the highwall mining machine was a large truck engine. Surrounding the engine was a dizzying array of different gears, pistons, conveyor belts, crushing and grinding wheels, and control panels.

Stepping back to gaze at this monstrosity, I worried that I had overdone it. This thing looked like something a madman might create, something born more of a fever than a brilliant mind. And yet, that ostentation would serve it well. The general wanted bigger and better, and he would get it.

I felt bad about waking Cai, but I needed her to see what I had made.

She rubbed her eyes and looked it over.

Her first words were: "This is nothing like the designs."

19.2

I admitted that it was very different.

"It is improved," I continued. "But I may have taken too many risks. There are some aspects to this machine that push the limits of what I am capable of creating. Sometimes the imagination is more forgiving than the steel itself."

Cai got up and walked around the highwall machine.

"I can't believe you did this, Tunde. Is it finished?"

"It is very close."

"All in one night?"

"It is not yet morning," I corrected. It sounded more like a boast than I had intended so I repeated that I was not yet finished. "But we can turn it on."

"Yes." Cai rubbed her hands together. "Let's."

"Should we call anyone in to watch?"

I do not know why I was feeling so confident in my abilities. In hindsight, it was either because I was delirious or I was simply too eager to show the general. I wanted my people to be free, and I hated the idea of waiting a single day longer.

"How about we just check it out together?" Cai said.

Motioning for her to step back, I walked over to the highwall machine and threw the switch. The machine immediately hummed to life. The sound of it was as deep as the roar of a lion; it created a rumbling bass sound that vibrated every inch of the work shed. It was working!

"It looks amazing, Tunde."

I opened my mouth to thank Cai and tell her that we had reached the final step when suddenly the engine made a hideous sound. Metal ground against metal and there was an explosive pop. Oil and dust spilled across the floor of the work shed. I closed my eyes as the highwall machine belched, and, with a final grotesque squelch, its gears ground together and the engine seized up before dying.

The machine was broken.

Cai said, "We can redesign it? Build it again tomorrow?"

"Do not worry," I said. "Nothing works the first time."

I started picking up tools but found myself gripped by an anger that suddenly felt overwhelming. My friends, it is very rare for me to lose my cool. I think of myself as a very measured and even person, someone with a genuinely balanced temperament. But when I do lose my cool, I also know that it is not in my best interest to leave it bottled up.

"I need a break," I told Cai, setting down my tools.

One of my wrenches fell off the table. That is when I lost whatever modicum of cool I had been able to maintain. Hearing the wrench clatter against the floor of the shed made my blood suddenly boil. I kicked it with a vengeance and sent the heavy thing spinning under a worktable.

Cai was taken aback. She did not jump, but I could see the deep concern in her eyes. All of us have a breaking point. I think I was most shocked at how long it took me to reach mine, considering what we had seen since we had arrived.

"You okay?" Cai asked. "You've been under so much pressure. And you've taken this all on by yourself."

"Thank you," I said. "I just need some time to think."

"Should we meet back here in a few hours?"

I nodded in the affirmative.

Then I stepped outside and I ran.

19.3

Sometimes, when you have reached a wall, the best thing to do is to walk in the other direction for a while.

It is amazing what stretching the legs can do for a sore ego.

The air was cool and fresh. A steady breeze was blowing the fetid mine air away. The sky above Akika Village was clear, and the stars were out in all their glory.

On the horizon, toward the mountains, an electrical storm was rumbling closer. I doubted it would rain—this was the wrong season—but it would give my rambling some nice lighting effects.

I made my way out of the village and down a narrow wadi where a river used to run. It had been dry when my father was young, but my grandfather, I was told, had once caught a huge fish in it. This fish, he claimed, had whiskers like a cat. I do not know if the story is true, but I loved the idea of walking where once a strange fish had swum. That fish started an avalanche of questions—Why was the river dried up? Why was the tantalum under our village?—but they all solidified into one overriding question: How was I going to get the highwall machine working?

I remembered the Game, how I worked on Efiko without Rex and how my frustrations were once again boiling over. Yet this time I was not angry with my best friend. I missed him. Sorely. I was worried about his welfare, and, surely, I realized, this was why my mind was not running smoothly.

I was distracted.

It was not a state I was intimately familiar with. The few times in my life when I had trouble focusing, I was able to quickly refocus. How was it, then, that being up against such daunting stakes I could not get my mind to concentrate?

Perhaps it was not me but the highwall machine itself?

Could I be losing my edge?

No. I refused to believe that. This was merely a step. Life, my mother had always told me, is a process. You must go step by step; there is no other way.

I climbed out of the wadi and made my way up a hill studded with cactus. A few nocturnal creatures scuttled away from me as I reached the top of the hill and gazed down into the valley below. In the daylight hours, it was a home for gazelle. I would come here sometimes and watch them mill about, attempting to calculate how their formations moved. I wondered, could there be a mathematical formula to describe the herding behavior of gazelle? Surely there was.

Tonight, however, the valley was silent.

But it was not empty.

Two hundred meters away a fire was burning beneath a shea tree.

Someone was camping there.

19.4

In my country, fires are to be shared.

They are like meals, and sitting at a fire alone is a sad situation to be in.

We are not cowboys who dream of solitary lives beneath the stars!

I walked down into the valley toward the fire and wondered if it was a herdsman from a neighboring village or perhaps a hunter who was tracking a lion.

It was neither.

It was Werey.

She was sleeping when I walked up. I did not want to frighten her, so I sat across from her on the other side of the fire and cleared my throat as loudly as I could. Werey did not respond to that, either.

"Ms. Werey," I said.

She snored loudly.

Werey was clad in a patterned blouse and an *iro*. A snake roasted on a spit in the middle of the fire. It was well past edible, consisting now of a long rope of charred scales. The fire spit, and Werey coughed, choked, and then hacked in her sleep.

"Werey!" I shouted, growing more concerned.

She grumbled something and opened her eyes. She did not seem surprised to find someone had joined her at the fire. On the contrary, she stretched and yawned.

"Why do you come to my fire?" she asked in northwestern Yoruba dialect.

"I was just out for a walk," I answered in English. "Your fire was inviting."

"Fine. But you cannot have any of my snake."

"That is no problem."

Werey leaned forward and pulled the serpent from the flames. As she rolled it off the stake, the blackened meat crumbled in her fingers. She ate what little meat remained and it left a greasy, black stain on her fingertips.

I wondered about her people. Though she was the last, she was stronger and more fiercely intelligent than anyone in Akika Village gave her credit for. This was her land. This was her way of life. When the cities have burned and the countries blended into other shapes, her way of existence would still be here. It was not a life of earthly wisdom so much as it was a life of refined survival.

Yoruba artwork

"I know you," Werey said as she picked snake bone from her teeth.

"Yes," I said. "We have met several times."

"No. I know you."

"You have heard the stories of my time in America?"

Werey laughed. "I do not care for stories of America. I have as much interest about what happens there as I do about the surface of the moon. In my lifetime, I will see neither."

"You do not know that." I smiled. "Perhaps you will go to the moon."

Werey was not in a humorous mood. "No," she said. "This has nothing to do with travel or mysteries. I know you because I know that look on your face. You are broken, exhausted. That is why you are wandering around by yourself in the night."

I could not deny it was true. Though *broken* was a bit much.

"Do you have any advice for me?" I asked.

"I do not."

I considered getting up and leaving her to her fire and darkness.

"But," she said, "my people do."

19.5

Werey cracked her knuckles, cleared her throat, and placed herself in the storyteller mode.

When a storyteller begins a story, they reach back and connect with their ancestors. This is the well the story comes from. The same well from which Werey was going to draw up a story that would change my entire life.

"There is an orchard," she began, her voice deeper than I had remembered it. "It is hidden from sight, in a cleft between two jagged mountains. The elders of my people used to tell stories of the orchard. They claimed it was in Benue State, but that is wrong. It is closer to Akika Village than most people realize."

I did not want to interrupt, but I had, in fact, heard this story before. Or at least I had heard the version that the old man two houses over used to tell us. He claimed it was a myth. Werey seemed to think not.

"Getting to the orchard is not easy. It requires walking through the desert where you will find poisonous serpents like carpet vipers and puff adders."

I looked down at the bones of the snake she had ingested and wondered. . . .

"It takes a day and a night to make your way to the cleft in the mountains. During the night, you do not want to sleep beneath the baobab trees. Do you know why? It is because the moonlight brings them to life. They walk and can crush you with a single step. If you do find the cleft in the mountains, you will move through it. The climb is difficult, of course."

"Of course."

Werey ignored that and kept on with her story: "If you find the orchard you will be rewarded with a beautiful sight. There is a clear stream that bubbles up out of the earth, and on the banks is the most incredible collection of fruit trees you could imagine. There are juicy mangoes, huge atili, and delicious June plums."

My mouth watered just hearing this short list.

"But you cannot take any of these fruit," Werey continued, leaning in over the fire to add to the dramatic effect. "If you do, even if it is a single seed, you will never leave the orchard. The exit shifts away from you at every turn."

"I have heard this story," I told her. "But I like your version of the telling."

"The chief of my people and his brother found the cleft to the orchard," Werey said, her tone as solemn as the moon above us. "They kept its location a secret, but one day they left the village with large sacks, determined to cheat the orchard and bring back the magic fruit there. They were never seen again. Shortly after this, my people grew despondent. They had lost their chief, they had lost his brother, there was fighting in our camps. Family turned against family, and even the animals were on edge. Five of our hunters left our home to go to the big city by the ocean. The rest of my people followed them. But I was the last to go. It was so many years ago now. . . ."

Werey paused, reflecting. The only sound was the crackle of the fire.

"It took me several weeks to track them all down. Weeks of wandering the concrete streets, my feet sore from the unnatural feel of the fake stone, made me doubt my own mind. I heard voices and saw things I knew were not there. Each of my people that I found, it was the same thing. They were ghosts lost in this shell of a village. The buildings and streets swallowed them up. They no longer sang the songs their elders taught them. They no longer knew the dances of their ancestors."

This was the end of her heartbreaking tale. We both sat in silence.

Finally, I met her gaze and nodded that I understood.

"Werey," I said, "I do not know if you realize this, but you have just changed the entire history of Akika Village."

"How is that?"

"You have just told me how to fix the highwall machine."

20. CAI

After Tunde left, I tried to work on what I could in the shed.

But I actually spent most of the time strategizing how we'd roll the highwall machine out. We'd arrived planning to fool the general, but now we had to build something that could change the lives of every member of Tunde's village.

I never doubted that Tunde could actually build the highwall mining machine, but we needed to ensure it worked even better than we'd promised. They say that in business, the most effective part of the sale is the presentation—Tunde would ensure the machine did what he intended it to, and I would ensure that it looked every bit the game changer it truly was.

Even though Tunde had been frustrated by the initial test, what was sitting in this room was remarkable. Not so much for what it did but for the fact that it existed at all. It energized me to see our plans turn concrete. We had something tangible to show the general, something tangible to motivate ourselves.

I picked up pieces and started reorganizing the floor of the shed.

Wherever Tunde was, I wanted him to come back to find the place ready.

I didn't get very far.

I was cleaning up our blueprint table with my back turned to the workshop door when it creaked open.

"Tunde," I said, "I tried to get everything—"

"Cai."

It wasn't Tunde. My heart stopped as I turned around to find my father standing in the entrance to the workshop. He was wearing slacks and a jacket. But his shirt was open at the top and his tie was tucked into his jacket pocket. This was the closest to disheveled that I'd ever seen him. There were heavy bags under his eyes like he'd gotten about as much sleep as I had.

"Excuse me?" My natural instinct was to act as though he was mistaken.

"I know it's you. I saw you when I arrived and . . . A father knows his daughter. Only, I couldn't believe it. We're thousands of miles from home, in a remote village. My brain could not process the reality of it."

For the first time in a very long time, I didn't know what to say.

I took **off my sunglasses.**

"Are you Painted Wolf?" my father asked. "The hacker?"

"I'm more like a journalist."

My father let out a big sigh. It was like I had just admitted to him that I was a bank thief. He sat down at a workbench and ran his hands through his hair.

"So you're here because . . ."

"The general is destroying this village. I know you see that. You said so yourself. I'm here with my friends to stop him."

"How?" My father seemed exasperated. "How did you get here? You were at the program that your cousin told us about in China. And now you're not there, you're here and you're the notorious blogger the authorities are looking for. The one who could go to prison for decades. Help me, Cai, I don't understand. . . ."

My father was deeply confused, and my heart hurt seeing him like this. It hurt even worse knowing I'd done this to him. If I wasn't Painted Wolf, I might have let the overwhelming emotion of that moment break me down. But now it only made my resolve stronger. When I see a problem, I react logically. I had to bring my father into the fold. Both to ease his discomfort and ensure he didn't blow my cover.

I walked over to my father and sat down beside him.

"I am here under a false name," I said, "Chen Jiang. I'm pretending to be a savvy business investor. My partner, Rex—the general thinks his name is Damian. He's the one who went to India with Kiran. We had a plan before we got here. But it went out the window the minute we saw what the general had done to the village. Now **things are more complicated**. . . ."

My father mulled this over for a few long, anxious moments.

"I don't know what to say, Cai. . . ."

"I just need you to understand that I did all this because it was the right thing to do. It still is. You raised me to understand right and wrong. You taught me to call out injustice and corruption when I see it—"

"I never meant you should put on a disguise and climb buildings!"

"I am making a difference, Father. Those people I exposed are going to jail. The deals they tried to set up have fallen apart. Regardless of what the press says, what I do has made our world better."

"And I don't doubt that," my father said.

"Then . . . what?"

"It's how you do it." He reached over and put his hand on my shoulder. His touch was instantly soothing. I could sense the emotions welling up in my chest, but I held back my tears and closed my eyes.

"It's so dangerous," my father continued. "You could be killed. Worse."

"Like shame? Are you worried I would shame our family?"

"No . . ." My father paused, then continued, "Well, at first, I did think that. I was very angry. Worried that this would ruin my career and my goals. All I've ever done I've done for you and your mother but . . . That's not true, either. I'm not here in Africa for you or your mother, I'm here because of my own **greed**. My own desire for power. I let my bad ambitions guide me instead of my heart or my mind. I will help you however I can, Cai. But I am afraid the general has me in a corner."

"Then you need him to be stopped just as much as I do."

"Yes," my father said, his eyes trembling, "I suppose that's true."

I leaned over and we hugged. The emotions, the stress, the fear, I let all of it come tumbling out with the tears. He held me tight, and though I didn't look up, I could feel his body shake as he tried to push back the emotion overwhelming him.

We sat like that for a minute before I pulled away and wiped my eyes.

"So," my father said, "what do we do now?"

"Tunde is building the highwall machine to help his people. We want it to impress the general, to prove to him that we are worth the capital. The general surely told you about the rhodium?"

"Yes."

"There is no rhodium. Well, maybe there is, but we certainly didn't discover any of it out here. We're tricking the general into crossing the border into Benin. We're going to manipulate his GPS data so he doesn't realize the mistake he's made. When he's safely over the border, we'll have United Nations troops arrest him."

My father cleared his throat and then stood. He walked over to the highwall mining machine and looked it over. Then he turned to me and asked, "Can this machine actually do what you've told the general it can?"

"Not yet. But it will."

My father nodded.

"Well," he said, "then we've got a lot of work to do."

With that, he gave me the sweetest smile I'd ever seen on his face.

20.1

Seconds later, the door to the workshop exploded open.

Tunde barreled in talking a mile a minute. He didn't see my father; his eyes were on the floor and then on the blueprints. He tore through them, babbling about mountains and a hidden garden, or something.

"That is the key! You see here, I was designing it all wrong."

"Umm, Tunde . . ."

He looked up, eyes wild with whatever new revelation had taken hold of him. He seemed confused to see me without my sunglasses. I motioned with my head across the room to my father. Tunde looked and then stepped back, mouth agape.

"It's okay," I said. "He's with us."

"With us?" Tunde was still stunned.

"I am going to help you," my father said. "Cai has told me about your plans. This machine is very impressive, but to ensure that the general and I buy into it, you're going to need a little help."

Tunde walked over to my dad and extended his hand. They shook as Tunde said, "You should be very proud of your daughter. I would not be home today if it were not for her. She has saved me several times over. Now she will help me reclaim my village. Painted Wolf is **one in a trillion**."

My dad looked to me. "I know."

"Okay," I said as I pushed my sunglasses back on, "let's get back to work. What were you talking about when you came in here babbling, Tunde?"

"I had a revelation," Tunde said. "I have learned from you. Last night, after our defeat, I met with Werey in the valley to the north of the village. We sat and talked and she told me a story. . . ."

"Hang on. Werey?"

"The old lady everyone thinks is crazy."

"I know but . . ."

"Sometimes the best ideas come from outside the box of traditional thought. She told me about this mythical orchard and it is hidden away in a secret valley. If you go there and try to take the bountiful fruit from this valley, you will never be seen again. What I am saying is the valley is magical and the fruit is a temptation. I suppose it is like the Garden of Eden in a sense but this . . . You are not following me, are you?"

"I'm trying," I said, "but maybe just tell me what the idea is."

"My design has the working parts revealed. You can see everything."

"Okay? I thought that was the point. They need to see it work."

Tunde laughed. "That is exactly what I thought, too!"

"But it's wrong?"

"Very much so. This story of the valley with magical fruit is very clever. People have been telling this story for hundreds of years because it has two important things: a moral lesson and a mystery. Obviously, we cannot build a moral lesson into this machine. That would be silly."

"Yes, that would be."

"So," Tunde said, "we are missing the second. We have no mystery here! You described what the highwall mining machine would do to the general over dinner. I was so bent on trying to show everyone what I had designed, that I cut some corners. The machine doesn't work properly because I weakened the engineering to make everything transparent. So the general could see every gear and piston working. I was giving the viewer too much. We need more mystery! We need a black box element to the design. Not only will it allow me to better reinforce the moving pieces but it will provide the necessary mystery. As any stage magician knows, the less the audience sees, the more they will believe."

I took a moment to glance over at the highwall machine. It was quite a contraption, so many moving parts, so many complicated pieces, but I could immediately see where he was right. It didn't look like the next-generation thing we wanted Tunde to make. Even if it worked perfectly, it still didn't have that design element it needed. It needed to be **something** people **would gawk at**. Something that no investor worth their salt would willingly pass up.

"So," I asked, "what do we do?"

"We are going to build in some black boxes, metal shielding to hide the works. Nothing too obvious, just places where the audience will have to wonder what is going on inside. To hook him, I need to build in the mystery."

I woke up the next morning in a bit of a haze.

It took a long shower and some fruit to wake me on my way to the open office space. I got down there around seven.

Already, there were three people working. They looked up at me, but none of them smiled. They just went back to working.

I sat at my workspace and stared at my reflection in the monitor for a few seconds. I hated the clinical feel of the lab. And none of the brain trust people had any idea how to properly welcome someone. Truth is: A week ago, Kiran had been threatening to have us locked up in prison. And this place felt just like a jail cell.

I couldn't start coding with that thought hanging over my head.

So I got up and tried to find my way back to the front door. Kiran said he was cool if I went for walks. He even suggested it. That sounded like a good idea. I needed to get some fresh air and hear something other than the clattering of fingernails on keyboards.

Thing is, the place was kind of a labyrinth.

I tried to retrace my steps but got lost pretty quickly.

I wandered down several winding passageways that all looked the same, antiseptic white paint and tiled floors. The lighting was all LEDs embedded in glass cubes on the ceiling to give off some otherworldly "natural" light.

Then I was in a glass walkway that I had no idea existed.

It was suspended two stories over the street, and below me I could see people pushing carts along the sidewalks and vendors staring up. At first I thought they saw me, and I waved, but they didn't. Took a few seconds for me to realize the glass was mirrored on the outside.

They were looking at themselves.

On the other side of the walkway, I went down a spiral staircase to what looked like an immaculate white garage. At its center, in a stall, sat a small black car. I doubted it was one of Kiran's around-town cars. The thing looked experimental.

"That's the Becker," a voice said.

I turned around to see Lea behind me.

"You're the new guy?"

"I'm Rex."

"I'm Lea." She smiled. "Huerta, right? Kiran's been talking about you. And he almost never talks about people. So you must be something special."

"I think I just rub him the wrong way."

"That's the secret, huh? If you irritate him he likes you? Dang, I never thought of that." Lea motioned to the car. "It's a next-generation self-driving electric car. Kiran is certain it's going to be the future. I worked on its camera systems. Pretty proud of it, if I do say so myself."

Lea and I were the only people in the garage.

It seemed like a good time to ask her a few questions.

"So what's the deal with this place exactly?" I began. "Do we have set hours?"

"Nope," Lea said. "You can come and go as you please. Seriously. Miguel takes off every other afternoon at two and wanders around the city."

"And we're working on what? Some sort of intelligent—"

"No, silly," Lea said. "We're taking your program to the next level."

"WALKABOUT? I kind of considered it already done."

216

Lea laughed. "Kiran says nothing is ever really done, it's just abandoned. We're working on a piece of something huge. That program you designed is kind of like the spine of it. There are black box labs in other countries working on the muscle and the flesh. That sounds kind of weird but . . . but we're working on the nervous system."

"So it's what? Frankenstein?"

"It's crucial to the creation of the Rama program."

"Of course," I said. "The brilliant Rama program. I have no idea what it even does. I mean, like *really* really does. And yet Kiran wants me to upgrade my program to be a centerpiece for it. He work pretty hard to convince you?"

"No." Lea grinned. "Not hard at all."

"Lovely."

Despite Lea's ingratiating smile and warm affect, she was just as punch-drunk over Kiran as the rest of the brain trust. They might as well have had IN KIRAN WE TRUST tattooed on their foreheads.

This "visit" was going to be more painful than I'd imagined.

I knew my only option was to make sure I took control of the situation.

Cai had showed us how it was done in Nigeria. She flipped the tables on the general and made him ask us to build Tunde's machine. I realized that was the sort of brilliance I needed to use in India. Kiran had dragged me halfway across the globe to make sure my program melded with his—I was going to flip that around.

WALKABOUT 2.0 was going to be owned by WALKABOUT 1.0.

Lea led me back to the workroom before she took off to who knows where.

The second I got back to my desk, I booted up the computer and dove into the familiar waters of the WALKABOUT program.

It was like walking into a garden that you'd grown but left unattended for a few years. Strange lines of code had appeared.

217

Others, ones I'd slaved over, had been whittled down to near nothing or chopped down completely.

I knew Kiran was monitoring everything that went on in Maidan.

If he wasn't looking over my shoulder with a hidden camera, then he was logging every single keystroke I made. I had to find a way around it.

The answer was easy: I took the computer offline and then rebuilt its hard drive. Took maybe an hour. Afterward, the machine was faster and spyware free.

I knew it wouldn't last.

The second I logged back into the Maidan network, it'd be infiltrated.

So I did everything I needed to before then.

I typed in the code I'd written on the scrap of paper in my room.

If they were going to use my program as the foundation for Rama, then I was going to have my own way into it.

21.1

I'd be lying if I didn't admit some of the Rama code was pretty intriguing.

It was clever.

Actually, Rama was more than clever.

If it had been in the hands of anyone else, it might have been something of a game changer.

Looking over the code, I could see how people could be wildly excited about it. Rama offered a new Internet, a new way to communicate across the globe for free. And it was entirely democratized. Everyone talks about Tor networks, the onion router that keeps the dark Web dark, but this was the complete opposite: a crystal-clear Internet that grew organically with its users.

At least, the prototype was exceptional.

There was, however, one thing that bothered me. While Rama was designed with the end user in mind, a very simple interface that tracked nothing, there was an underlying matrix that didn't make sense.

Rama was designed to connect people, and yet it had its own "cognitive structure," a learning algorithm associated with artificial intelligence.

But this AI wasn't like the ones we use every day. It wasn't *one* AI at all. In fact, it was a collection of hundreds of small, simple AIs. They weren't active, not yet. But it was clear that when they were, they'd form a sort of hive mind—each individual AI feeding a particular stream of information to the next.

It all looked really hypothetical, like something a think tank would be playing around with for a few years. Exactly like something a brain trust might develop. Regardless, I was intrigued enough that the day passed like a blur. I didn't eat; I didn't even take my eyes from the screen once.

When I finally looked up, it was dark outside and most everyone had already left. Lea included. I was alone in the workroom.

My legs were cramping so I decided to test what Lea had told me. She said I was free to leave, to wander the city at my leisure.

So I went to my room, grabbed my hoodie and a nutrition bar.

Then I walked to the front door. It was unlocked. I looked up at the camera mounted on the wall above the door. A flashing red light told me it was on, recording, tracking me.

I pushed the door open. No alarms went off. Nothing happened at all.

"Okay," I said aloud, hoping any nearby microphones would pick it up, "I'm just stepping outside like I was told I could, nothing fishy going on. Just going to stretch my legs and see the city for a few hours. Back later."

The camera stared at me like a doll's eye. Again, nothing happened.

So I left and the door closed behind me with a dull thud.

Leaving the impeccably clean and overorganized environs of the lab and stepping out into a city that held itself together by concrete and chaos was a shock. So was the heat. I thought it was oppressive during the day, but the night wasn't much better. The city didn't cool down at night; it just released steam.

I had no idea where I was going to go.

I didn't want to run into anyone else so I made a plan to avoid all the places that Lea had mentioned. I wanted to get as far away from Maidan as I could, and, honestly, the idea of getting lost was really appealing.

There was just so much I still had to process.

Leaving Nigeria in the heat of our takedown of the general was a slap, but leaving Cai so soon after she was sick was like a kick in the face. This weird part of me imagined that somewhere in Kolkata was a hidden street that might lead all the way back to Africa. Some magical thoroughfare that would take me back to my best friend and the girl I was in love with.

Clearly, I was delirious.

21.2

I probably looked like a madman, too.

I had the video slide show in my head playing back and forth through every moment I'd had with Cai since the moment I saw her at the Game. I knew getting all nostalgic wasn't going to get me anywhere.

So I walked.

I walked with no sense of direction.

I stopped when I came to an intersection, looked both ways, and turned toward wherever looked most interesting. I didn't really take any of the city in. I was too caught up in my thoughts to notice the commotion around me.

If you asked me what I saw that night, I couldn't even tell you.

Famous buildings?

No idea.

Flowering trees?

Nope.

Street magicians sawing people in half?

I wish.

Guys selling wigs from a baby carriage?

Well, yes, actually I did notice that.

It was midnight when I realized I should probably try to find my way back. I honestly had no idea where I was, though, and if I could have taken a cab or rickshaw, I couldn't have told the driver where I wanted to go.

Typical Kolkata rickshaw

A secret lab hidden in a random building? Oh sure, I know that place.

I stood on a corner across from a flower shop and tried to get my bearings. It was useless. I was so hopelessly lost that someone would actually have to come and find me. I realized that could take days.

I might actually starve to death in the middle of a city.

That's when I noticed a pay phone.

It would have been so easy to pick it up and phreak it. Phreaking a phone is when you can fool the phone into thinking you deposited however many coins were required to make a call. I could phreak this phone in a second.

I crossed the street and stood a few feet from the phone.

Did Kiran really have spies everywhere?

I was beyond lost. Was it really possible that someone followed me?

There's no way. Look at this city! Just pick up the phone. . . .

I reached for it but stopped short.

I wanted so badly to call Cai, to hear her voice and know that she was okay. Even if we spoke for three seconds, even if it was just her answering and saying, "Hi," I would have given anything for that.

But first, I had to call my parents.

I needed them to know I was okay.

Kiran is just trying to spook you, Rex. He can't see you.

Still, I looked around to be sure no one was watching me. The street was largely empty. The few people milling about weren't exactly staring at me. And I couldn't see any visible cameras on the rooftops or the telephone poles.

I figured one quick call would go unnoticed.

Kiran isn't some superhuman. He can't see you right now.

I reached for the phone but realized it was simply too risky.

I noticed a young man with a broom a few yards from me. He was smoking a cigarette and leaning on his broom, lost in thought. If I was going to make a phone call, I would need to be creative about it. I'd have to social engineer this guy.

I walked over to him.

"Hello," I said. "Do you have a cell phone?"

The young man nodded.

"I'm, ah"—I dove back into my inner Painted Wolf and tried to remember how this sort of thing would go—"I'm an American, with an electronics company. Are you familiar with OndScan? We're best known for our browsers."

I motioned to the OndScan logo on my shirt.

The young man said, "Yes. I know the company."

"Great. Well, we're on the streets of Kolkata today to roll out a new app. It's a protection thing and it's totally free. Once it's downloaded to your phone, it'll ensure no one can hack into your calls or your online communications."

"Does it cost money?"

"No," I said, "it's entirely free. We're putting it on people's phones to test run it. In a few weeks' time, we'll give you a call and ask you some informal questions. If you agree to let us survey you, the app is completely free. What do you say? It's a limited-time opportunity. Expires at midnight tonight."

The young man pulled his cell from his pocket and handed it to me.

"Thanks," I said. "Will just take a few minutes to set up."

His cell was a four-year-old Nokia smartphone. But it'd work.

I got into the settings and was able to rewrite some of the security codes. It was pretty ancient stuff, and, honestly, I did the kid a favor by making his cell pretty much hack-proof. Even though it only took me two and a half minutes, I pretended that I was having trouble.

"I just need to call my boss real quick to clear this up," I said.

The young man nodded his okay.

I dialed my uncle's phone number in Mexico.

It rang three times before, "Hello?"

Ma's voice chimed through the static.

223

Speaking in Spanish, I told Ma it was me.

She shrieked and instantly broke into tears.

"I'm okay, Ma," I said, turning from the young man and praying he didn't speak any Spanish. "I'm in India. I've got a plan to get you home."

"India?" Ma was perplexed.

"It's very hard to explain."

"Start explaining right now," she said, her tears subsiding. "What happened in New York? The news has said so many terrible things about you."

"And none of it is true, Ma. I promise you."

"But why are you on the run?"

"We have to be," I said, the cell shaking in my hand. "I told you in Boston that we've been framed for doing something we didn't do. I never meant for it to ruin your lives, to get you deported. I just wanted to find Teo. . . ."

"Have you?" Ma asked, her voice breaking.

"Not yet," I said.

Ma silently cried again, but I broke in.

"I came very close, though," I said. "I found an apartment he's been living in. I must have missed him by days. But he was there, Ma. He was there and he was working. I'm so close. I told you I'd find him, and I know that I will."

"You found an apartment?"

"Yes," I said, "I found his apartment."

Overcome with emotion, Ma slipped off the phone.

I turned to the young man and put my hand up to show him I'd be just a minute longer. He looked a little impatient.

Papa came on the line then.

"Rex?" he asked. His voice almost made me cry. "Is that you?"

"Yes, Papa," I said. "I'm okay. Please tell Ma that I'm fine. I'm fixing everything. You should both apply to return to our house, to California. I had someone fix—"

Suddenly the line went dead.

I looked at the cell. It was dead. Battery drained.

I turned around and handed the cell back to the young man.

"Battery just died," I said. "But everything is in order. You won't notice the app on the home screen, but it's running in the background. Like I said, we'll be calling you in a couple weeks for a follow-up."

The young man shrugged and put his cell back in his pocket.

To be honest, I had some serious concerns about Kiran having tracked me. The second the street noises came roaring back in, I got paranoid.

You just took a huge risk, Rex.

I wondered about the consequences. Maybe each of Kiran's brain trust members were allowed a few infractions before anything serious happened? Like a three-strikes-you're-out kind of thing?

If he was going to pull the plug, did it mean calling the authorities?

How much worse could it even get?

"Rex?"

The voice was high-pitched and singsongy.

And it was coming from right behind me.

21.4

I spun around to see a young girl standing to my left.

"I wasn't making a call. I swear. I just . . ."

I stopped short. This girl was maybe thirteen years old and had her hair pulled back in a tight ponytail. She was wearing a red sari and had no shoes on.

"You are Rex, aren't you?"

"Tell Kiran that I wasn't making a call. Just testing."

"My name is Sindhutai," the girl said, extending her hand. "Don't worry, I got really paranoid about the phone call rule, too. He doesn't have any real way to enforce it; it's just one of his psychological control things. You're safe."

We shook hands.

"Should I know who you are?"

Sindhutai shook her head. "I was part of the brain trust. I'm a hyperthymestic. I have what people call a photographic memory. As of right now, there are only twenty-seven people worldwide with memories as good as mine."

"Wow."

"That's what most people say."

"Why aren't you with the brain trust anymore?"

"I don't trust Kiran," Sindhutai said. "He made a lot of promises to me and my parents. He came through on most of them, but I realized pretty quickly that he speaks out of both sides of his mouth. He said he was healing the world, or something. I realized he wasn't. So I left."

Hang on, something's not right here.

"Sindhutai," I asked, "how exactly did you find me?"

"I followed you from the lab," she said. "But that's not important right now. I work with someone who wants to ensure that Kiran doesn't succeed. We have information we think is important. You worked out a back door program to WALKABOUT 2.0. But you made a mistake."

I whipped my head around, certain Kiran was standing behind me.

He wasn't. The street was empty.

"How do you know that?"

"We're looking out for you, Rex. You hid the back door program in code devoted to acoustics. Only you put it in the wrong line of code. Every night at midnight, the computer security systems do an automatic sweep for stray code. They'll find and delete your back door program. You need to move it into the amplitude lines. Understand?"

"Yes."

My brain is going to explode in ten seconds. . . .

"Why should I believe you, though? I've never seen you before. This could just be another one of Kiran's crazy psychological games. A way to freak me out."

"It's not about believing me," she said. "You have to trust me. We want you to accomplish your goal and help you get out of here. But there's still more to do."

"More like what?"

"The back door program is a good start," Sindhutai said. "But there is one more thing you need to add to it. We want you to put in a kill switch, a program that will disable the whole system from an external site."

"That'll be hard to hide." I laughed.

"We know you can do it."

"Wait. Wait. Why didn't you do this when you were there?"

"I didn't know how."

"And the person you're working with?"

Sindhutai shook her head. "We've been waiting for you."

God, that sounded ominous.

Sindhutai turned and waved to a man in a mirrored motorcycle helmet on the other side of the street. He jumped onto a filthy street bike, revved his engine, and raced over, coming to a stop inches from me.

Sindhutai looked at the bike. "He will take you back to Maidan. But first . . ."

She handed me an envelope. Inside was a postcard.

The front was a photo of some Indian shrine.

On the back was a short sentence written by hand in very blocky letters. The handwriting was weirdly familiar. It looked a bit like my own. A little bit like Teo's.

Don't be ridiculous, Rex. You're letting your hopes get in front of your logic.

The message itself was quite simple:

IT IS TIME TO MEET. I WILL SEE YOU TOMORROW NIGHT. BE AT THE BOTANICAL GARDENS IN SCIENCE CITY AT MIDNIGHT; WAIT ON THE BENCH JUST INSIDE THE SOUTH ENTRANCE TO THE PARK. SEE YOU THERE.

"Who is this from?" I asked Sindhutai, completely perplexed.

"My coconspirator," she said. "See you tomorrow."

The guy on the motorcycle revved his engine again. He seemed a bit impatient. Sindhutai told me to get on.

I climbed onto the back of the bike.

And with that, the bike thundered off into traffic. I had to hold on to the driver tight so I didn't go tumbling off into the street. His leather coat was heavily padded and stunk like exhaust, and his boots were covered in mud.

He also drove like a maniac.

The motorcyclist had clearly never heard of traffic laws.

He sped through every single intersection, regardless of the color of the light. Sometimes there weren't any lights. Didn't matter. He was on a mission to get me back like he had something much better to do with his time.

I hadn't been on a bike since I was a kid riding around with Teo. A few minutes into our wild ride through the city, I began to relax. The feeling of weaving through traffic, while entirely different, felt comfortingly familiar. It reminded me of Teo's apartment. Of how close we'd really come.

An hour later, I was standing in front of Maidan.

"Thank you for the ride," I said. "Here, let me see if . . ."

I fished around in my pockets for some money, but I knew I didn't have any.

No matter, the motorcyclist ignored my gesture, revved his bike's engine again, and then sped off into the night. I waved good-bye.

The front door to Maidan opened and Lea popped out.

"Who was that?" she asked.

"I have no idea," I said.

22. TUNDE

My friends, we finished the highwall machine in record time.

Working furiously, we were able to have the machine run without error five times before I gave it my Tunde stamp of approval. I knew that the next time it would be switched on, the general would be watching.

But I had so much optimism flowing through my veins. Now that we had an inside man, I felt as though there was no way the unveiling of the highwall machine could fall through.

While I worked with Mr. Zhang, Cai had gone back to the village proper to get a read on where the general was. She is like an emotional barometer and can sense even the slightest disturbance in the mood of the people she watches.

Sure enough, she came back with unfortunate news.

"Kwento is on his way over," Cai said as she stepped into the workshop.

"How long do I have before he gets here?" I said as I put down my tools.

"Maybe two minutes."

"Okay." I cracked my knuckles. "I can do this."

"It gets worse," Cai said, glancing over at her father. "The general has moved up the demonstration day. He is desperate to impress me and get to that rhodium deposit. I ran into Naya in the village. She stormed over to me and told me we had to have it ready tonight. Also, the general is looking for you, Father."

I wanted to react by panicking, but I did not.

Clearly, Cai was rubbing off on me. Instead of shouting and having my heart rate triple, I took a deep breath and let it out slowly. Then I said, "Okay. We can deal with all of this. I will talk to Kwento. Mr. Zhang, you should leave by the back door. Cai, we just need to finalize a few things."

"You sure you're okay?" Cai asked, a bit taken aback.

"No," I said, "but I will be."

As Mr. Zhang crept out the back door, I stepped out of the workshop into the gleaming daylight to see Kwento arrive with several of my people. I recognized them as the men who had gathered in the mine. They were under his sway.

"Tunde," Kwento said, "my men are getting anxious. Yesterday, while you were closed off in this shed, we were worked without rations. Several people fainted and had to be dragged into the shade to recover. Is the machine ready?"

"It is. I will be demonstrating it to the general tonight."

Kwento turned and looked back at his men.

"And this is going to work?" Kwento said. "You will not pull some prank and then escape Akika Village under the cover of darkness. . . ."

"I would never," I said. And, my friends, my anger at this suggestion did make my blood boil. I actually stepped up to Kwento, a man a good two feet taller than myself, and put my face as close to his as I could.

"I love my people and my village," I said. "How dare you suggest I do not."

Kwento stepped closer to me. His face was only inches from mine.

"Why is it that when I walked in here, I saw the Chinese man leaving?"

I glanced over at Cai but then turned to face Kwento.

"Do you know how to build this machine?" I asked him.

Kwento shook his head but did not step away.

"I have been working day and night," I continued. "I have not slept, to ensure that this machine works. And I am doing it for my people! There is no monetary gain for me. There is no prize waiting at the end of this. There is something even more precious. If I fail, then our village falls to the general."

"That is what I am stopping," Kwento spit.

"And you will die," I said.

A tense moment passed before I said, "When you are brawling, do I step into the ring and tell you how to punch? Do I tell you to hurry up and knock that man down? No. I know you are a fighter, and I trust that about you. I am an engineer, Kwento. I make things. You need to trust me to do it. Sometimes, I might need occasional assistance, but you are not the one to doubt who I turn to."

Kwento considered what I had said, then stepped away.

"Just know that I will be watching," he said.

"Of course," I replied. "So is everyone else."

Kwento signaled to his men and they turned around and left the workshop. As I watched them go, I realized how close we had come to losing everything.

If I had not been ready, they would likely have risen up to take the general down that very evening.

Surely, they would have lost.

We all would have.

22.1

While Cai and I were preparing the reveal, a curious thing happened.

We were busily polishing the highwall mining machine and clearing the workshop when I noticed Naya standing in a field opposite the building. She was talking into a phone and seemed even more animated than usual.

"What do you think is going on there?" I asked Cai.

Cai looked and shook her head. "Probably just making someone else's life miserable. I'm glad she's not in here staring at us. Can't stand that girl."

"She does not have her entourage," I said. "That is unusual."

"Naya does seem to stop by a lot," Cai said. "I think she likes you."

"What?" I yelled without realizing how loud my voice was in the shed.

"Seriously," Cai said. "Maybe she has a crush on you. That would explain why she seems to be coming around at random times."

"That is ridiculous," I said. "Besides, she is walking away from us."

Through the window I could see that Naya was crossing the field. She looked as though she was being surreptitious, as though she hoped no one would see her vanish into the trees.

Cai noticed this very clearly as well.

"There's something different going on here. I think we should pay her a visit."

We managed to leave the workshop quietly and make our way around Naya so she could not see us. We hid behind several trees and watched her as she shouted into the phone loud enough that we could hear what she was saying from several yards away.

"This will not do! I need for my father to send them away. If they succeed tonight, they will derail everything!" Naya said. "It is now or never."

As we moved closer, I could see that the phone she was talking on was what people refer to as a "burner cell." A cheap, prepaid cell phone that can be disposed of easily after a call. These are phones used by criminals and are largely untraceable. On our drive to Akika, Naya had used a smart phone. There was no way she was suddenly downgrading to a toss-away phone unless she had a very good reason.

233

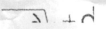

"No!" Naya said. "My father is wrapped up in this. I am telling you—"

She stopped short, eyes wide, as we stepped out into her line of vision like lions emerging from the long grass to the horror of a trapped gazelle.

Naya hung up the phone.

"What are you two staring at?" she asked, furious. "If my father finds out that you are stalking me and not working, he is going to be most unhappy."

"And what if he finds out you're tricking him?" Cai asked.

"I do not think you know what—"

"I think we do," I interrupted. "Who do you really work for?"

Naya scoffed and tried to push past us, but we stepped back in front of her.

"Tell us who you were talking to or we tell your father," I said.

"Go ahead," Naya spat.

"You're mistaken if you think that phone is safe. I can crack it. In fact, I recorded your phone call just now," Cai said as she lowered her sunglasses and pointed at the camera lens embedded in the side.

"I believe you called your father an idiot," I said.

Naya was not a person who was used to experiencing defeat. She fought it with every nerve and fiber of her body. But we had her entrapped and she knew it.

A few seconds of silence passed as Naya dropped the burner phone to the dirt and ground it to pieces with her heel. The phone came apart easily, the screen cracked, and the plastic snapped. Still, even in this state it could be salvaged.

"You two have ruined my operation," Naya said.

"Operation?" I asked. "Who are you with?"

"Terminal."

22.2

Hearing that word was like being hit by a battering ram.

It sucked the very air from my chest and left me dizzy. My friends, I thought the last twist to our story was enough to knock me sideways.

"The general's daughter works for Terminal?"

Cai was stunned as well.

"My father is a monster," Naya said.

"You have been quite a monster yourself," I reminded her.

"Only to get in his good graces. He has never really wanted anything to do with me. He sent me off to boarding school in Europe when I was five. I have only been home a few weeks over the course of the past thirteen years. He never visited me. Never even bothered to send a card."

"So this is how you get back at him?" Cai asked.

"It is not about me," Naya said. "This is about a larger goal. My father is just part of a bigger process, a whole lot of people doing bad things around the globe. Terminal found me and told me I could help them. I had an in that no one else could match. We are going to bring the general to his knees and expose his partnerships. The world will do the rest."

I was not sure if Naya was to be trusted, but I did not trust her before.

"So we have a common goal?" I asked.

Naya shook her head. "You both think you are so clever, but you are a distraction. I was close to getting what I wanted before you showed up. And you are so clumsy! Even with your fake passports and doctored résumés, I could tell you were hiding. I tried to convince my father, but he is not a detail person. However, it did not take me long to put the pieces together. You are the LODGE. Terminal knows

235

everything about you. You are just children running around trying to be spies and heroes. You are going to get hurt in this game. If I were you, I would just pack up and leave."

"That's not going to happen," Cai said.

"So there you have it," I added. "It seems we are at a stalemate. We both want the same thing, but we have different ways of getting it. What was your plan, Naya?"

"The only way to stop my father is to destroy him."

"Spoken like a true Terminal disciple," Cai sneered.

"And you think giving him what he wants will help?" Naya said.

I did not want to reveal our larger plans so I just nodded.

"It will not change anything," Naya continued. "The general is a greedy man. Since we are at a stalemate, how about this? I will not expose you and you will help me. Maybe Terminal will take you in."

"What are you planning?" I asked her.

I was growing increasingly frustrated with Naya. She was in my village, among my people, playing a game with all of our lives. I did not like it one bit. I believe she saw the intensity of my expression, because she sighed and then told us exactly what it was she was up to in Akika Village.

"My father runs a scamming operation called Counterblast," she said. "They have access to a library of malware that goes beyond anything a bunch of Russian hackers can dream up, stuff that would take a team of very good programmers ten years to create. He keeps it in a soccer bag in the big tent where all of his electronics run. A dozen hard drives with the most sophisticated programs imaginable. My father is tricky; no one suspects that bag has more than old tennis shoes. Terminal wants it. They want to take Counterblast over and use it for good."

"For good?" I could not believe such a thing was possible.

"The only way to change the status quo is to blow it up," Naya said, climbing onto her high horse. "Getting that data is like waking up on Christmas morning and finding a nuclear bomb under the tree."

"Why don't you just take it?" Cai asked.

Naya said, "You know my father; he is not a trusting person. He keeps that data very close to the vest. I have had to put on quite a show, the adoring daughter, to get into his good graces. I was hoping I would have that data and be out of here this week. But I did my job too well and now he relies on me to keep an eye on you. I cannot take the data until you two are gone."

"Listen," Cai said. "We can help each other. You continue to convince the general to trust us and we will be gone in a day. We will help you however we can before then."

My friends, I can tell you one thing for certain: We would keep Naya and Terminal in the dark about our plan to trap the general, but I would also do everything I could to ensure Terminal never got ahold of that data.

"Why should I trust you two?" Naya said, narrowing her eyes.

"You already said it yourself," Cai continued. "We've complicated matters. Our showing up has made things more difficult for you. Tunde and I need your silence, and you need our cooperation. Even if we don't like it."

Cai put out her hand.

Naya took it and they shook.

Then Naya turned to me. "This machine works, right?"

"It better," I said.

I walked with my father toward the mine.

It had taken several hours but we managed, with the help of Kwento and his men, to get the highwall machine out of the workshop and onto a flatbed truck. It moved so slowly, we just walked alongside.

The sun was just setting. The sky was bright orange, and the few clouds drifting about looked like they'd caught fire. It was the magic hour indeed.

"Are you going to tell Mom?" I asked my father as we walked.

"And give her a heart attack?"

"Might be better than having her find out later. The thing is, Father, there is still so much for me to do. Even if this works and the general is locked up, my friend Rex is in India and I need to get him back."

"The tall American?"

"Yes," I said. "He's part of our team."

"Kiran's told me a lot about him," my father said as he stepped over a prickly shrub. "He says he sees himself in Rex. Kiran has such grand visions of what he wants to do, but, I'll admit, I have only seen tiny slivers of them."

"Then why work with him?"

"Even the lowest branch is happy to be on the tree. I don't know, I was looking for a way to get us to a nicer apartment and a better car. You will go to university soon, and I want you to be able to choose where you go."

"There are scholarships, Father. . . ."

We walked in silence, the tires of the flatbed truck crunching the ground beside us. Already, soldiers and villagers had gathered in the field, anxious to see what their hometown hero had created.

"I think Mother would understand," I said. "She'd be upset for a while, but she'd come around. I think if she knew, she'd worry less."

"And what about me?"

"What? What about you?"

My father slowed. "Are you going to tell her about me? I have failed her and you; this business with Kiran and the general is shameful. I have wanted out of it for the past few months, but I'm in too deep. It's gotten to the point where I can't extract myself without losing everything."

"I'm going to help you get free of this, Father."

"Even if the general is removed from power," my father said, "Kiran is only growing stronger. He won't let me just bow out. He'll see it as a slight. He can be **a vengeful person**, Cai. I've seen him do terrible things."

"And that's not going to happen to you," I continued. "We'll find a way to fix this. To make it right. You've already started by helping me and Tunde."

My father reached over and squeezed my hand.

Just before we reached the field, my father pulled an envelope from his jacket pocket and handed it to me.

"I should tell you," my father said, "even if the general crosses into Benin and is arrested by UN soldiers, he is likely to avoid charges unless there is evidence at the site. I think I can provide that."

"How?"

"I will turn over everything that I have."

"Father . . ." I suddenly grew very concerned. "You can't implicate yourself."

"We don't have a choice, do we? I **need to do** this, Cai. The only way out is to clean the slate. To expose him, I have to expose myself. Everything is stored in a cloud account. I will download all the files I have as well as the general's files I can access. He keeps a lot of the data associated with his other schemes there. I have seen malware programs as well as scamming data. If I download it all onto hard drives and we turn these over to the authorities, maybe it will go a long way to clear my name."

I nodded to my father. Then, noticing the time, I grabbed his elbow.

"You need to go," I said. "The general will be expecting you to be with him. If he or his people see you here with me, they might suspect something."

"Ah." My father smiled. "You are very good at this."

23.1

Tunde stood beside his parents.

Behind them, a white sheet covered the highwall machine.

It looked pretty dramatic; this massive, angular lump could have been anything. Tunde certainly had nailed the mystery aspect he'd been looking for. People milled about, looking at the covered highwall machine from every angle. Tunde smiled and nodded to them, ever the charmer.

Ten minutes later, the general's car arrived. It was another black car with the same driver who'd brought us from the airport. Naya was the first to step out. She glanced over at Tunde and me. It was quick and I doubt anyone noticed, but it was clear what her intention was: She wanted us to know she was watching.

Not as the general's daughter but as Terminal.

If this worked, she would get us out of her hair that much sooner.

The general climbed out of the limo. He was wearing an ornate uniform. Each shoulder dripped with golden tassels, and his breast sparkled with as many medals as the fabric could carry. My father followed behind him, acting very much the part of the loyal partner.

"So what do you think?" the general asked me as he approached.

"It looks . . . intriguing."

My father spoke up. "It is quite ingenious, but I haven't seen it work yet."

"Well," the general said, "that is why we are here."

Soldiers set up three folding chairs near the highwall machine. They graciously allowed me to sit beside them. I looked over at Tunde as I sat and folded my hands in my lap. I had to act as though I was ready to be disappointed. It was difficult. Everything was riding on my reactions, and, sitting there beside my father, with the whole of Akika Village staring on, I had to bury my churning emotions.

"I told you I would deliver the finest highwall mining machine ever devised," Tunde began. "Well, I am happy to report that I have succeeded beyond our wildest ambitions."

The general said, "That is what these ears like to hear."

With the skill of a magician, Tunde pulled the white sheet from the machine.

The crowd gasped seeing it.

It was difficult to describe, but the best comparison I can give is that it resembled a road-paving machine. It was about twenty-five feet in length and had a series of flat conveyor belts that led from one large bucket to another. There were also tanks of fluid and about two thousand miles' worth of cable and wire.

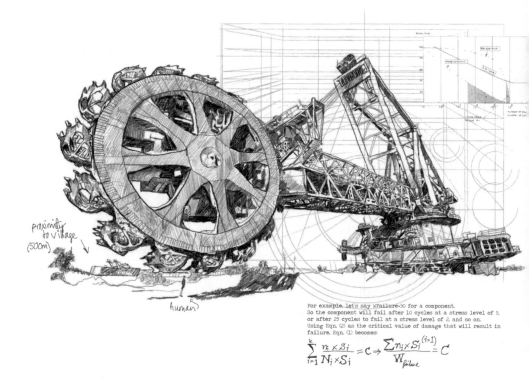

proximity
to village
(500m)

human?

For example, let's say WFailure=50 for a component.
So the component will fail after 10 cycles at a stress level of 5,
or after 25 cycles to fail at a stress level of 2, and so on.
Using Eqn. (2) as the critical value of damage that will result in
failure, Eqn. (1) becomes:

$$\sum_{i=1}^{k} \frac{n_i \times S_i}{N_i \times S_i} = C \rightarrow \frac{\sum n_i \times S_i^{(i \ne 1)}}{W_{failure}} = C$$

Tunde's highwall mining system

If you'd seen it in the street of a major city, you would have assumed it was something that had crashed there. A wreck. But in that field just outside Akika Village, it looked like something driven in from the future.

"I do not have much to say," Tunde shouted to the crowd, speaking to the general directly. "General Iyabo asked me to make a machine that will do the work of one hundred men. I did and now I will show you how it works."

Before he switched the machine on, Tunde looked to Kwento.

Kwento was grinding his teeth.

While I was pretending not to be too impressed, I could feel the tension in the air. Tunde needed this highwall machine to work to save his people. Kwento was relying on it to stop an impending, and surely deadly, revolution. Naya wanted it to work so we would leave. I was desperate for it to work so I could get the general over the border and my father to safety.

Everything hung on this very moment.

Under his breath, Tunde whispered, "Here we go."

Then he pressed a series of buttons and the machine revved to life. It ran on palm oil, so the engine was quite loud. There were several backfires and black puffs of smoke before it ran smoothly. Tunde then climbed into a seat in the "cab" of the machine, and he drove it like a tractor to the nearest mine wall. With a flick of a switch, the massive spinning blades on the front of the highwall mining machine roared to life. The wall of the mine sparked as the machine's blades bit into it. The crowd gathered in close to watch what the machine would do next.

In the few places where we could see the machine's activity, the ore rode around on the conveyor belts before being crushed, then heated, and finally vanishing inside a holding drum on the back of the machine. I leaned forward, pretending to be particularly interested in the process.

Secretly, however, I was overjoyed! It was working so well.

After five minutes of the highwall machine's rumbling, Tunde switched it off and walked to its end to where the holding drum was. It was nearly as big as Tunde himself. He unlatched it and the drum swung forward, emptying its contents on the ground before us. The drum was overflowing with tantalum ore.

The crowd cheered.

"General Iyabo, Mr. Zhang, and Miss Jiang," Tunde said as he approached the general, my father, and me, "I would remind you that this is a demonstration machine. With the proper tools and access to higher-grade machining, we could make something much more sophisticated."

"So," the general asked me, quite pleased, "what do you think?"

I considered for a moment, letting the silence sink in.

"The machine is well built," I said, standing up. I dusted off my hands as I approached the highwall machine. I walked around it, studying it carefully. "I watched Tunde build this. We all know he's an impressive worker. Very devoted. This is quite an impressive engineering feat considering the time he had."

"But is it impressive enough!?" the general asked as he stood up.

I nodded.

"I am convinced that you are a worthy business partner, General," I said. "In the morning, I will take you to the rhodium deposit. With Tunde's genius and your direction, we will be very, very successful."

The general clapped and the villagers broke into applause.

Kwento went over to Tunde and squeezed his shoulder. They spoke quietly for a few seconds before Tunde hugged his parents and then shot me a discreet smile. I still had to look like a business partner who was certain what I was doing would work. Inside, however, I wanted to jump with joy.

The general walked over to me and we shook hands.

"I have a feeling we will be great partners," he said. "I am pleased that you did not trust Kiran and chose to come to me directly. I know that he has the wealth and the **technological wizardry**, but I have something even more impressive: I know how to get people to do what I want."

I nodded as though I agreed completely. But I wanted to tell the general that he had no idea who he was messing with. While he might be a powerful man in Nigeria, Kiran was a brilliant puppet-master. All of us were deceiving each other, playing a dangerous game with the truth.

"Excellent," I said.

24. REX

Five minutes till midnight, I found the stray code Sindhutai had told me about.

Luckily, none of the brain trusters were paying any attention to me.

I was seriously sweating and stressed.

A single string of code could have blown my whole mission.

I moved it to the amplitude line fifteen seconds before the computer security system ran its automatic sweep just like she said it would.

That was a close one.

I leaned back in my seat and sighed loud and long. Olivia glanced over at me and then shook her head. I'm sure I just looked like an amateur.

"Does anyone sleep around here?" I asked as I got up.

I didn't get a response.

I went to my room and tried to sleep but ended up just tossing and turning in bed, the adrenaline taking forever to make its way out of my system. I stared at the ceiling and let my mind wander. It didn't wander far: Cai's face kept materializing in front of me.

Four hours later and beyond exhausted, I gave up on sleeping and went downstairs to have breakfast with the brain trust.

If I thought that might give me a second wind, boy, was I wrong.

The meal consisted of fresh fruit, breads, nuts, cheeses, and eggs. For the most part, it was a silent meal. The kind that really distracted people have. Where everyone's doing their own thing. Kiran didn't join us. When I asked about it, Olivia said he rarely if ever came down to eat.

"Maybe he's a breatharian?" I suggested, half kidding.

I didn't get a single chuckle.

Kiran had certainly picked a focused bunch. I wasn't sure if it was because they were so committed to the cause or because this was just their superpower, but they were in the zone twenty-four-seven. I could appreciate that level of concentration. Thing is, being around people lost in their work is kind of boring.

Well, more than kind of.

Truth is: If I hadn't made an effort to actually speak to the brain trusters, none of them would have even acknowledged my existence.

I need to get a kill switch into the system and get out of here.

A back door program would be easier to write and it would give me access to the system, but once it's opened, it can be tracked. If I wanted to shut the system down, it might take minutes. But a kill switch takes only nanoseconds to work.

I wasn't sure what Sindhutai's agenda was, but I wanted to make sure that whatever kill switch I coded, it would be difficult to execute. I wasn't just going to hand over a potentially dangerous program to some random girl who stalked me. This would be as much for me as it was for her.

Sindhutai was right about one thing, though: Hiding the kill switch would be difficult. I had to take my machine offline and cover the screen as best I could without calling attention to myself. I was as certain as ever that Kiran was watching and listening in. If he wasn't, then the brain trust certainly was.

I had gone to India to be a spy. I needed to step up my game Cai-style.

I'd gotten the back door into WALKABOUT 2.0, but adding

the kill switch, she'd like that. I wanted to tell her firsthand and was desperate for news about how things were going in Nigeria. I wanted an update, even if it was just a minute or two.

If Sindhutai was telling the truth, I could even use a pay phone.

Digging through reams and reams of my old code, I realized that I'd have to pull a Painted Wolf with the kill switch. I had to hide it where Kiran wouldn't look and maybe distracting him with something else would do it. I decided to decrypt two of the three lines of code that Kiran was desperate to unlock. It would take him closer to making Rama a reality, but it would also shift attention from the new problem I was adding in.

Still, as my fingers were racing across my keyboard, I got the sinking feeling that I was playing with fire. We'd struggled with giving the general what he wanted, and so we'd put flaws in the jammer. This wasn't quite the same. To place the kill switch, I was giving Kiran exactly what he wanted. If he cracked the third line of code and I didn't get the kill switch activated in time, we could have big trouble.

It was a risk I had to take.

I kept on working until my fingers were numb. By the time the kill switch was complete and safely tucked into a random bit of operating code, it was nearly eleven at night. As soon as my machine was online, I knew Kiran would see I'd given him two of the locked lines of code. He'd probably be thrilled. I didn't want to be there to hear him ramble on about how I'd done the right thing.

I scrambled from my computer to see that the room was empty.

Obviously the brain trust wasn't working late.

I wondered if I'd missed something, maybe a thrilling Kiran lecture. Regardless, no one bothered to let me know. It didn't matter. I was busy; I was keeping up my end of the bargain. And having everyone gone meant my leaving would go largely unobserved.

That was good because I had a mystery meeting to catch.

247

Finding Science City on a map wasn't difficult.

Getting there, though, that was going to be a whole different can of worms.

Taxi or bike wasn't exactly feasible.

I had no money, and even though the maps all showed the route—and it looked like a straight shot—I knew this place well enough now to know that in India, there are no straight shots.

I could take a train. There were schedules and reliable service, but, again, no money meant I was walking.

And I was fine with walking.

But it would take me hours to get there and then hours to get back.

I didn't have hours.

So I needed an alternative, and that's when I remembered the Becker.

This fancy, next-level electric car was just sitting in a garage gathering dust. As far as I could tell, no one was ever using it. I was sure I could not only hack my way into the vehicle but that I could take it out on the streets and have it back without a scratch. I'd never, technically, driven a car. But how hard could it be?

I sneaked my way down to the garage.

And opened the door to find Lea standing there with a smile.

"Good evening," she said.

Of all the people and all the times! How bad is my luck!?

"Hey," I said. "How, uh, how's it going?"

"Excellent," she replied. "Every day at Maidan is a great one."

I started mentally rattling off ideas of how I'd get her out of this room. Time was ticking down. From the maps, I figured it'd be a forty-minute drive to the botanical gardens. I needed to get moving and fast.

Putting on my Cai hat, I thought back through what I knew about Lea. She loved it here. She loved what she was working on. But mostly, she was totally in awe of Kiran. And I could use that to get her to give me the Becker.

"When was the last time anyone used the car?" I asked.

Lea thought for a second. "It's been a few months," she said. "There are a few hiccups in some of the self-driving programs. The car keeps stalling."

Bingo. This was my in.

"Want me to take a look at it?" I asked.

"Oh, that's okay. This is Kiran's baby. Means everything to him. He just—"

"I'm pretty sure he'd be okay with the guy who created WALKABOUT just having a peek at it," I interrupted. "Besides, he flew me all the way out here to do some work. I'll throw this in as a favor. It can be our surprise. He'll love it."

The thought of impressing Kiran made Lea light up.

"Are you serious?"

"Of course," I said. "He'll be pumped. You and I will figure out the problem, and if we can fix it, think of how psyched Kiran will be. We'll tell him together."

Leah suddenly frowned, overthinking it. "I don't know. I mean, you just got here and he hasn't shown you the car yet. Maybe it's better if we waited. . . ."

I had to get her out of the room and get into that car. Pronto.

You're losing time here, buddy. Seal this deal now!

"He hasn't shown me the Becker because it's not working, right? That's got to be the reason. Here's the thing, though: We can say it was your idea. You asked me to work on it because you know how much it means to him."

She mulled that over.

Tick . . . tick . . . tick . . . Come on, Rex.

"If he's upset, and he won't be, then I'll cover for you," I scrambled. "I'll tell it exactly like it was: I wandered in and told you I could fix the car. I'll tell Kiran you warned me not to mess with it. But listen, none of that is going to happen, okay? What's going to happen is we'll get the Becker up and running and then you're going to look like the brain trust's A-number-one."

"I don't know. . . . It just seems . . ."

"Come on," I pushed. "It'll be cool. You'll see."

That worked. Lea opened up the Becker and handed me the keys.

Whew. Did it.

I climbed into the driver's seat and scrolled through the touch screen on the dash, pretending to look for some problems. The car's software was impressive. All of it OndScan patented designs. All of it very Kiran in its simplicity. Still I quickly found a few coding mistakes.

"See these here." I pointed them out to Lea.

She looked them over, but it was obvious she didn't see what I saw. I went through the program and fixed every flaw I found. Most of them were minor. Like really minor. But, as I explained to Lea, when they add up, they were surely the cause of the glitches. I finished in three minutes flat.

Damn, I'm good but still, tick . . . tick . . . tick . . .

The clock on the dash told me I had only thirty minutes.

"I'm just going to need to drive it a little. To make sure," I said. "Just far enough to see that we've got it calibrated right and get it working."

Lea frowned. "I'm not sure that's such a good idea."

Oh no, here we go again.

"We're almost there," I said. "Imagine how psyched Kiran's going to be when you tell him that we got the Becker running. I'll tell you what, he'll be most impressed with the fact that you did it on your own. You had the initiative, you took the risk. Kiran loves people who take risks!"

Lea brightened at that thought.

"Yeah, okay," she said. "But just a short drive."

"Of course," I said. "Thing is, I'll need you to stay here. You'll watch out for anyone. It'll be fun. Like we're spies. You radio in to me, tell me if you see anything suspicious going on and I'll zoom right back over here."

Lea seemed to like that. She nodded and got out of the car.

I switched it on.

The engine purred, so soft and quiet it was like the engine on a toy car.

Ma was uncomfortable at the thought of me driving and, as Papa pointed out, we didn't have a spare car lying around. He needed the one car we did have, a truck, for work, and with his hours there wasn't time for me to go gallivanting around with my buddies in it.

Still, cars are relatively simple machines.

Despite all the bells and whistles, an electric car was the same as a gas-guzzler. You pointed it in the direction you wanted to go and hit the accelerator.

Even better, this one would do all of that itself.

I was pumped. Here I was, in a car that would take me to my mysterious benefactor, and in a matter of minutes I'd know what was really going on. For the first time since I'd gotten to India, there was a wave of optimism bubbling up in me. It made me giddy, almost like I'd imagined Tunde felt every morning.

Lea rapped on the window. I opened it.

"How do I radio you?"

"Huh?"

"You said to radio you. If anyone comes around, you know?"

"Of course," I said, forgetting I'd added that bit. "You can just radio into the car. Looking through the code, I saw there's a two-way radio over Internet Protocol. The number's in the manual. But, seriously, don't worry. Back before you know it."

With that, I flashed a smile to Lea and rolled up the window.

I pressed go on the touch screen; the car shifted into reverse and eased out of its spot. The garage door opened, and then, seconds later, I was in the street. I cracked my knuckles as though that did anything other than make me feel cool and reached over to program my destination into the mapping software.

I waved to Lea as the garage door closed and then took off.

Thing is: The Becker was not a race car.

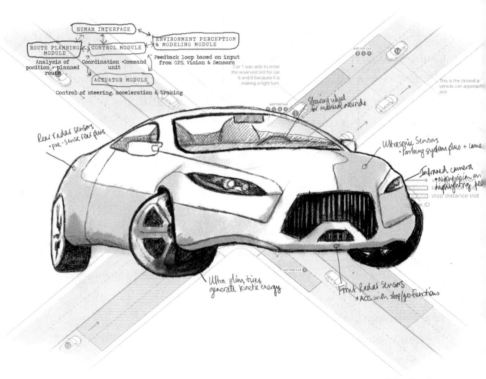

The Becker

If anything, it was more cautious than I'd anticipated. It obeyed the speed limit, not that I saw it posted more than a handful of times, and took every turn as slowly as possible. Several times, I wanted to wrench control from the Becker and give it a little more gas.

Especially when the honking started.

Despite the hour, the roads were packed. People, cars, buses, carts, motorbikes, and bicycles offered endless varieties of potential accidents. The Becker navigated it all with surprising ease. It was impressive.

But still painfully slow.

24.2

At 11:48 p.m., the Becker pulled up in front of the botanical gardens.

It was closed, but people were milling about in front.

I exited the Becker and ran as the doors locked behind me.

"You stay," I said to the car, and it honked once as it armed its alarm system.

I walked briskly around the perimeter of the gardens to find an entrance. There was a gate at the back. It had a simple combination lock. There's an easy trick to cracking these; I'm not going to tell you how to do it, but I can do it in five steps.

Lock off, I stepped into the gardens.

The sound of street traffic disappeared as I made my way down a wide path lined with palm trees. The clouds were low overhead and the air was muggy, which gave the place a heavy feeling. Crickets were going nuts in the undergrowth.

I found the bench ten seconds early.

The next hundred and eighty seconds felt like a millennium.

My only companions were several rats I saw skitter in from the street and make their way to some rat hangout beneath a rotting log.

No one showed at midnight.

No one showed at 12:05.

Or 12:10.

Or 12:15, or 12:20, or 12:30.

I was crushed.

If this was one of Kiran's overly complicated plans of getting back at me or convincing me he was working for the betterment of humanity, it was an obtuse one. Maybe it was designed to break my spirit.

Regardless, I had to get back.

They'd notice I was gone and limit my excursions.

Or worse.

I waited five more minutes before I stood up, stretched, and looked around, desperate to see someone, anyone, walking toward me from the darkness.

Goddamn it, why do I get so hopeful. . . .

I was ready to return to Maidan. Whatever this detour had meant, it had been effective in at least one area: I was tired, beaten down.

I knew it was possible that my mysterious sponsor had run into trouble—maybe there was an accident?—but I would be lying if I said I didn't feel sorry for myself.

With that, I walked away, back toward the gate.

The voice caught me off guard.

So clear, so familiar.

"Rex . . ."

24.3

Teo walked out of the shadows.

He held the mirrored helmet in his hand and wore a padded leather jacket. Of course, Teo was the motorcyclist.

That was why he seemed so familiar!

But my logic had gotten in the way of my hope.

He looked different. His hair was longer than I'd ever seen it, and he had it tied back in a messy ponytail.

Still, the interceding years had been kind.

All of Teo's teenage awkwardness had been hammered out, and he'd filled out the lanky kid I remembered from back home. I stood there stunned, unsure of whether I should hug him or hit him.

Teo extended his arms.

We didn't need words. We just hugged.

He was solid. He was here.

Finally . . .

It had all led up to this moment. Two years of agonizing over him. Two years of watching Ma and Papa breaking down, aging rapidly like they'd been in a war. Two years of having my entire life focused on my brother's ultimate fate.

"Why the hell didn't you tell me who you were earlier?" I said.

"I didn't think you were ready."

I couldn't help it. I pulled back my right fist and punched him in the face.

Teo reeled backward, holding his lip, and said, "That's why."

"You kind of deserved that," I said. "Though maybe not that hard."

Teo sat back on the bench beside me and rubbed his face. I felt a twinge of regret about hitting him, but it passed pretty quickly. Having that anger out of my system relaxed me. God, it was so good to see him.

"How did you find me?" I asked.

"I've been keeping tabs on you, Rex. I followed Kiran here after the Game. I was hoping you'd find my apartment and maybe you'd follow the bread crumbs I'd left. When you showed up, I knew it was time."

"What about the tweaks on WALKABOUT 2.0? Hiding the code?"

"You talk out loud when you think," Teo said. He pointed to the USB he'd left behind, the one I wore around my neck. "Outside of the tracker, it also has a tiny microphone. I assume you found my lab and got the sticky drives?"

255

"I got even more. I downloaded, or whatever you want to call it, all the data from those gel disks. That is such crazy tech it's—"

"Excellent," Teo cut me off. "Where are they now?"

"In Nigeria, with my friend Tunde. I haven't had time to review all the data on those disks, but we have them safe and sound. Well, maybe not so safe, but we have them. I'm guessing you created a biological computer, is that it?"

"Yes."

"That lab was pretty plush, Teo. If it wasn't Kiran, who funded you?"

Teo took a moment to figure out what he was going to say. He had to choose his words carefully. I wasn't going to jump down his throat, but he knew he was going to disappoint me.

"Terminal," he said. "But I'm not with them."

"You just take their money. . . ."

"We can talk about that later," he said. "We need to get out of here. I have a place on the other side of the city. We can go there now, grab my stuff, and then catch a flight to Beijing. There's one leaving at six—"

"I can't go to Beijing," I said. "I need to go back to Nigeria. My friends are there. I'm sorry but I can't just leave them. They need help."

Teo looked disappointed.

"You're a good friend. Always have been," he said. "But you're a very popular person, and I need your help, too. There's a working prototype of the organic computer at an apartment just outside of Beijing. It's up and running as we speak. I need for you to program it. And we have to do it soon. It's the only thing that can stop Kiran. I had a passport made for you and a plane ticket—"

"Why the urgency? Organic computers aren't exactly known for their computing power. Kiran's running quantum machines. . . ."

And that's when it hit me.

Kiran's work at Maidan was all about machine intelligence.

All the code the brain trust was adding to WALKABOUT 2.0 involved communication and visual systems.

He was building a deep-learning program and . . .

"An organic computer is a computer Kiran can't touch," I said aloud as the thoughts coalesced into something coherent. "Once he gets Rama online, there won't be any air gap between machines he can't breach. WALKABOUT 2.0 isn't just some second-generation Internet. It's the infrastructure for a digital revolution that will send us all back to the Stone Age. Kiran's building a deep-learning program that will run Rama. When it's live, it will be linked into every single wired device on the planet. All but one . . ."

"My organic machine," Teo said.

"We have to stop him."

"And we will. Together. Let's go."

I stood up, shaking my head.

My heart was all over the place.

Despite everything, despite finally finding my brother, I couldn't abandon Tunde and Cai. Even if, deep down, I knew that they could do it without me, I had to go back and make sure.

"I'm sorry," I said. "I need to help my friends first."

Teo thought for a moment before he stood up and said, "How about we make a deal: I'll go to Nigeria in your stead."

"You?"

I didn't know what to say. It sounded crazy and amazing at the same time. I knew he'd be able to help Cai and Tunde. And I knew that whatever Kiran was developing in China, I could crack it. I wanted to trust him with every fiber of my being, but . . . I wasn't sure I could. Teo could read the doubt on my face.

"I'll go to Nigeria and help your friends, Rex," he said. "You go to China and help me. When everything in Africa is settled, we'll all come and meet you. It'll only be a matter of days at the most. I'm serious. You trust me, right?"

"I . . . I don't know. . . ."

"I'm your brother."

"And you left us."

Teo looked like he was going to get emotional but swallowed it back down. "I know I did," he said. "I hurt you and Ma and Papa. I hurt you guys bad. I didn't mean to. . . . Things just got out of control. . . . I'll explain it all to you soon. But right now I'm asking you to help me. . . ."

Teo gave me the same pleading look he'd given me as kids. The look he'd shoot across the kitchen table when he wanted me to run outside with him and get into mischief. God, how I missed that look.

"Okay," I said, and we shook hands. "But we can't wait until morning."

"We'll go to the airport now. I'm sure we'll find a flight. Oh, here."

Teo handed me a burner cell phone.

"I've programmed a few numbers into it. I'll give one to your friends and I'll have one myself. That way we can coordinate everything—"

"And not lose touch again," I said.

Teo smiled and nodded. "Of course."

As we walked to the botanical garden's exit, I once again felt that powerful pull of brotherly love. It was so good to have him back, so good to be walking side by side. We stepped out onto the street, and I smiled seeing Sindhutai waiting beside Teo's motorcycle. She gave a little wave.

"You certainly found an excellent assistant," I told Teo.

"Best mind Kiran let go," he said.

I shook hands with Sindhutai. "Thank you."

"Good luck," she replied. "If you ever need any additional help, feel free to reach out. I don't have a cell phone or a computer, but if you're ever in Kolkata, I'm sure I'll find you."

I climbed onto the back of the motorcycle as Teo put on his helmet.

"I have a lot of stuff to tell you," I said. "So much has happened."

"I know," Teo said. "I know, little brother."

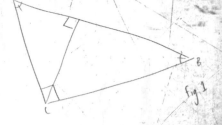

25. TUNDE

It was nearing dawn and neither of us could sleep.

Though we had accomplished amazing feats, we still had a final obstacle to overcome. My friends, we still had to get the general across that border without his knowledge. To pull off that feat, we needed to have the new settings that Rex had programmed into the jammer activated. Timing was going to be quite tricky. Especially as getting to the jammer would require sneaking into the tent where the general stored all of his most valuable technology. I mentioned this to Cai, but she seemed unperturbed.

"We did it before," she said. "We'll do it again."

"You and Rex did it before," I clarified. "I am not as good at your spy craft."

"No better time to learn than now."

My friends, I will not lie to you, I felt a tinge of excitement at the thought of this daring mission. We had outwitted the authorities in Boston and New York. We had gotten onto a plane via a complicated series of subterfuges. Surely, I thought, I could get into this tent. It should be no problem.

While we made our way through the village, I was happy to see that none of the soldiers were on patrol. Perhaps they were sleeping in? Regardless of the reason, I figured it would bode well for our plans.

As we approached the tent, Cai and I discussed what we should tell the soldiers. We both agreed that the best approach was to act as

$$A^2 + B^2 = C^2, \quad C = A\sqrt{A^2 + B}$$
$$C^2 - A^2 = B^2, \quad C^2 - B^2 = A^2$$

though we were inspecting equipment prior to showing the general the location of the rhodium deposit. Cai explained that it was a psychological tactic: We would suggest that, having already proven ourselves with the highwall mining machine, it was now up to the general to prove himself a worthy partner.

It was a risky suggestion, but Cai is nothing if not a lover of risk taking.

There were three soldiers standing in front of the tent. One of them, a younger man, recognized Cai and nodded to her. As we walked up, he said, "Sorry, but General Iyabo has told us not to let anyone in today. I ask that you turn around and head back to the village now."

The soldier was not mincing words.

Cai, of course, took it as a challenge. "This is exactly the thing that I wanted to hear," she said. "Excellent work."

The young soldier looked to his friends, a bit confused.

"Did you happen to see our demonstration at the mine?" Cai asked. "We have developed some very advanced technology, and the general has some of it in this tent. Today is a very big day for me, and I want to ensure that everything is being protected properly."

"As you can see, it is," the soldier said.

"I would, however, like to check for myself."

The soldier shook his head and placed a hand on the gun on his hip.

"Would you like me to ring the general?" Cai asked curtly.

She was not going to play games with this soldier. But he was not bending, either. I will tell you that my concern was growing. Not only was this standoff quite risky, but we needed to get to the jammer. If we could not get into that tent, the entire plan might fall apart. I shuddered at the thought of what fate would befall us if that occurred. My village, my family, my life . . . All of our lives were, right that second, hanging in the balance. I opened my mouth to dive into the conversation when someone stepped out of the tent holding a huge cup of steaming-hot coffee and rubbing his eyes.

"What is going on out here?"

It was Mr. Zhang. He looked quite angry, as though he had not slept in many days, but when he saw Cai, his expression softened. The young soldier stepped aside.

"Sir," the soldier said, "they are asking to enter the tent but—"

"For what reason?" Mr. Zhang asked me.

"We want to ensure that our equipment is functioning properly," I said, making it up as I went along. "We have a very big day today, as you already know."

"Yes, yes," Mr. Zhang said, nodding to himself. "Fine. Come on in."

The soldiers were taken aback, particularly the younger one, as we walked into the tent alongside Mr. Zhang and let the tent flaps fall closed in their faces. As soon as we were inside, Cai hugged her father. He put a hand on my shoulder and squeezed it tightly. "How can I help?"

Ah, I was nearly overcome with happiness! I wanted to do a little dance right there in the center of the tent but I chose instead to contain myself. We still had much to do. Cai asked her father about the jammer and he pointed to a corner of the tent where it was stored. As I turned the jammer on and switched the programming, Cai and her father set up his cell phone so we could control the system. He told her that when they were on the road to radio back to his vehicle and give him a call sign.

"What do you think it should be?" Mr. Zhang asked.

"How about . . . walkabout," Cai suggested.

I will admit that I clapped inside my head hearing that.

Two minutes later, we were finished.

"We still have two remaining problems," Cai said. "The first is that we need to get the jammer into the back of General Iyabo's vehicle. It has to be with us to work."

"I will take care of that," Mr. Zhang said.

Cai kissed her father on the cheek.

"And the second?" Mr. Zhang asked.

"Naya said there were hard drives, all of the general's Counterblast data, hidden in a soccer bag. It's somewhere in this tent, stuffed into a corner or something."

I found the soccer bag in a corner beneath a pile of coats. The bag was well hidden, tossed aside as though it was nothing, just as Naya had said it would be. *Ah, General Iyabo is a clever man.* He hid one of his most precious commodities in plain sight like a wealthy man dressing as a hobo to avoid his creditors!

Now we had the jammer and the hard drives. Surely, we finally had everything we needed to bring the general to his knees and free my people.

Omo, it gave me shivers of delight.

25.1

Back at my house, Cai and I studied the maps very carefully.

We found a rural spot in Benin less than two miles over the border.

With the precise site lined up, Mr. Zhang used his satellite phone to contact an acquaintance of his in New York. This acquaintance had diplomatic ties and linked Mr. Zhang with a United Nations official. The official wasted no time and alerted teams of police and UN soldiers in Benin.

They would be waiting for us across the border.

They said they would be there by eleven in the morning.

We set out for the site three hours later, shortly after ten a.m. It took so long because the general was in something of a foul mood in the morning due to his overindulgence the night before. I believe he had had one feast too many, and the indigestion made him even more cantankerous than usual.

Hopefully, it was to be the last feast he would have in a long time!

We loaded up in a convoy of military vehicles. Cai, Naya, and I sat in the lead vehicle. The general followed behind us in a second car with Mr. Zhang, and the rest of the soldiers and my people followed him in a series of trucks and *danfos*.

We had gone about ten miles over very rough road when I leaned over to Cai and whispered, "We need to turn on the jammer now."

She nodded to me and reached up to tap the driver on the shoulder.

"Sir?" she asked. "Can you please put the radio to the general's car on?"

The driver held up his radio and pressed the talk button.

"Yes?" a voice replied through a veil of static.

"This is Chen Jiang," Cai said. "I need to stop and stretch my legs up ahead. Maybe just get out of the car for a bit of a walkabout. Over."

There was silence for a moment before the voice returned.

"That is fine. But only for a minute."

Cai turned to me and gave a nod.

The driver slowed the car to a stop, and as he got out, the general pulled up alongside us. The convoy was halted behind. The back window of the limo the general was riding in opened, and he leaned out.

"Everything okay?" he shouted.

"She needs to stretch," our driver said.

As the two spoke, Cai opened her door, stepped out, and walked around the vehicle, stretching her legs. "I'm fine," she told the general. "I have been cooped up as we were working the last few days. I just like to get up and stretch every few miles."

"Just do not take too long," the general said. As he rolled up the window, I noticed Mr. Zhang sitting beside him. I caught his eye, and just before the window had fully closed, he nodded to me. The jammer was active. We were good to go!

Cai climbed back into the car and the driver looked at us very annoyed.

Naya glared at me.

"You two are very suspicious," she said.

"Just health conscious," Cai replied with a smile.

25.2

As we approached the border with Benin, Cai asked to look at a satellite phone.

"Can you bring up our current GPS coordinates, please?"

The driver held up his phone to show us the GPS readout.

The jammer was working!

"We are close," Cai told Naya. "Just three more miles ahead."

Naya radioed back to her father, and he accepted the information without argument. Surely he was not feeling well, because I had never seen him pass up a chance to argue.

Being in the wilds of my country, there would be no signs announcing our crossing the border into Benin. We would simply follow the rutted and dusty road over the invisible border until we arrived at the right location.

With every yard we traveled, I grew more and more anxious. I wondered if the UN authorities would put on a big show or if they would be subtle. I certainly hoped it would be the latter. The last thing we needed was for them to accidentally disclose the plan by a show of force or a roadblock.

And then a second concern popped into my head as we watched the dirt road spread out in front of us unbroken. What if the UN troops or authorities were not waiting for us on the other side?

Cai could see the concern on my face.

She looked over at me. "We're fine," she said quietly.

Sure enough, approximately eight nerve-racking minutes later, we crossed over the border into Benin. No one in the vehicle seemed to notice. But the driver slowed the car as we came over a rise and in the distance we saw a figure standing in the middle of the road, waving.

"Who is this?" the driver asked.

I was dumbfounded. From a distance, I cannot say that I recognized who this person was. For a second, I got the distinct sensation that he might have been Rex in disguise, but I knew it could not be. This figure was taller than my friend. And, yes, I know that is hard to believe, considering Rex is what I have heard people refer to as a beanpole! It was a silly thought and I let it pass quickly. Surely, this was one of the UN peacekeepers dressed in civilian clothes.

"That is our mining expert," Cai told the driver. "Just go ahead."

Naya got on the radio to her father. "We are being waved aside by some man in the middle of the road," she said. "I am told he is with them."

"Be on alert," the general replied.

The driver pulled a weapon from a holster on his side and placed it in his lap for easy access. Whoever it was that was flagging us down, I sincerely hoped they were being very careful.

When the car pulled up to the individual, I saw that it was a young man. He was tall and had long black hair pulled into a ponytail. He was dressed in what Westerners call "business casual" and looked quite clean cut. I had no idea who this person was, and judging by the expression Cai displayed, she did not know him, either. The young man leaned in the window.

"Sir," he said with an American accent, "you'll want to turn here and follow the path just down the hill. The location is at the bottom, by the tree grove."

The driver turned the car and we continued down the rugged path that the young man had pointed out.

"Where are we?" the general asked over the radio.

Naya looked at her GPS.

"One and a half miles east of the Benin border," she said.

He did not respond, obviously satisfied with that.

The convoy rumbled to the end of the path by the grove of citrus trees, and there we found a tent had been set up. Cai pointed to it and told Naya, "Here is the location. We have champagne and light hors d'oeuvres waiting inside."

The driver, clearly hungry, stopped the car and got out.

We all left the cars and followed the general, Mr. Zhang, and a battery of soldiers into the tent. As we walked inside, I saw Mr. Zhang use his cell phone to shut down the jammer and the GPS modification program. With a simple swipe, the jammer ceased operating and the normal GPS signal was reestablished.

Even though we had been in Benin for the past ten minutes, now it was obvious to anyone who wanted to look.

What we found inside the tent was not what I expected. There was a long table at which sat a man in an elegant business suit. He was surrounded by at least twenty-five armed peacekeepers in the distinctive blue UN helmets.

He stood as we entered.

"General Iyabo," he said, "my name is Dr. Lucas Gigaba."

"What is this?" the general shouted, enraged.

"You are under arrest for war crimes," Dr. Gigaba said as several of the UN peacekeepers moved in and took the general by his arms. It was an incredible sight. To see my persecutor, the man who would lay waste to my people and my village, taken into custody nearly made me swoon with emotion!

Omo, this was one of those moments when time seems to slow down and you become a witness to history. My heart was aflutter and my mind was a mess of competing ideas. It was nearly impossible for me to believe what I was seeing. This was a moment I had not even dared to dream of!

"But you have no jurisdiction! This is Nigeria," the general roared.

"No," Dr. Gigaba said. "You are in Benin."

To prove his point, Dr. Gigaba held up his cell phone and displayed a map of our current location. It clearly showed we had strayed into Beninese territory.

I have no shame, my friends. I burst out clapping and hollering!

I even did a little dance. My own private shindig of celebration.

Well, I thought it was private. Cai saw me and grinned at the sight.

As General Iyabo was handcuffed, the UN peacekeepers moved in on his soldiers and disarmed them. We heard a commotion outside as the others were taken into custody as well. The general was defeated on that day and not a single shot was fired. It was truly a joyous day.

And yet as my nightmare was ending, another was just beginning.

"Wait . . . What are you doing?"

I spun around to see Cai racing to her father. She was pushing away several soldiers who had surrounded Mr. Zhang and were attempting to handcuff him.

 26. CAI

"He's with us," I yelled to Dr. Gigaba.

The UN soldiers ignored me and continued to arrest my father.

"Cai . . . ," my father said, "I will be okay. If you protest too much . . ."

His expression told me he had already resigned himself to his fate. That broke my heart. My father had been punishing himself for what he had done, but I had assured him I would fight to clear his name. I still knew that I could.

"You can't arrest him," I said. "He's got proof of the general's crimes."

"He is a wanted man, part of the general's circle. Where is this proof?"

"Outside," my father said. "The **data in the soccer bag**."

I bolted from the tent.

The morning had been such a roller coaster of stress and pummeling emotion. I was so happy to see the general fall, but I had never, not in a million years, foreseen my father being taken down with him. It was an emotional blind spot. But I knew I'd have more than enough time to kick myself about it later.

First, I had to get that soccer bag with the general's data.

Unfortunately, I wasn't the only one looking for it.

When I got to the car, I found the trunk already open. Naya was vanishing into the distance on the back of a motorcycle. On her shoulder was the soccer bag.

I screamed at the top of my lungs before I started running after her. Even at my fastest, I knew she'd make the border in no time flat, long before any of the UN peacekeepers could join the chase. Still, I kept running. My lungs burning, my feet slamming into stones, but it was no use.

I got to the top of a small rise to see the motorcycle speeding off into the distance. Naya was long gone. And with her went the proof that my father was just a businessman caught up in something way over his head. Even worse, Terminal now had all of the malware and scam data the general had been stockpiling.

"Cai."

I turned around to see the friend Rex had sent standing there with his hand outstretched. "Rex has told me a ton of amazing things about you," the young man said. "It's a real honor to meet you."

"We have to go after her," I said, breathing hard. "Don't just stand there."

Rex's friend gazed off into the distance and shook his head.

"She's practically over the border already. Even if—"

"I thought you were Rex's friend!" I shouted.

"I'm his brother. Teo."

Teo grinned. But I could feel nothing but rage right then. It's a little embarrassing to say it, but I **punched Teo in the face**. He stumbled backward, holding his hand to his left cheek.

"Ouch!" he shouted. "God, you and Rex are just the same."

"What do you mean?" I asked, shaking my fist.

Teo rubbed his cheek and squinted. "I left Rex about twenty hours ago. He's in China now. I have tickets for you and Tunde. We can go meet him; I have passports and tickets for you. We have a ton to do there."

"After we get my father back," I said.

We ran back toward the tent. I wasn't ready to give up on catching Naya yet, and I had to keep pushing back the creeping realization that there was nothing I could do. Just before we reached the tent, the UN soldiers ushered my father outside. Dr. Gigaba walked alongside them, talking into his cell.

The UN peacekeepers

"Please," I begged Dr. Gigaba. "Let him go."

"I am afraid I cannot do that, miss."

"Where are you taking him?"

Dr. Gigaba took a moment to look me in the face.

"The general will be taken to The Hague to stand trial. We have an agreement with the Chinese government, and Mr. Zhang will be sent to Beijing."

My father was led away in handcuffs behind General Iyabo, and I ran alongside them, pleading with whoever else I could find who would listen. Dr. Gigaba seemed sympathetic but only slightly. He was there to catch the bad guys, and, in his mind, my dad was one of them.

"Cai," my father said just before he was placed into the back of a large UN truck, "I'm going to be okay. Get the hard drives or find a way into the cloud to get that data. That will prove everything."

"Is there a password?"

"You know it already," he said just before the door was closed. "It's your name. Take care of your friends and your mother."

The door closed and the truck peeled out.

The general was loaded into a second truck by several armed men. He shouted and spat and stared hard at me as they shoved him inside. Before he could say anything, the door was slammed in his face and the truck took off.

I watched them go until the dust had **vanished**.

Tunde walked up to me with Teo, but I was too upset to listen.

I needed to speak.

"We have to go back to your village," I told Tunde. "Naya has the information that my father pulled together, and if we hurry, we can catch up with her."

"She is not going back to Akika Village," Tunde said.

"We still have to try!" Turning to Teo, I said, "You can drive, right?"

Teo was able to hot-wire the general's car, and we were on the road five minutes later. The drive back was nerve-racking. I kept telling Teo to hit the gas, but the road wasn't exactly ideal for racing.

"We're going to wreck this car's shocks," Teo said as he punched it.

"Shocks can be replaced. My father can't."

I suppose I was naïve in hoping that Naya would still be in Akika Village. I assumed we'd catch her packing up her stuff or drive up on her just as she was setting out again. As we pulled into the village, I rolled down my window and asked the first person we saw on the road, a young man, if he'd seen Naya. He said he'd seen her drive past but that she didn't stop. Just tore through the town.

"Do you know which way she went?" I asked him.

He pointed into the far distance to the east.

"Cai," Tunde said, "the road from my village branches just two miles from here. From there, it branches a dozen more times. Even if we drove as fast as we could, there is no possible way for us to track her down. I am sorry, my friend, but we need to figure out another way to get that information."

I closed my eyes and Tunde squeezed my hand.

"It will be okay," he said.

I pulled myself together as we drove the rest of the way into Akika Village.

It seemed most of Tunde's people had gathered around our car as we pulled up. We got out of the car and Tunde climbed onto the roof of the car. He gave a loud whistle to catch the attention of his people. They all turned to him, silent, anxious.

"**The general is gone!**" Tunde exclaimed. "*He no go lai to lai come back.*"

The people surrounding the car erupted in cheers and shouts of joy.

Despite the crushing knowledge that Naya had escaped, I was still so delighted to see the joy in the faces of the people of Akika Village. The road ahead would be hard. Their village had been overrun and their landscape obliterated. But at that moment, the air was filled with nothing but happiness.

Part of me couldn't believe we'd actually done it. Traveling halfway around the globe, pulling off a con that just two weeks ago I never could have imagined working. But it did. And that's all that matters.

Tunde climbed down from the car and made his way through the surging, delighted mob to me and Teo. He hugged me and then Teo, beaming like always. "We did it, my friends!" he said. "We actually did it. So what is next?"

"You should be here," I told him. "Spend time with your family. You deserve a break after all this chaos. Seriously, I don't think you've had a good night's sleep in way too long."

"I do not need to sleep," Tunde said. "I need to find Rex."

Tunde looked to Teo, and Teo nodded.

"You're sure?" I asked Tunde.

"Of course. **We are the LODGE**, are we not?"

"Fine, let's get our stuff together," I said. "We're going to China."

My trip to Beijing was convoluted but, thankfully, uneventful.

I took two different flights and had a four-hour layover. Fortunately, I was able to sneak into one of the traveler clubs, the ones reserved for cardholders and people with special passes. They had a decent buffet and several large-screen televisions.

The TVs were tuned to Chinese news, and that's where I first saw it. Success in Nigeria. There was footage of General Iyabo being led from a tent in the desert to a waiting UN truck. I couldn't believe it.

I actually jumped up and cheered. Right there in the club.

All the businesspeople around me stared in horror. I was certain I was going to get kicked out, but I sat back down and lay low. No one came round to bug me.

The TV was muted and the closed-captioning was in Chinese, but I didn't need to understand what the reporter was saying to figure it all out. General Iyabo was going to The Hague. He'd be put on trial. I studied the footage when it repeated to see if I could catch a glimpse of Tunde or Cai. But they weren't there.

Still, it felt so good to know that it had worked.

Ten minutes earlier, I had gotten a text from Teo on the burner cell he'd given me.

It was simple and direct. It said:

> **With your friends. All good.**

Thank God.

Tunde's village was once again safe. *Whew*, talk about taking a load off my shoulders. After reading the text, I nearly sank into the couch I was sitting on. The next text was even better. It was from Cai.

> **We did it! Can't wait to see you! ;)**

That one made me jump up and clap.

I felt like Tunde with all the public celebrating. A few people sitting nearby looked over at me and shook their heads. They must have thought I was crazy.

Crazy lucky!

I tried to text Teo and Cai back but nothing went through. I didn't worry too much about it, though. They told me they were okay and I trusted that Teo had things under control. If he didn't, well, Cai certainly did.

I had two hours before their flight was supposed to arrive.

I people-watched for a while before my mind drifted back to India and Kiran.

I wondered what he was doing. Not only had I left the Becker parked outside the botanical gardens, but I'd simply disappeared without even as much as a wave good-bye. I felt bad for Lea. I kind of threw her under the bus. But she'd be okay. A true believer like her would always find a place at Kiran's side.

Was he going to try to hunt me back down?

Did he have any idea that I'd hidden programs in WALKABOUT 2.0?

The guy's not an idiot. Of course he probably suspects you did.

I hid the programs pretty well, though. Even if Kiran suspected

I hid something in the code, it would take him a really long time to find it. I doubted he'd find them before Rama went live. Well, that was my hope anyway.

Regardless of my subterfuge, I knew I'd see Kiran again.

It was only a matter of when.

As Cai, Tunde, and Teo's plane pulled in, I stood waiting with several discarded flower bouquets I'd found in a bin near the bathrooms.

They were in surprisingly good shape. The flowers had opened fully and their scent was nearly overwhelming.

As soon as Cai saw me she ran over and we hugged.

I actually lifted her up off the ground like they do in romantic movies but ended up stumbling backward and falling into some guy's luggage.

Teo got a laugh out of that, but Tunde helped me up.

I gave Cai the flowers, but she seemed distressed.

"I saw it on the news," I said. "Everything go okay?"

"The general is gone, but Terminal stole the general's data and my father was arrested," Cai said. "We need to stop Terminal and then get him back."

"Your father? Terminal?"

I was nearly speechless.

"Naya," Tunde said. "She took the proof."

The general's daughter. Unbelievable.

"My apartment is only an hour away," Teo inserted. "There are more than enough computers there to access the cloud data you need, Cai."

"And Kiran?" Cai asked. "How do we stop him?"

Teo said, "We beat him at his own game."

"I like the sound of that," I said, putting my arm around Cai and then pulling Tunde in close. "What do we need to do next?"

Teo ran his hands through his hair and cleared his throat. Then he looked out through the glass at the skyline of Beijing, shimmering in the distance.

"Something really, really crazy," he said.

Damn, here we go. . . .

"I bet Kiran is pretty pissed off that you just up and ran," Teo said. "He's going to come after you guys with a vengeance."

"I'm counting on it," I said.

"No," Cai said, breaking into a wicked smile. "This time, the LODGE is coming for him."

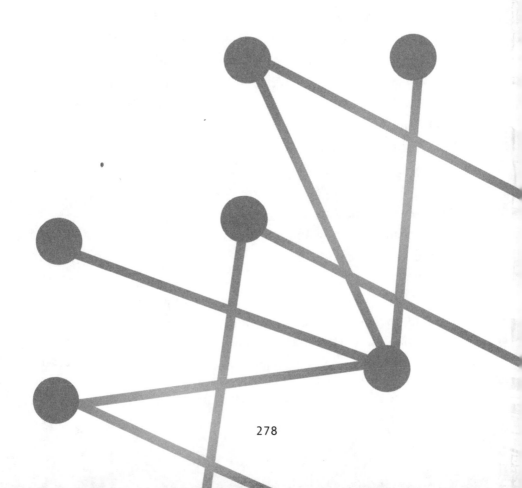

ACKNOWLEDGMENTS

To my warrior partner Keith Thomas and
to my brother Everardo Gout . . .

To James Manning, the bad hombre artist and Australian madman
who visually captured with me how Cai, Rex, and Tunde see the
world . . .

To Holly West and Jean Feiwel, the Amazonian Scribblenaut
Goddesses who I will gloriously follow into any battle, and to
everyone at Macmillan who is truly as responsible for this book
series as I am . . .

To my family, who is, as always, the
gravity that keeps me in orbit . . .

To Brian David Johnson, who keeps reminding me
that the future is a brilliant opportunity . . .

To Ken Hertz, who, despite the insanity I drive him to on
an almost daily basis, begrudgingly guides me through this
wonderful, weird life . . .

Thank you all.